THE MYSTERY OF TREEFALL MANOR

An Inspector Graves mystery

For Corinne,

So, he commanded them to hack and fell
The ancient oak-trees and to lay them well

"The Knight's Tale"
The Canterbury Tales

CONTENTS

PROLOGUE
1 – AN INVITATION TO MURDER
2 – POETRY BY THE POND
3 – AT THE MANOR
4 – BUMPS IN THE NIGHT
5 – ENTER THE DETECTIVES
6 – MURDER OR SUICIDE?
7 – DISCUSSIONS IN THE DINING ROOM
8 – THE EIGHT POINTS
9 – CURIOUS, THE THINGS PEOPLE DO
10 – ELSIE TELLS HER TALE
11 – THE LETTER AND THE WILL
12 – LYING AND TIGERS
13 – RAIN AND FIRE
14 – THE THIRD DEATH
15 – THE TRUTH
16 – THE WHOLE TRUTH
17 – AND NOTHING BUT THE TRUTH
EPILOGUE

PROLOGUE

*I'd take my soul and sell it to the Devil
To be revenged upon him! I'll get level.*

"The Miller's Tale"
The Canterbury Tales

The stare which met Jayne Brown was cold and expectant. Alexander Grimbourne was unaccustomed to his staff asking for an audience with him; having one demanded was unheard of. As Alexander looked at the thin maid, her hands clasped over her soiled apron as she stood in the centre of the study, from behind his desk, he could detect no outward sign of nervousness. This both rankled and intrigued him. In fact, a knowing smile twitched at the corner of her mouth. It was the smile of a bad card player who, despite being unable to hide their excitement, knows they hold the winning hand.

Alexander raised his bushy eyebrows as he spoke, "Well, Miss Brown, I assume you have marched in here to say something. Spit it out!"

Jayne, not wishing to rush her moment of importance looked around the room at the expensive paintings and solid furniture.

"You're very rich aren't you, sir?" said Jayne as she eyed a gilded picture frame.

"My wealth is no secret and no one's business! Now tell me why you have disturbed my morning, or you will spend your afternoon looking for a new job!"

The chuckle which escaped Jayne appeared to be triggered more by joy than impudence though Alexander glared in reply, nonetheless.

"Oh no, Mr Grimbourne, I fear it is not *I* who shall be looking for a new job."

Jayne looked at her master, waiting to see if her words would alter the stony expression on the man's face. The silence of the room was disturbed by the creaking of the chair as Alexander leaned his tremendous bulk back against it. He stroked his chin as he looked at the girl standing before him. Her greasy hair was parted in the middle and her complexion was pale and lifeless. After a moment's contemplation, Alexander said, "Miss Brown. Would I be correct in surmising that you have a piece of information about my household that you wish to share with me in exchange for financial compensation?"

"Not just one piece of information, sir. Indeed, there is more than that," replied Jayne, her mouth twisted into a sneer.

"I'm listening, but I am warning you, girl! You had better not be wasting my time ..."

Jayne glanced at the solid oak door, ensuring it was closed before continuing to speak. Her voice sank to a whisper. Alexander's cheeks darkened more and more with each word she said, the anger boiling inside of him turning his face to the colour of bloodied pus.

The forest was ancient and dense. The grey light of the moon overlaid the forest canopy like a layer of dirty snow. The two figures beneath the heavy branches were enveloped in almost total darkness. A solitary magpie sat near to them, silent and ignored.

"What is the matter? Why this urgent meeting?" asked the hooded figure, the cold night making their breath cloudy as though they were smoking an invisible cigarette.

"He knows," replied the other as they rubbed their gloved hands together furiously.

"How? We have been so careful!" strained the voice of the faceless figure.

"Not careful enough it seems. That little witch Jayne told him this afternoon. She found a letter I wrote for you before I had a chance to send it. She's been nothing but trouble from the moment she arrived, always rooting about, sticking her nose in other people's business."

Somewhere not far away a creature scurried, crunching dead leaves as it went.

The magpie cocked its head, its whiteness blurring in the darkness like a grey glow.

"What are we to do?" asked the hooded figure.

"What can we do? Our options seem rather limited, don't you think?"

1. AN INVITATION TO MURDER

*He sent a servant, bidding him to call
His daughter to him, and with ashen face
Deathly and cold, gazed on her lowly grace.*

"The Physician's Tale"
The Canterbury Tales

There is no such thing as winning or losing, there is only won and lost. The truth which haunted him. He remembered the sneering grin of the prosecutor as he whispered those words when the verdict was delivered. Defeat had been thrust upon him when victory had looked assured. The surprise witness, the damning testimony, his own conceited arrogance... but now, four years later he was sure he had learnt his lesson. Yes, thought Edmond Osborn, today in the chamber had gone well, almost perfectly in fact, but he wasn't counting his chickens; he had not won *yet*.

The lawyer was sitting in his favourite fireside chair in the corner of his Mayfair club, swirling a crystal of port. He stared into the ruby-red elixir, his thoughts twirling and sinking into the dark depths. The short walk to the establishment had been quickened by autumn wind and rain driving him encouragingly from behind. Before him lay a newspaper which he had been flicking through for ten restless minutes before neglecting it to focus on the maelstrom in his mind. The exhilaration of the day had caused his mind to replay old defeats and glories. He compared his past cases with his current one, seeking a pattern, a similarity, anything that could help him ensure a successful outcome.

Ed was so preoccupied that he failed to notice the appearance of a tall, elderly gentleman at his side who was giving him hearty salutations. Ed, awakened to the present with a shake of the arm, tossed the broadsheet aside and invited the aged Lord Sampson to join him for a drink. After all, Lord Sampson may have retired from the bar but as a former Lord Chief Justice, his opinions and views still held great weight within the circles of the Law, and with those who upheld it. Ed, a young barrister who had already shown great promise, knew it would be wise to humour this great guardian of the courts in the interests of his own career.

"I saw your picture in the newspaper yesterday. This Trevelyan business seems to be of great interest nationally," said the esteemed gentleman. "How is the case going? A perfectly simple affair if you ask me. Hang the scoundrel! That's what I say! A truly despicable crime. I don't know what has become of us since the war. Forty years ago, when I was on the bench, I never dealt with half as many crimes as you young chaps do nowadays."

"Yes, quite," replied the handsome young man. "A tricky case for the defence. I think we got their backs up today though. They were a bit stumped when we called the cook to give her evidence this morning."

Lord Sampson smiled at the man's competitive nature. He too remembered many cases going well only to fall flat on their face at the last moment. Ed, not wanting to dwell on an ongoing case, decided to change the conversation to safer ground and uttered a few inviting words about the weather. Lord Sampson took the reins of the conversation as forcibly as he did enthusiastically. Rain, rain, and more rain. Anyone listening to his monologue would be forgiven for thinking a flood was coming to rival Noah's, such was the good Lord's forecast of the matter. However, Lord Sampson's ramblings came to an abrupt halt when a smartly dressed waiter came to their table and presented Ed with an envelope upon a silver tray.

Mr Osborn Esq.
Member
The Pitt Club
London

Ed opened it, produced a letter, and read through it with a puzzled expression on his face. He read it again,

1st October 1926

Mr Osborn,

It would be my sincere pleasure if you would honour us with your presence and be my guest (Sunday 10th October) to occasion the wedding of my only daughter Ruth to Lord Frederick Taylor M.C.

If arriving by train seek the porter at the station and he will arrange for a car to collect you.

If convenient come Friday (8th), a room at the Manor shall be prepared.

Sincerely,

Alexander Grimbourne
Treefall Manor
Swinbridge
Rockinghamshire

"How peculiar," said the young man.
"What is?" asked Lord Sampson.
"This letter from a Mr Grimbourne. He has invited me to his daughter's wedding at his manor in Rockinghamshire."

"Well, what is peculiar about that?"

"Well, only that the lady's betrothed is a dear friend of mine. I had a letter from him just last week and he never mentioned a love interest, never mind a fiancée."

"Ah well, perhaps it was love at first sight. I'm told it can happen, you know."

"Perhaps," replied Ed, his voice carrying little conviction. "I say, you should know who I mean. Lord Taylor. Though I doubt you will have seen much of him in the House, he doesn't spend much time in London, prefers the country air."

"Ah yes, Lord Taylor, young fellow like yourself, terrible shame about his father, he was much respected, died before his time," said the Lord in a mournful tone that only our elders can master.

"Yes, I never met his father. He died whilst Freddie and I were serving at the Front together, a twist of fate possibly. Freddie missed the first day of the Somme because he was home for the funeral. We lost many good chaps that day."

"A terrible business," muttered Lord Sampson.

"Anyway, this letter upsets my plans, I shall have to go and sort out a few matters. Awfully nice speaking with you Lord Sampson, I hope to see you soon." And with that, Ed Osborn strode to the door of the Pitt Club, picked up his umbrella and hat from the stand and once more braved the London downpour.

Alexander Grimbourne had just finished writing a letter and had placed it within its envelope upon the out-tray of his desk, when he rang the bell summoning his secretary. As he waited, he surveyed the study in which he sat. The carpet was a deep red and luxuriously soft underfoot. In fact, the whole room shone with expensive taste. Gilded candlesticks, a marble fireplace, a rich mahogany bookcase which took up an entire wall, a fine chandelier in the centre of the ceiling. At the rear of the room, opposite the casement windows sat Alexander behind the enormous antique desk. The master of the manor, small against the room's ornate grandeur. As he sat, he was reminded of Jayne Brown. He looked at the centre of the carpet where she had stood and thought about the revelations she had spewed.

After a few moments of quiet reflection, Alexander's train of thought was interrupted by a timid knocking upon the old oak door.

"Come in."

Slowly pushing the heavy door, the threshold of the room was broken by a dark haired, meek looking man. George Campbell stood nervously with his head bowed as if he were a prisoner before Genghis Khan, his fate undecided.

"You called, Sir?"

"Yes Campbell, I did. Have the invitations for the wedding been sent out?"

"Yes Sir, I sent them earlier this morning and a few last night."

"Excellent," said Alexander, his lip curling into a smile. "I have another letter for you to send, in the tray there."

"Thank you, Sir. Was there anything else, Sir?" replied the young secretary eager to leave his master's presence.

"As a matter of fact, there was..." replied Alexander Grimbourne in a tone of fiendish delight.

Elsie Barter, middle-aged and mother of six, was dusting the panelling of the walls in the hall outside Alexander Grimbourne's study when she heard raised voices coming from inside.

Much to the honest cleaner's annoyance the verbal exchange was indistinguishable, the words muffled by the thick walls and solid door of the ancient house. However, the articulate woman correctly identified the master of the house as being the owner of the louder of what she thought to be two voices. This was a shocking scenario for Mrs Elsie Barter to comprehend for, although it was common enough to hear Mr Grimbourne raise his voice in anger, she couldn't possibly imagine who would be so courageous, or stupid, to reply in the same way.

Alexander Grimbourne had a fearsome temper, as the entire household knew. In his view, he was Lord of Heaven and Earth, creatures great and small, he was judge, jury, and executioner. Many staff members of the household had felt his wrath and their tenures had thus been short-lived. He looked with contempt on all those around him whether they were family, villagers or even the local clergy. No one was above his scorn, as Mrs Elsie Barter knew well.

After a few minutes of painful straining to make out what was being said, but without any joy of success and having edged reluctantly closer and closer to the great door with a fear of being somehow detected from within, the noble Mrs Elsie was disturbed from a different direction. Soft footfalls were making their way gracefully down the stairs above the cleaner, giving her just enough time to retreat a few steps away from the study door, lest anyone should get the wrong idea entirely. Thus, Mrs Elsie, a picture of innocence, looked up with a wonderful toothless smile at the young lady of the house as she descended almost mournfully to the ground floor.

"Ah, dear Ruth, how wonderful you look today. You look more and more like your darling mother every day, God rest her soul!" cried Mrs Elsie with great sympathy and warmth.

"Yes, thank you, Elsie," replied Ruth absently, her attention was fixed on the door of her father's study. "I say," continued the lady, the colour fading from her cheeks. "Who is my father with?"

"I'm sure I don't know dear, why can *you* hear voices? My

hearing is not what it used to be, but I shan't complain." Mrs Elsie stated. However, just as this short dialogue was completed, the answer both women sought was presented. The great door flew open and out stormed George Campbell, his face scarlet and his forehead dotted with beads of sweat. If the secretary saw the other two people in the hallway, he gave no indication of this as he rushed past them in a blind fury and turned the corner out of sight.

Mrs Elsie's fine brain was going hammer and tongs trying to figure the meaning of this extraordinary scene, and this difficult thought process was duly conveyed in a look of helpless confusion upon the poor woman's face. In contrast with this, Ruth although as equally in the dark as to the meaning of the argument as the cleaner, relaxed her shoulders and some colour returned to her beautiful face. She looked almost relieved.

"Oh my!" cried Mrs Elsie, disturbing Ruth's frantic thoughts, "I wonder what that was about? A bad business no doubt!"

"Oh, I'm sure it's nothing to worry about, Elsie, we all know my father can be a little trying at times, Mr Campbell probably just forgot to run some errand or other and father just got a bit prickly about it all. A fuss over nothing, I'm sure," whispered Ruth, forcing a smile.

"Yes, I'm sure you're right, of course," replied Mrs Elsie, giving her most convincing smile.

"Anyway, I shall leave you to get on with your work, we don't want you to be getting into trouble as well now do we?" said Ruth playfully and, with that final remark, she walked down the hallway on her way to the kitchens. As she went past her father's study, she glanced in, the door still being open from Campbell's dramatic exit. Alexander Grimbourne was sitting behind his desk, his hands clasped in front of him, staring straight ahead towards the windows that looked out to the gardens. His mind seemed adrift in an ocean of thought, but the slightest hint of a smile could be seen on his face, a smile that Ruth shuddered at seeing. It was a smile of malicious intent.

'*Poor George,*' thought Ruth as she turned the corner and proceeded away from the study, before her mind returned to other, more pressing matters.

2. POETRY BY THE POND

Said John, 'Alas the day that I was born!
We've earned nowt here but mockery and scorn.

"The Reeve's Tale"
The Canterbury Tales

Over a week after these events John Grimbourne, only son of Alexander was taking his daily walk through the woods. He moved slowly, limping on his left leg. It was early afternoon, and the sun was falling from its zenith, its rays unhindered by cloud as they made their way onto the green landscape of the Treefall estate. Despite the pleasant sunshine, there was a cool autumn breeze in the air and the grass glistened from morning rain. John had rather sensibly chosen to wear a thick woollen scarf along with a hunting jacket and mud-splashed hiking boots.

Walking quite aimlessly, albeit with his limp, his mind devoted to troubling matters, John approached an old tree stump beside a large pond, a favourite spot of his on the family estate. Deciding to rest his leg, he flung his satchel down on the ground and sat on the stump, gazing at the golden shimmer of the water as it slithered like a snake with the gentle lapping of the tiny waves. After a few minutes of unsatisfactory reflection, he decided to banish unhappy thoughts from his mind for a time and instead do what he loved doing most, in fact the only thing

THE MYSTERY OF TREEFALL MANOR

he loved doing: writing poetry. Reaching into his satchel, he produced a leatherbound notepad, which he rested on his lap, and then a flask of tea.

Surveying the scene in front of himself, John opened the flask and took a sip. The tea was strong and milky: a perfect tonic. The escaping steam clouded his glasses momentarily, the sun's bright rays mingling with the white steam created for John an almost holy vision, like the entrance to heaven. After setting down his flask and allowing the mist to clear, John took a pen from his pocket and opened his notepad. He cast a critical eye over his latest work as he always did and rubbished himself as a poor poet.

> *The fish in the stream knows no rules,*
> *He only swims against tides to pools,*
> *An easier life I cannot see*
> *Yet would I exchange my life with thee?*
>
> *Among life's sorrow there must surely be joy,*
> *But to seek without finding will only annoy,*
> *Where does the fish seek his meaning?*
> *In the reeds, the soil or is he dreaming,*
>
> *Of walking abreast with four legged creatures*
> *And exploring the hills, trees, and all earth's features?*
> *Forthright endeavours men want to be found*
> *But what can men do while their hands are bound?*
>
> *To break the shackles that hold us tight*
> *Takes courage, valour, and a heart to fight,*
> *But the fish in the stream knows no rules,*
> *I wonder if he knows that men are fools.*

'Awful,' thought John. 'I doubt Wordsworth would ever have thought to rhyme 'creatures' with 'features'.'

All thoughts of poetry played on his mind: which words he could substitute, the absolute agony of alliteration, the meaning of verse and its subtlety. He considered the construction of his next poem, a poem to rival Kipling… if only.

John knew that poetry must be true, it must wrench the heart, it must suffocate and stifle the reader, it must be for the poet himself and no one else. It is art; heart and soul must go into it otherwise it is worthless no matter how clever or sophisticated it sounds.

With a sigh he threw down his pen and stared intently at the water. A heron pecked among the water lilies at the far side of the pond, its proud neck straining with intent upon the flora. Ducks bobbed up and down on the water's surface, nonchalant as to where they were and uncaring if there was ever to be a tomorrow.

'Oh, to live a life like thee,' John thought, and a sad smile passed over his lips. Bravely, he took up his pen again and wiped the mud from it on his jacket sleeve. Looking at the heron, he thought about its majesty, its ancestral link to a bygone age where feathered reptiles would roam the sky without fear of bow or gun, where predators bigger than elephants would stalk the lands in a prehistoric age, where game was fair, and fair was game. *'Still,'* thought John, *'love didn't exist before animals' blood became warm, even if life was much simpler.'*

Sitting on a tree stump in the open-air contemplating nature, God, demons and dragons, John was as far away from present as could be. He did not hear the man behind him approaching, nor, for that matter would he have wanted to, given his desire for solitude.

John liked the noiselessness of his surroundings, being able to breathe freely and deep, to think without limitation or constraint, to mourn without interruption. A nervous cough disturbed his dreaming like a twig snapping in the forest. John turned abruptly, his startled face breaking into a half smile when he looked into the face of his sister's betrothed.

Frederick Taylor offered John a sheepish smile, his hands resting on a fine walking stick. His initials were inlaid with gold on an embedded crest, and a short, cut deer antler formed the handle. He seemed embarrassed, no doubt acknowledging the fact that his appearance was uninvited yet feeling it would be rude to pass his future brother-in-law without presenting himself lest his presence should be noticed. Freddie lived on the adjoining estate, though his rambles rarely took him over the Treefall land.

"John, I was just passing, I didn't expect to see you. How is the poetry going?" said Freddie with half an eye on the weathered pages of the notepad. It was now John's turn to be sheepish.

"Oh well, I don't know if one could call it poetry, sometimes it is simply good to get out into the air and jot down a few things, you know? Whatever comes to mind."

"Excellent. And what is coming to mind today? Or is it bad form to ask?"

"Well Freddie, I was just thinking about the nature of things, you know, the scope in which we animals live. I was looking at that heron by the reeds and was thinking of the laws of his life and ours, the rules by which we must abide."

"Interesting, but surely one cannot compare an animal to a human? After all a heron does not live by any rules, it has no one to govern it."

"But it lives by the rules of nature, the rules of nature dictate its life's intent, to live and breathe and procreate, to sustain its species for future generations to come. It is true what you say, a heron cannot break the law, for there is no law which it has sworn to uphold, but it is tied to the law of nature whether it likes it or not, much like ourselves."

"I doubt very much whether it likes it or dislikes it. It is a heron and is a simple creature," replied Freddie.

"I do not doubt that you are right in what you say, and I don't wish to argue the point, it only makes me wonder why *we* are so different. Human beings I mean. Why are we specially chosen to have intelligence when other animals are not? Can men not be fools too?"

"Animals are not fools but they are not wise either, they are what they are," replied Freddie. "It is a human's curse to behave wisely or foolishly and to not know the punishment (if there is one) or reward (if there is one) of their actions until the day has come. Or so I believe," said Frederick solemnly. John, struck by the sincerity of the words just heard nodded in comprehension.

"You missed the war, didn't you?" continued Freddie.

"Yes. Damned leg. Since birth, don't you know."

"Yes, I believe your father mentioned that."

"He's not likely to ever forget it. The shame of having a cripple for a son." John replied, his voice thick with bitterness. "I tried to join up and do my bit of course but the War Office wasn't having any of it."

"Perhaps for the best. An awful time. It is hard to know what is just and what is not sometimes in war," stated Freddie, looking at the mud around his feet.

"So, do you believe that animals are just, Freddie?" said John resuming the earlier thread of conversation.

"Animals are just in *their own* nature but should not be compared with a man's nature. A dog may share the same hereditary genes as a wolf, but a dog will rarely attack a child as a wolf might, although they share common ancestry."

"But a human may attack another human, or animal for that matter, whether provoked or unprovoked," John replied after taking another sip of tea.

"Yes of course, we are our own masters in that regard." said Freddie.

"Yes, that is the key which is what makes us so different. If a fox slaughters a coop full of chickens, it has no conception that is a wrong thing to do because it has no moral meter and will not be judged by a higher power. Humans on the other hand know that murder is wrong yet sometimes do it anyway because not all humans believe in a higher power, and so believe the only punishment they will receive is through the courts. If they are caught that is."

"Ha, and if you committed murder do you think you would be caught, John?" laughed Freddie.

"Oh no of course not, not unless I had to run away quickly from the scene of the crime," answered John self-mockingly, joining in with Freddie's laughter.

Freddie left John still sitting on the stump. When he looked back after a few minutes he could see John hard at work, his pen scribbling furiously upon his notepad. He hoped their conversation had inspired the poet. Freddie thought John to be rather odd at times but, found himself liking him no less for it.

Continuing on his way through the fields and woods towards the village Freddie didn't meet anyone else, he moved at a leisurely pace and, although he was in no hurry, he took an old narrow shortcut known locally as Poacher's Lane. This track cut through a large copse of densely packed oak trees, and only branched off in one place which led to Treefall Manor. Freddie reached this fork in the path and stopped to look in the direction of the manor. The surrounding trees were thick and tall, allowing Freddie a mere glimpse of the roof and miniature turrets of the ancient seat of Grimbourne power, which was still some way off. Starting down the lane again, Freddie walked for a further fifteen minutes before reaching the edge of the village of Swinbridge. Poacher's Lane came to an abrupt halt behind the local watering hole, the Blue Boar Inn. The pub landlord was the only person in sight, busily chopping logs and tossing them in a nearby basket. His face was redder than a beef tomato and his chest heaved as he toiled through his labour.

This was the person Freddie had come to see and he was rather glad to be interrupting Samuel Mason from his chores before the stout chap keeled over and never poured a pint again.

"Excuse me, Mr Mason!" called Freddie, just as the subject of his attention drove the axe down with tremendous force, splitting the wood clean in two. Samuel Mason did not hear this call over the cracking din, and Freddie had to call again before he was heard, all the while making sure he was a safe distance from the swinging axe.

Upon looking up and seeing Lord Taylor standing a few yards away smiling pleasantly, Samuel Mason hastily removed his beaten cap from his head and made a slight bow, panting like an overexerted bulldog all the while.

"Good afternoon, my Lord."

"Good afternoon, Mason, I'm sorry to disturb you but I was wondering if I might have a word?"

"Of course, my Lord, how can I help?"

"Oh, nothing to worry about," assured Freddie as he noticed Samuel shifting his feet and twisting his cap. "Only you may know that I'm to be married in a few days and I was wondering, if it would not be too much trouble that is, whether it would be possible for you to open the inn a bit earlier? You see I was hoping my service staff at home could come down for luncheon and refreshment?"

"Oh, I see," replied Samuel whilst stroking his moustache. "Well, I wouldn't have thought that would be a problem, how many are there?"

"About ten or so. I'm terribly sorry for the late notice, but with so much to organise it quite slipped my mind," replied Freddie.

"I suppose I could get young William to help me, he won't mind seeing as it's yourself, my Lord. But will the staff not be needed on the wedding day?"

"No, Mr Grimbourne's own staff will be taking care of most things and the wedding itself will be a relatively small affair. I thought it might be a nice idea for them to have a day off and to celebrate here, they've all been so devoted to me, and especially my late father, that I thought they deserved something of this kind. Just keep a tab of what they eat, and drink and I shall settle the bill the day after."

"Of course, as you wish my Lord."

"Thank you ever so much Mr Mason, they shall be delighted, I'm sure."

Despite the kind words and warm smile offered to Samuel Mason, the landlord felt that Lord Taylor was somewhat glum.

A tiny sparrow sat a short distance from the two conversing humans. He moved his head left and right in sharp movements pondering its next destination. The yard at the back of the Inn no longer held any interest to him and he fancied it was getting near lunchtime, so he stretched out his little wings and began fanning the air around him in preparation for take-off. In a few moments, he had soared over the heads of the two-legged giants and was circling the Inn. The air he could feel held no danger that day, and he could freely look around him as he floated on the heavy air. The stream ran clear and cold beside the pub, swerving this way and that until it was lost in thick woods in the distance. Choosing a different course, the little sparrow flew without haste over the village, weaving to avoid the rising smoke which poured upwards from several cottage chimneys. The tidy gardens below looked resplendent: the autumn sun illuminated the valiant flowers which battled the frosty nights and stood proud in the day in a plethora of colour. Tabby cats could be seen stalking beside the hedges or lying in some bright patch, savouring the last sun rays of the year. The sparrow climbed a little further then stopped for a rest on the church spire, his microscopic frame held above the world of man and beast. Far below an old widow clad in black tended the grave of a lost lover of long ago. She bent low, labouring over her work, her wrinkled hands wiping the rough headstone clean.

The treetops swayed in a gentle breeze and off again went the little sparrow surfing on the wind. Down, down, up, down, this way and that, over the sleepy village of Swinbridge until finally the winged creature stopped on the roof of the village railway station. Sporadic blasts of smoke could be seen in the distance, getting bigger as they came closer, and with them the low rumbling of the carriages as they trundled toward the platform.

The train stopped amid a whirlwind of smoke and screeching, half a dozen or so passengers descended from it, reaching and pulling their luggage with the help of the conductor. Among these was Ed Osborn. He had travelled with only one suitcase and stopped to stretch as he stepped from the locomotive. Ed decided to ignore the instructions in the invitation he had received, he chose instead to make his way to the grand old house on foot, and to stop at a pub for lunch. He was in no hurry to get to Treefall Manor, after all, he was unexpectedly invited and the only person there he would know was his old friend who would probably be busy with wedding plans. No, he thought, much better to go to the local inn and get some information as to what he could expect to find.

Ed walked slowly, taking deep breaths to expel any London smog still lingering in his lungs. He looked all around him, admiring the vibrancy of the flowers and the gentle chirping of the birds. Ed was no stranger to village life, his childhood memories consisted of playing in fields and picking wild berries in the summertime. Swinbridge, he decided, could be plucked into the sky, and dropped into any rural part of England and it would not look out of place.

It was an hour past noon when Ed arrived at the Blue Boar Inn. The sign above the door read '*Samuel Mason. Proprietor. Licensee*'. Upon entering, Ed scanned the small saloon: the only other occupant was an elderly man sitting in the corner who looked like he was asleep. In front of him was a pint of ale, barely touched, and beside him was an old collie who lay with his chin resting on his front paws. He looked up at Ed as he entered without raising his head, his eyes sad, as though he wished to see something more of the world other than the inside of this public house. Behind the bar stood a large man with a red face and white moustache. He seemed a little out of breath but was listening intently to what the woman he was talking with was saying.

The old woman was babbling at a rate of knots, choking for breath between exclamations. Despite the rapidity of her words, it seemed to Ed that the man behind the bar (whom he correctly assumed to be Mason) had no difficulty understanding her. Ed, still being at the door, was too far from the pair to make out exactly what was being said but as he approached the bar his ears pricked as he caught the words 'Grimbourne', and 'poor girl' and his curiosity was aroused.

Upon seeing this intruder gingerly make his way to the bar, the conversation died like a candle flame being struck by a strong draft, and both man and woman turned to give the stranger a welcoming smile.

"Good afternoon," was the greeting which was issued from the landlord and was duly returned in kind by the newcomer who could feel every inch of his person under scrutiny by the small creature on his right.

"How can I be of service sir?" asked the proprietor.

"I'd like a pint of bitter if you would, and perhaps a bite of luncheon if any is available?"

"Of course. We have some game pie freshly prepared by Mrs Barter here," said Mason indicating the small creature who hadn't said a word, despite her mouth being open, and who was still voraciously examining the tall stranger. Ed eyed Mrs Barter critically then smiled and said that game pie would be delightful.

"What brings you to these parts, Sir? I haven't seen you around here before," said the publican as he tugged on the beer pump.

"I'm here for a wedding. I'm to be a guest at Treefall Manor under Mr Grimbourne." At these words, Samuel and Elsie exchanged a quick glance with one another and the landlord put the pint pot on the bar top with more force than Ed deemed hospitable. After gruffly asking for payment for the refreshment, Mason turned from the stranger to talk with Elsie about some trivial matter. The abruptness with which the mood of Mason seemed to change aroused curiosity more than annoyance from the lawyer, and he became resolved to find out the cause of this swing. Pondering over the few words spoken between the two men, Ed affirmed that the quiet hostility displayed must surely be aimed more at Mr Grimbourne than at himself who was, of course, a mere stranger in these parts, and indeed the attitude of the landlord had changed at the mention of Grimbourne's name. Deciding to interrupt the conversation between the man and woman in order to glean some information about his soon to be host, Ed politely asked, "What kind of man is Mr Grimbourne? I'm afraid to say I have never met him."

Samuel Mason slowly turned toward the visitor, his red face redder than a few minutes previously. He eyed Ed for a few moments, as though unwilling to believe his testament before spitting out the words, "He's the devil, and we all know where the devil belongs," before turning once again to Elsie. This time though he did not resume speaking to that fine woman but stopped like a statue, his eyes seeing nothing, momentarily deep in thought. He eventually turned again to Ed and said in a gentler tone than before, "If you have never met the man, why has he asked you to be his guest at his daughter's wedding?"

Wondering whether the change of tone was due to a feeling of guilt at the harshness of the original words or whether the landlord did not believe his statement, Ed simply replied with the truth: that he was a friend of Lord Taylor's though he hadn't seen him for some time.

The room held silence for a little while as the local man and woman exchanged another glance which was now becoming habitual, and Ed thought he saw a hint of a smile of the landlord's lips. He said now more pleasantly "Lord Taylor is a fine man though what he has done to deserve a father in-law such as that I will never know. There was certainly no love lost between Lord Taylor's father and Grimbourne and that's a fact. You just missed him. He was here not an hour ago making a few arrangements."

"Does Freddie enjoy a good relationship with Mr Grimbourne?"

"I'm sure I don't know Lord Taylor's personal feelings on the matter, but I cannot see how such a good man could like such a bad one."

"Now, now," said Elsie joining the conversation for the first time. "Mr Grimbourne has always been very good to me, giving me work after my poor Alfie's accident and whatnot. There's not many as would be so kind to a helpless mother of so many! I'm *very* grateful!" Ed could not help but feel this statement from the woman was purely for his benefit in case her employer heard of this conversation and it looked black against her, Ed being a stranger. After all, it was perhaps best to protect oneself. Samuel Mason on the other hand would not guard his tongue against Ed's host. He continued his damning assessment.

"It is a miracle that man's cruelty has not rubbed off on his children, thank the Lord that it hasn't."

"How many Grimbournes are there? I really know nothing about them," replied the curious lawyer.

"Well, there is Alexander as discussed, his eldest, John, a bit of a quiet type, keeps himself to himself and there is nothing wrong with that, I daresay. Other than that just Ruth, a wonderful girl, poor thing is terrified of her father. I hope Lord Taylor takes her far away once they are married, though I doubt he will."

"Is there not a Mrs Grimbourne?"

"There was. She died before the children reached their teenage years. She was a very nice lady." Ed looked at Elsie during the last part of this speech, she was staring at the landlord solemnly, gently nodding her head, agreeing with Samuel on the character of the late Mrs Grimbourne.

"Apologies Mr…?"

"Osborn."

"Yes, Mr Osborn. I forgot to fetch your pie."

3. AT THE MANOR

But how they made the funeral fires flame,
Or what the trees by number or by name
-Oak, fir-tree, birch, aspen and poplar too,
Ilex and alder, willow, elm, and yew,

"The Knight's Tale"
The Canterbury Tales

After his reflections by the pond, John Grimbourne walked back to the Manor, his pace determined by his cursed appendage. The weather was still fair although a little colder now in mid-afternoon. He approached the grand house from the rear, the three-tiered mansion cast its shadow belligerently, careless of trees, plants, and John himself. An island in a sea of forest, the lonely breeze sighed.

John's sleeping hunger was awakened by the aroma of soup which drifted from the kitchens. The cook, Betty, may have been old and somewhat batty but there was no doubting her abilities in preparing dinner, John thought to himself, shivering slightly in the shade.

Leaving his muddy boots in an old shed and putting on a pair of soft leather slippers, John walked along a short path to the pantry door through which he entered. He had exchanged sticks in the shed and was leaning heavily on his favourite ash crook, his leg feeling sore due to the uneven ground over which he had travelled. He was making his way through the wide hallway towards the stairs beside his father's study thinking about an afternoon of rest on his bed and maybe some light reading when the door to the study swung open.

"Good afternoon, Father," said the son dutifully.

Alexander ignored the politeness of the remark and glanced at the stick which he had heard thudding down the passageway.

"I was expecting a guest to have arrived, a man called Osborn, he was to ring up from the station but may have walked. Take the car and go and find him in case he has gotten lost." With the orders given, Alexander turned back into his study shutting the door behind him.

John bowed his head and lamented the death of his afternoon rest.

The engine of the Triumph Fifteen saloon purred as it started from the gravel path outside of Treefall Manor. Despite his leg, John could drive with ease; it was one of the few pleasures in his caged existence. He weaved the motor along the path that stretched for a mile or so out of the family estate, flanked on either side by mighty oaks. The trees shut out the light and one felt as if floating down a river in a huge gorge. Passing through the open gate leading on to the village road, John looked left and right but there were no other vehicles on the road and no sign of the man he had been sent to find. His father had given no description of the man, the prior interview being very abrupt, but John knew everyone in the village by sight, if not by name, and a stranger walking around was sure to catch the eye. John turned right, Treefall Estate being at the very end of Swinbridge village. He drove slowly up the main road surrounded now by cottages on either side rather than trees, over an ancient stone bridge beneath which trickled the stream known as the Swin, and still no sign of Mr Osborn appeared.

Unbeknownst to John, Ed was just taking his last sip of ale and was wiping his mouth with a napkin ready to continue on to the Manor when the Triumph saloon drove past the pub and continued in the direction of the train station at the extreme end of the village. John drove further on down the main road and waved at the vicar who coming out of the church beside him. When he got to the train station he pulled up and looked around, though this Mr Osborn was nowhere to be seen, and John realised his task was becoming an increasingly difficult one. The stationmaster and porter were polite and eager to assist but proved to be no help at all. They hadn't noticed a man leaving the train and, as John did not have a description of Mr Osborn, their memories couldn't be jogged.

John imagined his father's wrath at his failure as he got back into the saloon. Even if Mr Grimbourne had been wrong about what time the train was due, or indeed which train the visitor would be on, John knew that such trifles were irrelevant, and that blame would be placed solely and sorely at his feet.

Driving slowly back through the village in order to delay the inevitable scene which was to be played out in the manor study, John sighted a stranger leaving the Blue Boar Inn.
The gentleman was smartly dressed and was walking proudly and leisurely carrying a small tan coloured suitcase.

"Hello there," called John as he pulled the car up to the side of the road and opened the door. "Are you by chance Mr Osborn?"

"I am," replied Ed eyeing John's withered leg as he struggled out of the car.

"I am John Grimbourne, my father sent me to look for you as he was afraid you may have gotten lost."

"Oh, I see," said Ed as he shook John's hand. "Your father advised ringing up but as the sun was out, I thought I would take a stroll and have a look around this pretty village. There aren't many delightful little cottages such as this in London, I should really get out into the country more often."

"Yes, I'm afraid we may take our little part of Eden for

granted sometimes. Please, allow me to take your case and I shall run you up to the house, we are near the end of the village now, but the road is still quite long."

"Thank you, have many other guests arrived?"

"No, I believe you are the first, the rest I think shall be here tomorrow evening, though there won't be many; it is to be a small wedding. The arrangements seem to have been made so quickly I'm afraid I've been lost in the whirlwind and am quite in the dark as regards to any sort of itinerary. Father has had poor George putting the show together with typical vigour. Am I correct in assuming that you are a friend of Frederick's?"

"Yes, that's right, we were together in the war, and we usually catch up in London when Freddie is down, which is rare enough these days. He appears to have developed a sudden phobia of the capital, I haven't seen nor heard from him in quite some time, barring the infrequent letter, though I now suspect falling for your sister may have something to do with it. It was quite a shock hearing of this sudden engagement."

Though not phrased directly as a question, the tone in which Ed said these last words was inviting. John opened his mouth to reply then thought better of it, giving out a little cough instead which sounded like a puppy trying to bark. Sensing John's quick hesitation Ed said, "What a wonderful motor, what does she do?" and the remainder of the short journey was passed pleasantly as the two men extolled the virtues of the Triumph Fifteen as it cantered on to Treefall Manor.

Ruth sat in the library, her head resting on one of the wings of an armchair which was tucked in a corner facing the door. Her eyes were open, looking ahead yet focusing on nothing. Ruth's soft hands caressed a necklace which hung below her throat as she stared into the abyss. At the end of a thin golden chain dangled a red ruby. Ruth's fingers toyed with the jewel, as though the answers to her worries lay within the cold fire of the stone, if only she could claw through it.

A cheerful humming interrupted Ruth's contemplation. The droning was coming from down the hallway and was getting louder. Ruth sat still, hoping that she wouldn't be disturbed but fortune did not favour her. Jayne Brown entered the library, oblivious to the occupant in the corner. She walked directly to the windowsill where she placed a vase of flowers, the yellow heads drooping under their own weight. Still humming, she leaned on the ledge and gazed out of the window to the tree covered land beyond. Tiring of the landscape, she looked down at a black polished table beside her and her attention was caught by an intricately decorated dagger which lay in a cradle made of wood. The hilt of the weapon was studded with gems and Jayne slowly ran her forefinger over the smooth stones until she felt the cold metal of the thin curved blade.

"Be careful Jayne, that is very sharp," warned the voice from the corner.

Jayne spun on her heels then scowled as she looked upon Ruth who was sitting very still.

"It is not *I* who should be careful!" spat out Jayne.

"What do you mean by that?" asked Ruth in a voice composed of anger and fear.

The girl took her finger from the blade before replying. She looked at the necklace which Ruth continued to paw and said in a mocking tone, "Oh, nothing, your highness! I wouldn't dream to threaten precious little Miss Grimbourne, the most beautiful lady in Rockinghamshire!"

"I think you had better leave now Jayne before I say something I regret."

"You can say what you like, your words mean nothing.

Everyone knows your father rules the roost and I think you'll find he is quite fond of me."

"That may be," replied Ruth who covered her ruby necklace with her hand as though to shield it from Jayne's gaze. "But all the same I think you should leave. The library is Mrs Barter's responsibility, you have no reason to be in here now that you have left the flowers."

Jayne laughed in response. She resumed her cheerful humming as she walked to the door where she abruptly stopped and turned to give a parting shot to the pale lady of the house.

"I think Miss Grimbourne, I shall take a walk around the gardens. I do like the gardens, although recently they have not been looking very well kept..."

Upon arrival at the ancient seat of the Grimbournes, John parked in a small, doorless garage partially covered by bushes twenty feet to the side of the house. Climbing out of the saloon whilst trying to conceal the difficulty that this presented, John promptly took Ed's case, regardless of much protestation from the latter who guiltily eyed the former's leg, which, despite being covered by trousers, was apparent in its deformity. It seemed to Ed as though there was no leg at all, merely bone which the trouser material wrapped around and clung to when the gammy leg was thrust forward or faced with a strong wind.

Ed followed the heir to Treefall Manor up the gravel path whilst looking at the great building before him. He could tell it was very old, the grey stone having been worn smooth by centuries of wind and rain. Much larger than a mansion yet much smaller than a castle, almost a cathedral thought Ed as he craned his neck to look at the miniature spires towering above him. How elegant they looked, four minarets perched on ancient stone, sitting defiantly, each one like Excalibur not yet plucked.

Yes, thought Ed, a cathedral in size but not in feeling, for there was no lightness or gaiety, no sense of the uplift and calm one gets when entering a palace of the Almighty. No, here there was no joy. A sadness seemed to lay thick, like a fog on the ground, punctuated by the shadows cast by the great oaks all around. Even on this sunny day, a battle was being fought between the falling sun against the house and trees which seemed to rise with every passing second. Darkness was winning. The young lawyer's pace had slowed so much with each absorbing thought that he hadn't realised he was now standing as still as the mighty spires at which he was staring. Only when John interrupted his trance and broke the silence by asking if he was alright did Ed become embarrassingly aware that he was standing stock still with his mouth hanging open staring upwards. Finding himself feeling like a mime artist when words failed to form in his throat, Ed gave a little cough, a mumbled something about the beautiful house.

The entrance to the manor consisted of four stone steps and a heavy set of twin oak doors, one of which creaked and unsealed, seemingly of its own accord as John placed his good foot on the first step. The crippled man was on the third level by the time the door was fully opened revealing a small, white-haired man who exhibited some surprise at John carrying the suitcase and made quickly to relieve the young master of his burden. The old man received a breathless thanks and turning, disappeared through the portico and down the hallway between two grand staircases with a rapidity that alarmed Ed.

"He moves at a fair pace for an old boy."

John chuckled the affirmative.

"Hodgkins has been with us for years, since before I was born. My earliest memories are of him roaming around the place with his shock of white hair. He seemed to float rather than walk, I fancied him for a ghost, I think."

Ed had passed through the small portico, empty except for a hat and umbrella stand alongside a little wooden bench and now stood in a great hall. A plush carpet with medieval design spread across the floor surrounded by the two staircases. The hallway, which the elderly Hodgkins had gone down, seemed to split the house in two, for its length was impressive, and several doorframes could be seen all along it on either side. Looking up to the mezzanine that conjoined the top of the two staircases, Ed could see the hallway replicated directly above, which he presumed separated the living quarters of the family and the staff. From outside the house, a third floor could be seen but how this was accessed wasn't clear, although the lawyer's judicial logic deducted more stairs at the rear of the house.

Looking around, Ed saw great pictures hung on the walls portraying similar looking men, all moustached and straight faced without a hint of a smile. The artists had all captured the same air of authority and hardness of glare; if the slight differences in facial features were not closely observed one could almost think the portraits were of the same man wearing different clothes of the ages, perhaps in a one-man play.

The windows were higher than the pictures, a great chandelier drooped from the high ceiling above where the two men stood, splaying light softly around the curving staircases. The eminent lawyer had stood in many rooms equally as grand and more ornate, but this space affected him. Again he was motionless; again he was speechless. It wasn't the grandeur which entranced him so, no, this room seemed to be trying too hard in some inexplicable way. No, here in this room was feeling, a foreboding. But was it the room or was it the house? Ed could not tell. Instead, he inwardly called himself a fool and once again turned to his host, a cracked smile beaming on his intelligent face.

"What a delightful room."

"Thank you, it's said that Arthur Grimbourne, my great ancestor himself laid the first foundation stone here in the Great Hall as it has come to be known. He had made his fortune from nothing and insisted on building the future with his own hands, as it were. And so, he did." John trailed into silence and Ed couldn't tell if his face betrayed regret or worry until the young heir broke the momentary silence. "Well, that's a tale my father tells better. He's quite the historian when it comes to the family roots and the examples, *we* should all live up to." Was there a hint of resentment in that last statement? Ed couldn't be sure.

Hodgkins appeared from the right-hand door at the farthest end of the corridor and glided towards the two gentlemen.

"Mr Grimbourne sends his apologies, he is presently taking care of some urgent business and can't be disturbed, but says he looks forward to being introduced at dinner. In the meantime, as a guest of Treefall Manor you may do as you please, feel free to explore the house and the grounds. John will show you around if you wish."

John's leg, which until now had presented a barely noticeable twinge suddenly throbbed as the butler uttered his last words. He regretted his earlier walk and lamented his poetic efforts. Still, this Ed seemed like a decent enough chap, he must smile through the pain.

"Thank you, please tell Mr Grimbourne that is very kind, although if I am to be permitted such freedom, I don't see the need to detain John any longer. He has already been too kind to me." Ed smiled and nodded at John as he said this, causing mild embarrassment to the man who wondered if his face had betrayed his thoughts when Hodgkins presented his father's orders. For orders they were, despite the golden lettering. If Alexander Grimbourne wished to see a guest, then time would be made to see them. After all, in the world of business he was at no one's mercy thus matters were only as urgent as his father decided them to be.

Hodgkins nodded, "Very good sir, the gong shall sound fifteen minutes before dinner is served," then floated back in the direction he came.

"I am quite happy to show you around, Mr Osborn, the house has a simple layout, but the grounds and woods are quite vast, it wouldn't take much to get lost."

"No, thank you, don't trouble yourself, and please call me

Ed. I shall take in the house and perhaps the lovely gardens I spied around the house as we drove up. I shan't wander too far."

"Very well, though first let me show you to your room."

†

John closed the door softly behind himself leaving Ed in the middle of a spacious guest room. They had walked up the right-hand curving staircase and went to the far end of the house where a smaller, narrower set of stairs took them to the third level of the house. About halfway along, John had opened a door on the left revealing the room in which Ed now stood. Now alone, he took a few minutes to look around. Several ornaments and paintings were spread evenly around, making the large room seem quite empty and bare. The curtains were parted, and the shutter window left slightly open, allowing a gentle breeze to freshen what Ed thought would have been a stale room a few hours before. There were few signs the room was frequently inhabited: cigarette smoke had made no impression on the ceiling or wallpaper despite an empty ashtray sitting alone on a bedside table. The bed itself had been placed headfirst against the wall in the middle of the room. The only other practical amenities were a small armchair in the corner by the window and a small basin sink beside a writing desk. It reminded Ed of his old room when he was in training for the Army.

His case was beside the bed, neat and perpendicular to the wall. The old boy must have taken it up the back stairs as himself and John were talking.

He strode to the window. The view showed a rolling landscape half covered by trees. He could see the shimmer of water on a large pond near the forest and gentle grassy hills on the other side. If he were in a room on the other side of the house, he would probably see the tops of the houses in the village, perhaps the train station far in the distance.

He thought he'd start by exploring the house. It was now well into the afternoon and Ed reckoned he had only a few hours to meander and get ready before dinner.

As he turned away from the window, something on the distant treeline caught his eye, a movement. Turning back, he looked through the window: a figure was crossing between the front line of the trees. For a few moments Ed couldn't think why this sight had caught his attention. After all, the landscape wasn't still: birds teemed and sang, baby waves lapped in the pond, even the few small clouds traversed across the sky at a slow pace, carried by the invisible breeze. It was something in the manner of the figure that had rung peculiar. Ed stared for a few more minutes, the figure was too far away for him to tell whether it was male or female, but he could make out dark clothing. Finally, Ed realised why this character was strange. It was the *way* the person moved. They were furtive, almost slinking, as though they didn't wish to be seen. 'Probably a poacher,' Ed thought as he turned to leave the room, making a mental note to inform John of what he had just seen.

A great many pictures hung in the hallways of the manor and Ed stopped to admire each as he passed. He did not disturb rooms whose doors were closed and, in this manner, proceeded to the library by way of a drawing room and a few sitting rooms which he thought quite needless. Though each room had its own individual charms and character he was particularly drawn to the library. It was the grandest room in the manor. Magnificent mahogany bookcases stretched from floor to ceiling so that, if walls existed, they couldn't be seen. A great velvet rug whose red colour was as deep as the ocean rolled out across the wooden floor. On top of it were two leather sofas and a small coffee table. The bookcases were immaculately carved, in just a few glances Ed spotted an orb, the sun, moon, stars and waves.

Over by the window was a polished ebony desk and chair. The black surface shone with reflected light. The desk was bare except for a blotting pad and a wooden cradle which held a glittering dagger. Ed picked up this curio of a foreign land and felt its weight in both hands. The blade curved along its length like a slithering snake. Ed pressed his fingertip against the sharp point softly, careful to not draw blood then, his curiosity satisfied, he replaced the dagger in its cradle, eager to examine the hundreds of books held in the room.

Leatherbound editions of all the great writers sat proudly on the shelves. Donne separated Shakespeare and Marlowe; Blake rubbed shoulders with Milton whilst the Bronte sisters had a family reunion on the higher shelves.

He perused some more, picking out a first edition copy of *A Study in Scarlet* and was about to sit on one of the comfortable looking sofas when he heard an old grandfather clock somewhere strike four o'clock. For a second, he thought dinner was being announced and that he had missed a chance to admire the gardens.

During his explorations, he had neither seen nor heard a soul. Doubtless the kitchen was a hive of activity, but the rest of the house was deathly silent. The library was on the first floor, opposite what Ed presumed were the family bedrooms. He went down the grand staircase once again and up the hallway to the rear of the house. On his right was the heavy door of Mr Grimbourne's study. Ed slowed as he approached out of curiosity to see if any sign of life could be heard but all was as quiet as the rest of the house.

When he considered the fact that a family wedding was looming, Ed thought it would be reasonable to see more bustle about the place. Seamstresses running to and fro, flowers being hurried about the place, champagne flutes clinking as they were unwrapped, all under the watchful eye of some monstrous matron type shouting orders. Instead, all was eerily still.

Turning left at the study, a short walk took him to the pantry door which opened to the garden. This was the same door through which John had passed after his walk earlier in the day, but the aromas which had stung John differed from those that now tickled Ed's nose. Old Betty had finished her soup and had now moved on to roasting a lamb. Scents of garlic and thyme circled around Ed's head as he walked along the path that led to the shed. The path forked, one tine leading to the little wooden shack whilst the other snaked left towards a dozen huge rhododendron bushes. There the path faded to grass, and one was free to wander the flowerbeds.

The gardens were alive with colour. Aster nestled beside crocuses, their purple radiance battling gracefully for supremacy. Shrubs and plants, many of which were unfamiliar to Ed, lay in beds in neat rows with space between for an admirer to walk.

Around all this flora was a natural fence. Judas trees encircled the majority of the gardens, leaving only a few gaps in which to walk in and out. The falling sun with its last rays caught the yellowing leaves of the trees. Ed looked at this effect of the sun and felt himself trapped within a ring of fire made all the more surreal because it lacked the heat of flames.

There he stood and smiled, for he was happy. He closed his eyes and soaked in the sun's feeble rays; he had left the stresses of city life behind him. He had finished a big case and, more importantly, he had won. His career was taking off. He liked London, yet, standing here with a clean breeze caressing his face, he was reminded of the joys of the countryside. Of the solitude. Filling his lungs with pure air and only birdsong polluting his ears. Yes, he was happy. Happy and hungry. Looking at his pocket watch, he saw evening had drawn on and it was time to go back to the house. He got as far as the rhododendron bushes when he heard voices. A woman was speaking. Her voice was low but betrayed emotion. She must have been only a matter of feet away in the thick bushes, yet she couldn't be seen.

Ed carried on slowly, careful not to make any sound. He was mortified at the thought of being seen in case someone thought he was there eavesdropping, but he realised he had a decision to make. If he stopped, whoever was talking might see him and would no doubt take him for a nosey parker. If, however, he carried on he would surely be seen once he had made his way past the shed. He decided he must place the old shack between himself and the mysterious voices. In a few quick steps he was beside the door of the shed and the voices had become more distinct.

"It's no good," said the woman's voice. "It is hopeless"

"Please my dear, don't fret, I hate to see you upset," replied a man, earnestly.

Ed could feel his face redden. Although accidental, the guilt of overhearing such a conversation weighed on him. He wondered if he could slip into the shed where he could neither hear nor be seen. It was quite dark now but there was still enough light left in the evening that he should be seen if exposed. Within a few seconds, he made up his mind: the pantry door of the house opened and an old woman wearing a stained apron came out holding a bucket. Ed, afraid that old Betty would see him half crouching, leaning against a shed as still as a statue would call to him or, being that she wouldn't recognise him, holler that a thief was on the prowl. He decided to take the plunge.

As he unbolted the door, he heard the girl say, "I am trapped. I shall never be free until my father is dead." She said this with such conviction that Ed's mind was so distracted he tripped on a pair of muddy boots as he entered the shed. His left foot stumbled, he reached his arms out to try to cling to something, anything, to stop himself from falling over, and at the same time trying make as little noise as possible, but his panic made the situation worse. He knocked over a walking stick that had been left beside he door and trod on a rake that clattered into two pieces. His arms found the sides of the shed and he managed to save himself from falling over by pushing against them. All was quiet. The stick and rake shaft lay at his feet. The silence was broken by a muffled voice saying, "what was that noise?"

He could not tell through the wooden walls whether the owner of the voice was the man or woman. He held his breath and closed his eyes until his red cheeks became redder.

He pictured the door swinging open or being ripped off its hinges and him being dragged out by his collar to shouts of "*Sneak! Thief!*", but the silence persisted for a few more moments until it was broken by a single solitary sound. A gong.

Under normal circumstances, the note would be barely noticeable to most ears, the noise travelling through stone wall, air, and the thin wooden shed. It was an almost imperceptible din, but to Ed it was a joyful boom. The next words he heard were welcome ones.

"I must go. The dinner gong has sounded. I must go before they realise I am not there."

Ed waited, rooted to the spot. He heard no word of goodbye or farewell. Were they gone then? He dared not open the door just yet. He must wait for a few more minutes.

He bent down to pick up the rake that he had broken. The shaft had a hollow at the top where the head had come out of when he stood on it. He pushed the head back in and though it was loose, he hoped the gardener wouldn't notice any damage.

Next, he picked up the walking stick and set it against the wall beside the door.

He held his breath and counted to ten. He opened the rickety door and scanned around. There was no one to be seen. With a hurried step he went back to the house and cursed for not giving himself enough time to change.

4. BUMPS IN THE NIGHT

You'll see him fall down dying at your feet.
Yes, die he must, and in so short a while

"The Pardoner's Tale"
The Canterbury Tales

The young Lord Taylor checked his tie in the mirror in his grand hallway.

Old Hodgkins had rung up earlier leaving a message that dinner would be at seven p.m. and that his Lordship's old friend had arrived and was currently admiring the house.

A brisk fifteen-minute walk was all that was required to reach Treefall Manor, but the terrain was not suited to evening shoes and chances were one in a million that he would arrive without a splodge of mud on his fine leather. He decided to take the car out, though did so rather begrudgingly as his habit was to walk as much and as far as possible, barring any inclement weather.

Eventually satisfied that his tie was straight he walked through the open front door where he saw his loyal Mr Singh waiting behind the wheel of a new Rolls-Royce.

Good old Singhy. The epitome of stability in the household. Freddie was comforted knowing that at least when

Ruth came to live, the staff would not be strangers to her and would do their utmost to make her feel welcome. Yes, he was blessed in that regard. Of course, if staff were not cutting the mustard, as it were, he was well within his rights to dismiss, but such an avenue seemed cold and not fitting with how he perceived himself. He was much like his father in that way. He remembered, years ago, a girl who worked in the kitchens who... goodness, what was her name?

"Singhy?" he said as the car lurched off the gravel.

"Yes, my Lord?"

"Do you remember that kitchen girl years ago who kept mixing the salt with the sugar when baking the cakes? What was her name?"

"Oh, now you really are testing me Sir, but if memory serves it was Emily, I think. Yes, Emily."

"Excellent Singhy, yes I believe you are right."

"Any particular reason for asking, sir?"

"No, no she just popped into my head is all. I was thinking of when Miss Grimbourne moves to the house, and the arrangements. Nothing to worry about."

"I see sir, very good. Nothing to worry about as you say. We are all very fond of Miss Ruth as you know."

Frederick felt reassured by the old man's sincerity. Yes, he was lucky with the domestic staff. Emily, that was her, a pleasant enough girl, but had a head full of hot air, or nothing between her ears as old Mrs Ferris the cook had said. Salt for sugar, custard for mustard. Freddie's father had tried to turn her into a parlourmaid after a while, until she nearly burnt down the house trying to set a fire in the drawing room. Wasn't there something else? Oh, yes, the old man tried to make her into a dog walker as though that were a job! Poor girl had tremendous allergies though. Terrible rash. Yes, that was the last straw for poor Emily, Lord Taylor gave her over to his cousin Harry after that in Surrey with ten pounds in her pocket. Freddie wondered where she was now.

Still, Freddie did not that I have any of those problems. He had a wonderful staff. Not like at Treefall Manor. That Jayne was just ghastly! And as for Elsie Barter, well, an anteater did less sniffing about than her.

The last of the day's light clung to the horizon as Frederick's car wound its way up the long drive of Treefall Manor. He was greeted at the door by Hodgkins, who took his coat and showed him into a drawing room where George Campbell was waiting beside a crystal decanter of ruby red wine.

"George, how are you?" said Frederick, ringing the other man firmly by the hand.

"Very well, Lord Taylor," replied the secretary who moved closer to Frederick, allowing Hodgkins access to the wine to fill glasses for the men, having somehow managed to stow away Fredericks's coat somewhere.

"I say, you have done a wonderful job preparing for Sunday. I had a sneak peek yesterday in the wedding room, it is quite unrecognisable," said Freddie.

"Oh, I'm afraid I can take little credit, the catering team from Rockingham have been excellent and of course your staff who have helped have been indispensable. I only hope all of the preparations haven't inconvenienced you in any way, sir? I'm afraid they might have been making a bit of a racket moving the tables and chairs and the like."

"Not at all old boy, not at all. It's quite miraculous really, given how quickly everything has had to be put together."

Hodgkins, having filled the glasses and poked the fire left the room.

The two men left behind remained standing and were quiet for a few moments.

"Are you alright George? Your wine will spill onto the carpet if your hand shakes much more."

"Oh Freddie, I can bear it no longer. He is a brute. I am glad poor Ruth is getting away from this house," said George, barely holding himself together.

Frederick put a hand on his shoulder, "Don't fret old chap, he has been working you too hard."

"If only I could come and work with you."

"You know you cannot. Don't torture yourself. I know you cannot leave this place but chin up, everything may turn out alright yet. Nothing lasts forever."

"It can't. It can't be alright; you have no idea. He is the devil who I must serve. I have no choice. My life is in his hands."

"I know sometimes things can seem hopeless, but we all have choices we have to make one way or the other no matter how hard. I think we should…"

The gong sounded. The sentence was left unfinished.

†

The dining room was ensconced in soft light. The candles on the long table were white, the wall mounted candles gave a yellow glow that flickered and danced on the wood-panelled walls.

When John entered, leaning heavily on a cane, three of the seven places set at the long table were occupied though the room was silent.

Alexander Grimbourne sat at the head of the table. George Campbell sat to his master's right, his shoulders slumped. John thought he may be ill such was the paleness of the young man's face.

Opposite George, and to the left of Alexander, sat Freddie who smiled at John as their eyes met. Freddie sat straight in a fine tailored dinner jacket, his fingers twirled a glass of wine throwing red flashes of light around his empty plate. This playful act was at odds with the oppressiveness of the atmosphere that John felt, or were it his own anxieties that weighed the room down?

John had only just pulled out his seat from the table when Ed appeared at the doorway, somewhat breathless. John eyed the slightly crooked necktie which the guest was wearing and correctly assumed that he had got dressed in a hurry.

"Father, this is your guest, Mr Osborn."

Upon hearing these words Freddie, who at that moment had been staring into the red depths of his chalice, raised his head and broke into a restrained smile. He rose and extended his hand to his friend, a courtesy which was not replicated by the master of the house.

"Good evening, Mr Osborn," said Alexander, as both Ed and Freddie seated themselves. "Welcome to Treefall Manor, I trust you were shown to your room and all the amenities you will require?" continued the stone-faced man.

"Yes, thank you. John kindly showed me all I desired," replied Ed, who appraised Alexander with an interested eye.

"Sorry I couldn't run over and see you sooner, I had a few last-minute preparations to take care of. It is very good to see you," said Freddie.

"Oh, that's alright," replied Ed as heartily as the heavy room allowed. "John mentioned in the car that I would see you tonight, are things coming along well?"

It was Alexander who answered, "Yes, it's all coming together marvellously, Campbell here has been a godsend at arranging everything."

The young secretary smiled feebly at this unexpected praise and winced as his master's hand clamped down on his shoulder. He looked up at Alexander, who grinned as he continued, "Yes, we would all of course be lost without George. I know Freddie would love to poach you from me but I'm afraid I'll have to be obstinate on the matter. Perhaps Ruth will find you a suitable secretary to see to your needs, but you can't have mine, Lord Taylor."

Freddie smiled at this ribbing whilst George blushed. Alexander continued to laugh as Ed studied him. Though sitting down, Ed could tell that the owner of Treefall Manor was not a tall man, though he was extremely broad. He had a neck like a bull and Ed could well imagine steam whistling from his nostrils in a fit of rage. His grey hair had dark roots and though greased to the side betrayed no sign of baldness. The man's demeanour was one of single mindedness and sour humour.

"Would you like some wine, Mr Osborn?" asked John almost in a whisper.

"Red please."

Freddie picked a bottle from a selection on the table and passed it to John who poured for George, Ed, and himself.

Alexander still had the ghost of a smile curled on his lip when the dining room door opened, and Ruth entered wearing eveningwear. The dress she was wearing was of a dark, soft fabric that reached her ankles. Her dark hair was tied back in an elegant fashion. She was followed by a young woman of similar age who was just as beautiful as her companion and whose dark red dress clung tightly to her alluring figure.

All the men stood to greet the two ladies, with the exception of Alexander, who remained still, only his eyes moved as they looked from face to face around the room.

"Good evening, ladies," said Freddie, who, now that all the places at the table were filled, made the introductions as he had previously been instructed to by Alexander. Firstly, he introduced the Grimbourne family: George, and the beautiful companion of Ruth to Ed who gave a small gracious bow at the kind words from his esteemed friend.

Ed, for his part was trying to work out which of the two ladies was his friend's betrothed. Certainly, Freddie was going to be a lucky man regardless of who was who as both of the young women were very attractive. The lawyer was not left wondering for long, however. After Ed, Freddie introduced Miss Penelope Dunholme, a friend of Ruth from when they attended boarding school together.

Penelope had long, fiery red hair and emerald eyes. Ed, much to his surprise found himself trembling when their eyes met. Her gaze was confident and playful, the kind that can cut a man in two.

John, miraculously in one piece, stammered a "How do you do?" to Penelope when she smiled at him and exclaimed how lovely it was to see him again.

"How long are you down for, Miss Dunholme?" Freddie said.

"Only for a few days I'm afraid. I must get back to London on Monday to continue doing nothing with my life, which takes up so much time yet is not as boring as it sounds. Francie Kildare asked me to lunch with her in the afternoon. She's horrendously dull but I haven't been to Liberty in an age so how could I say no? Of course, if she had suggested the Ritz, I would have told her I was going to church or to help out at a charity event or whatever but no! She hit my weak spot!"

"My dear, I don't think Francie would believe you if you told her you were going to church. She is not that stupid," said Ruth.

"Yes, she is, she's more than stupid. Besides, if she accused me of lying, I'd slap her in the face then go to see Father Gorman in confessional, say three hail Marys or whatever it is for hitting her and at the same time have made a fool out of her because I'd be in a church. It's a win-win."

The dining room door creaked open, interrupting the vivacious Miss Dunholme, and old Hodgkins slowly pushed through a silver trolley laden with soup dishes. A delicious aroma of garlic and mushrooms filled the room as the old butler served the table.

"Why would you have lunch with this woman if you find her so dreadful?" asked Ed.

"Well, the truth is, Mr Osborn, most people are terribly dreadful, but one can't go to Liberty alone, can they? Have some sense man. Besides, Francie isn't completely without virtues: she does give the most fantastic birthday presents."

"What did she get you last year?" asked Ed, unperturbed at having no sense.

"She took me to lunch in Liberty."

The soup was followed by French style lamb, smothered in a deliciously creamy sauce set on a bed of asparagus.

The conversation was dominated by Penelope, both by her speaking and being spoken to. George didn't listen to anything being said, instead he toyed with his food with his fork, but ate little. He didn't even notice that he was under near constant observation from his master who up until that point had himself paid little heed to the table talk but sat watching his secretary, smiling from time to time.

John listened intently and not without a pang of jealousy to all that passed between the two guests of the manor, for Ed and Penelope had discovered they each frequented the same establishments in the capital and had numerous mutual acquaintances. Indeed, it seemed extraordinary that they themselves had never been introduced to each another in some club in Leicester Square or Shaftsbury Avenue.

"Of course, I don't get out as much as I used to," Ed pronounced.

"Oh? But you're not old. Tied down to some dreadful woman you couldn't bear to bring here?" Penelope said boldly.

"No, married to my work as they say. Things have been rather busy of late, I'm lucky if my day is over by nine o'clock."

"You are a lawyer I believe, Mr Osborn?" interrupted Alexander.

"I am sir, a practice in Holborn; myself and two colleagues. I am pleased to say we have had some success in court of late."

"I know," smiled Alexander. "I saw your picture in the newspaper the other day after the Trevelyan case, a job well done, my boy."

"Thank you, sir."

"In the papers? Gosh, you must be the most famous lawyer in London," teased Penelope. "What was the case about?"

"Oh, it was quite straightforward really, the case got far more publicity than it merited."

"Nonsense," continued Alexander good humouredly. "There is no place for false modesty in this house Mr Osborn. You see, Miss Dunholme, Mr William Trevelyan is a very wealthy man, according to the papers, who murdered his wife."

"I'm surprised I don't know of him," said Penelope.

"Well, that is probably because he is an American

holidaying here," Alexander said, taking the interruption in his stride. "As I was saying my dear, this Mr Trevelyan is very wealthy but apparently not blessed with happy matrimony. He married a much younger woman who loves his dollar bills more than Bill himself, so they say. Anyway, to continue, one day a few months ago the maid opened Mrs Trevelyan's bedroom door one morning and found her dead in bed. Is that right, Mr Osborn?"

"Yes. That is correct."

"Thank you. Anyway, this old Mr Trevelyan was staying with some friends for the night fifty miles away or so and, though the lady was poisoned, Trevelyan argued it must be suicide. He rather cleverly claimed her motive for doing herself in was that he wouldn't grant her a divorce, thereby giving a motive for suicide but not for murder because, you see, my dear, he was under no obligation to divorce. From what the newspapers said they were practically living separate lives and so having her married to him was not causing him any such stress that would drive a man to murder."

"So why did he do it then?" asked Penelope as she caressed the stem of her glass.

"Perhaps, you could tell us Mr Osborn?"

"Well, it was pride," said the barrister. "You see, you are quite right Mr Grimbourne when you say that husband and wife were living apart, and again when you imply that the late Mrs Trevelyan had very little chance of extracting a dime from her husband and breaking free from him. However, William Trevelyan was a self-made millionaire who was ruthless in business."

"A man I can relate to, Mr Osborn."

"Yes, well, as I was saying, he didn't let business rivals or anyone get the better of him, he was a man who got his own way and that was that. So, for a young woman to decide that he was not worth being with, even though he had all that money and power, and for her to try and flee (for she had on several occasions), hurt the man's pride. He worried how he would look in the eyes of his friends as well as his competitors if he were seen to be made a fool of by a young girl he had chosen to marry. So, he decided to kill her, and, if it looked like suicide, it made his power over the poor creature look all the more real."

"But how did he do it if he was so far away?" asked Ruth.

"He put poison in truffle oil."

"Ah," interrupted Alexander. "A cowardly way to kill someone. Look them in the eye and see if you can get away with it."

"How was it that only his wife was killed and no one else?" queried Penelope.

"Only Mrs Trevelyan ate it. You see, Mr Trevelyan set the meal plan for each week on Sunday evenings. He went to visit his friends on the Tuesday afternoon and his wife died on the Thursday. Occasionally, he and his wife would dine together, when he was in the mood, usually just to torment the poor girl. If, however, Mr Trevelyan did not dine with his wife, then she always ate alone, such was her solitary existence."

"How did he then expect to get away with it?" Freddie now asked.

"Because he was counting on the fact that the police would think the poison which, was a slow acting barbiturate, would be in the lady's sleeping powder: perhaps she had taken too much of the stuff by accident. Even if the police did not think this, he never imagined the poison would be traced to the bottle of truffle oil."

"Why not? And how did he get found out?" asked Freddie, intrigued and appalled.

"Because the cook used all the remaining liquid in the truffle oil bottle when cooking dinner. She threw the bottle in the rubbish which was then collected first thing the following morning on the Friday. When the police asked the cook what she had made that evening and what ingredients she used, the cook told them that on the Tuesday morning the oil bottle had been full. The police then deduced that Mr Trevelyan must have emptied the bottle and put in the poison on the Tuesday in the early afternoon before he left for his friends' house. Therefore, knowing that when the cook made stuffed partridge with truffle oil on Thursday as set out in the week's meal plan, she would use all the remaining 'oil' and throw away the empty bottle, thus discarding the evidence."

"You must have had a hard time making that stick in court." It was George this time who joined in the conversation, his shyness conquered by his interest.

"We did to begin with Mr Campbell, you're quite right, although when old Trevelyan saw the cook come into the courtroom, he was white as a ghost. He soon crumbled after that and admitted to it all."

"Speaking of cooks, old Betty has lost none of her skill since I last visited, this meringue is light as a feather," said Penelope.

"Let's hope there is no truffle oil in it," said Ruth beside her.

"Speaking of crime," resumed Ed. "I think I saw a poacher from the guest bedroom window this afternoon. Some scoundrel lurking by the trees."

"It would be a fool who tries to poach on my land, Mr Osborn! Campbell, go and tell Hodgkins to have the coffee ready in the drawing room, this room has become too stuffy," commanded Alexander.

"Yes sir." George rose and tossed his napkin onto his plate. He looked at Freddie who was staring back at him with a stony expression.

"Is there much wedding preparation left to do?" asked Ed of Ruth as George slipped out the door.

"Not too much I don't think. As father said, George has been most helpful in preparing everything. I really have done very little."

"I should say!" teased Penelope, "I only received my invitation a week ago and that was the first I knew of any kind of relationship, never mind an engagement."

"Yes, well, it has all happened rather quickly, I suppose," replied Ruth, her cheeks reddening.

"When the heart wants as the heart wants, as they say,"

laughed Alexander, though Ed, who had been made curious by Penelope's remark, thought the laugh a very cruel one, as though Alexander was mocking his daughter and delighting in the misery which showed on her face. Ed looked at his old friend and their eyes met only for a second before Freddie quickly averted them and stared at his glass instead. There was certainly more to this engagement than love at first sight as old Lord Sampson had supposed, and Ed decided to interrogate Freddie at the first opportunity of being alone with him.

Penelope, sensing that her words had caused much tension yet not understanding why, quickly spat out a question as to what everyone's plans were for the following day and hoped the wedding would not be mentioned until she could have a heart to heart with Ruth.

John, sensing the beautiful redhead's consternation, answered feverishly, "Well, I for one have quite a busy morning. I am to walk to the Granger's cottage and see about getting some more chicken wire. Damned foxes played havoc last week."

"Is Treefall Manor a working farm then?" asked Ed, picking up the thread.

"No, we have very few animals and nothing larger than a useless old billy goat, but behind the house about a quarter of a mile is a little plot where we have some poultry and vegetables and things. We supply the village shop."

"You must keep your groundsman very busy then."

"That position is vacant," said Alexander. Did Ed see him give Ruth a quick look as he said it?

"Well, I must say, I'm looking forward to seeing more of the delightful village and this wonderful estate tomorrow."

"Me too. It's so long since I have visited Swinbridge. Getting away from London and into the country air will be a treat in itself," said Penelope.

"When did you arrive here, Miss Dunholme?"

"Only this afternoon."

"I must have just missed you arriving when I was looking around the house."

"You might have missed me, Mr Osborn, but I saw you."

"Oh?"

"Yes. In the library, though you had your back to me. I *was* curious about you as I didn't recognise you," said Penelope with a glint in her eye.

"Well, *I*," interrupted Alexander, "shall be working in the morning as usual. Then my solicitor Roberts shall be here around midday."

The older man left the latter words to hang heavy in the air. Ed and Penelope looked at each other to see if either could decipher any hidden meaning but each gave the other a blank, if, friendly look. It was Alexander's son who started to ask what all were thinking but only managed to stammer out a few words when his father cut him short and stated, "I'm changing my will."

✝

Ed could smell the delicious dark aroma of the coffee before his hand reached the door handle of the drawing room. The smell of the roasted beans in his nostrils acted like smelling salts, jerking him back to reality from the puzzling thoughts that had been occupying his mind. He was the last to join the rest of the company, as he had made a trip to the bathroom.

The mood from the dining room had now invaded the drawing room. Ed looked at John standing heavily on his good leg. He had foregone coffee and instead had gone straight to the whisky decanter where he still stood. The crystal tumbler shook ever so slightly in his hand and Ed noticed Alexander, who was the only one seated, watching his son.

Why had Alexander announced he was altering his will? How would it affect the family? Surely it was a simple matter of editing it to reflect the fact that Ruth was getting married and therefore needed less entitlement from her father. After all Freddie was a very wealthy man and a husband was to provide for his wife. Yes, that must be it, thought Ed. But why did Alexander feel the need to announce something so routine in that way and with that attitude? And why did Ed have an ominous feeling in the pit of his stomach?

Freddie, seeing his friend enter, gestured Ed over. He had not yet had a chance to speak to him alone and, though this large room wasn't empty, Freddie thought they could speak quite freely without being overheard by the ladies who were by the piano.

"Hello Ed, it really is marvellous to see you here, and quite a surprise too."

"How do you mean surprise? Surely you knew I had been invited to your wedding. And why didn't you tell me you were to be married?"

"Well, as a matter of fact I didn't know for sure you were coming until a few minutes before you walked into the dining room this evening. I gave Mr Grimbourne your club's address for an invite, but I hadn't heard from you. It was a shock to see Penelope too, although perhaps not as much. I'm sorry about not telling you about the wedding myself, it's all happened so fast, the last few weeks have been like a whirlwind really. I did mean to, but you see, with everything else it quite slipped my mind."

"Oh, Freddie, old boy, I'm not offended! Just surprised is all, after all we've been through together, I thought you would have mentioned it at least. But never mind any of that now. Ruth seems very lovely, is she the reason you haven't been down to London in such a long time?"

"Yes, in a way. Things have been very busy here with the estate and all, there is so much work to be done and I am currently without an estate manager to run the place."

"I'm surprised you found the time to fall in love."

"Well," replied Freddie, raising his eyebrows. "Our estates have always been next to each other and although our families have never been on what you would call intimate terms it goes to reason that a connection should be made. Of course, Ruth is rather lovely, as you say, and I have been acquainted with her since she was a girl... I suppose a man starts seeing things differently when he reaches a certain age."

"And her friend, how acquainted are you with her?"

"Penelope? I've met her once before in London. She is an old school friend of Ruth's, but I didn't know that when I met her and although they are in many ways chalk and cheese, they are really very close, I believe."

"How did you come to meet her?"

"Her father sat in the House also, he died very recently. The three of us lunched one afternoon, she told me her friend lived next to my estate."

"She really is a charming girl, tongue like a scimitar."

"Ha, I thought I saw you looking quite lovestruck at dinner."

"Keep your voice down!" hushed Ed.

Beside the piano, a not dissimilar conversation was taking place.

"Good Lord Ruth! Did you really want to get married without me there to throw confetti in your face?"

"No, of course not, but wait, how did you find out?"

"Find out you are getting married or that you didn't want me there?" said Penelope acidly.

"Oh, but it's not that I didn't want you—"

"Well, your father told me," cut in Penelope. "He wrote saying that you were to be married to Lord Taylor and that you would be needing a maid of honour, something I thought you would say to me yourself."

"Oh, I see, he didn't mention... then again why would he? My dear Penelope, of course you were in my thoughts, but it has been such a strange time, really, I haven't been able to think straight. Besides, it will be a frightfully small wedding and probably not much fun."

"Oh darling, how can you say that! It's your wedding, it will be fantastic! How many other guests will there be?" asked Penelope with enthusiasm.

THE MYSTERY OF TREEFALL MANOR

"This is about it, I think. A few of father's old friends arrive tomorrow but not more than three or four, it really is a small wedding."

"But why? Isn't a wedding meant to be something to celebrate and go wild over, with champagne and a live band and… oh! It ought not to be so small and the bride should not be so miserable! You barely said a word at dinner, and I haven't seen you smile since I arrived."

"Oh Penny, but I am so miserable…" The beginning of Ruth's soft sobs and tears were interrupted by Alexander Grimbourne, who, having sat and watched these scenes with quiet satisfaction stood and tapped his cup with a teaspoon.

"Ladies and gentlemen, the night draws on. Tomorrow will be the last day my daughter Ruth holds the name Grimbourne. I'm sure she will be glad to be rid of it. Celebrate in whatever way you see fit. Drink, dance, smoke; all of you enjoy your evening, I shall shortly leave you to it. Thank you, Mr Osborn and Miss Dunholme, for coming, I hope you have been made to feel welcome."

The collective crowd felt as though they had been released from their bonds. As Alexander implied, he would be leaving the little party, but none of them truly felt in the mood to extend festivities and most were at that moment thinking of their beds.

Ed was certainly yearning for rest, for it had been a long day, interesting, and not wholly unenjoyable. Yet as Alexander moved to leave the drawing room, he stopped by the lawyer and asked if he would like to see the wine cellar and the house from outside which he said was beautifully lit up.

Ed politely acquiesced, hoping this tour would not take up too much time. The master and guest left the drawing room which was halfway between the front door of the house and Alexander's study at the rear. They turned left along the corridor, soon reaching the study door, and continued along to the pantry door where John's walking stick sat, the mud at the bottom now dried.

The night was dark and cold. Turning left around the

corner of the great house Ed could just about make out the outline of a small, ancient door. This jerked opened when Alexander gave it a yank and light sprang out from the cavern beneath the house. They descended the stone steps and Ed felt the air become cooler.

The cellar was the same size as the drawing room. The floor was earthy clay whilst the ceiling was grey stone typical of what Ed had seen of the house. The walls were of green glass with sparkling reds and yellows; such were the hundreds of bottles which lined reflected in the electric lights which hung dotted around from the ceiling.

"Do you like wine, Mr Osborn?"

"I am no connoisseur, but I am not wholly ignorant on matters. That was a very pleasant Shiraz we had with dinner, I believe."

"You are quite right. Collecting wine has been a hobby of mine for a long time. Some of the bottles down here go back as far as the French Revolution. This is also the most peaceful part of the house. When I need to get away from my useless son and ungrateful daughter I come here. Don't look so shocked Mr Osborn, my son *is* useless, and my daughter *is* ungrateful so why should I say otherwise?"

"John seems a very capable sort of fellow," replied Ed vaguely.

"Capable? Capable Mr Osborn? John limps around here having been instructed to manage the estate, but he spends his time writing dreary, awful poetry whilst the estate goes to ruin. He has lived here all his life and still has no idea how the place is supposed to be run. You heard him earlier, he's going to get chicken wire tomorrow. Well, I saw the invoice for that chicken wire: he bought twice as much as is needed and paid twice the price he should have. We Grimbournes can trace our lineage to the Middle Ages. My ancestors supplied the wood that was used to build the ships that saw off the Spanish Armada. If you walk into half of the greatest Tudor buildings in this land you will pass beneath beams hewn from the Treefall Estate. Mr Osborn, the Grimbourne heritage is not made of wood as some people think. It is the Grimbourne men themselves, the men who cut the deals, undercut the competition, it is the name Grimbourne itself. Business acumen and ruthlessness is a trait common to all Grimbourne men going back hundreds of years. It is why we are successful; it is why we live in a commoner's palace. My son has none of these attributes. I knew the day he was born when I looked at him and saw that leg, I knew that he would grow and must choose a path. He would have to choose whether to master his leg, embrace it and thrust his chest out telling the world to go to hell or whether he would let the leg define him. He chose the latter."

"I see, and Ruth?"

"I love my daughter and want what is best for her, but like most young people she thinks she knows what is best for her. She doesn't. She knows her own mind and nothing else. I had the best governess when she was little, I sent her to the best boarding school money can buy, she has never had need of anything and yet she thinks I won't know her secrets? Listen to me Mr Osborn, this is my family, my house, hell, it's my village and I know everything."

The two men went back up the steps. Alexander was keen to show his guest the magnificence of Treefall Manor at night when it was illuminated by lights fixed to the walls and pointed from the ground. Ed suspected Alexander to be reiterating his rant in the cellar by showing off the manor. Despite this Ed could not help but be impressed when he looked at the building bathed in light. The manor seemed to have more than three floors, such was the height of each high-ceilinged room. The stone was faded with age and looked like the calloused old skin of the men who built it.

The two men were standing a few feet apart on the stone path that surrounded the house. Alexander was looking at Ed and speaking in a calmer tone than a few minutes before, when something occurred that shattered the still night.

†

Lord Frederick Taylor was the first on the scene. He ran out of the pantry door and looked around wildly, seeking the source of the terrific crash he heard moments before. Ruth, still in evening dress followed a few seconds after her fiancé.

"This stone, or piece of rock," said Alexander, who pointed towards the ground. "It came flying down from the roof or a tower or somewhere. It must have been loose. Good Lord it was close, if it wasn't for Mr Osborn here who pushed me out of the way it would have split my skull in two."

Ruth, who had never seen her father look less composed, remained quiet and looked at the piece of stone which had struck the solid path and bounced onto the grass verge. It had the diameter of a vinyl record and the thickness of a bible. Freddie picked up the rock and felt its great weight in both hands.

"You can see here by the difference in colour where smaller pieces have broken off as it struck the flagstone. I expect we'll find them in the grass tomorrow when it is light. This side here appears lighter in colour too as though this piece has separated recently from a much larger stone. You really are very lucky."

"Luck has nothing to do with it, your friend saved me, Frederick, it's as simple as that."

Freddie saw Ed blushing and looking very serious at the same time. He had seen him perform many daring acts during the war and, on more than one occasion, seen his friend make a split-second decision or instinctive movement that had saved a life. Freddie tossed the rock back to earth with a clatter. Penelope appeared from the pantry door showing none of the haste or concern demonstrated by Ruth or Freddie. She took a nonchalant drag of a cigarette and asked, "Is everything quite alright?"

John eventually caught up with the group, travelling as fast as his cursed leg would allow. Ruth answered his puzzled expression before words could fo in John's throat.

Alexander gave Ed a hearty clap on the back and walked into the house without speaking a word, leaving the others staring after him.

After a few moments of complete silence, Ruth turned and followed her father into the manor, taking Penelope by the hand as she did so. Ed fancied Ruth shot him a venomous look as she turned but wondered if perhaps his imagination was playing tricks on him in the aftermath of the shock he had endured.

"Shall I ring up Mr Singh and ask him to pick you up Freddie or would you like to stay and have a nightcap?" asked John.

"No, don't trouble yourself old boy, it is quite a pleasant night, I shall walk home."

"Are you sure?"

"Yes, I feel I need to walk off that delicious dinner. I'll run over tomorrow to see you both. Goodnight." Freddie rung both men by the hands and walked around the house to the path out of sight.

"I think I'll go to bed too, all this excitement has been quite tiring," said Ed.

"Goodnight, Mr Osborn."

☦

The stillness of the dead night remained. The grand old house slept in darkness. At midnight, John put his fountain pen down next to his empty tumbler and turned off his lamp. Sleep was hard to attain after the evening's events. John's mind was awhirl with thoughts and dreams. What if Ed had stayed his hand? What if? What if?

John woke with a start, his bedside clock faintly showed two o'clock in the darkness. He listened hard for whatever sound had dragged him from his slumber. After a few seconds, he thought he heard a creaking noise. He held his breath and listened harder, becoming more awake with each passing moment.

The noise was indistinct and numbed by the stillness of the night. Someone was awake and walking around on the ground floor beneath John's bedroom, although no sound could alert John to their purpose. Whoever was moving about was being very deliberate in their movements John decided, such was the periodic intervals between each noise.

Strange though he thought it was, John could not imagine any of the activity taking place warranting further investigation and he convinced himself a member of the household was probably fixing themselves a midnight snack. As usual John's withered leg woke a few minutes after his brain, with a slow, familiar throb. John rolled over and tried to go back to sleep.

✝

Ed had been a light sleeper since the war. The anticipation of a shell exploding nearby always kept his sleeping mind alert. The big arm of the little clock next to him stood at attention: it was four o'clock. The face of the timepiece could be seen through the dim moonlight which filtered through the thin curtains. Puzzled, Ed sat up in bed and rested on an elbow. Something had woken him, he was sure, but what? He lay listening in the silence. Yes, it wasn't his imagination, he could hear the creaking of floorboards. Someone was creeping along the corridor below his bedroom and towards the stairs. Curious, he thought, but not being familiar with the nocturnal habits of the household he decided to mind his own business and roll over.

5. ENTER THE DETECTIVES

'What!' said the priest. 'Can that be really so?
Mother of God! I beg you to proceed!'
'At your commandment, sir, I will indeed,'

"The Canon's Yeoman's Tale"
The Canterbury Tales

Elsie Barter hummed a tuneless ditty as she ran her duster over the bookshelves. The library was unoccupied save for the industrious woman and being pleased with her morning's progress, she decided to rest on a leather chesterfield for a few minutes. After all, she had dusted the same shelves the previous day so there wasn't really any need to do them thoroughly again was there?

Besides, Elsie knew she must slow down a bit; she certainly wasn't getting any younger. The stairs seemed steeper and the bookshelves longer every day. Of course, she wouldn't have to exert herself to the point of death if the young maids knew how to do their jobs properly! Their heads full of boys and dreams of marrying some rich Lord no doubt. Back in Elsie's day, hard work was in your bones! She would die of shame if she polished the silver the way young Jayne did last week. Jayne! That girl had developed a lot of airs and graces in the past few weeks. Elsie didn't know what had gotten into her! Answering back, slacking in her work, downright disobedience the like of which Elsie had never seen! No doubt some boy or other were behind it all. Of course, she had been sweet on William Hopkirk, but hadn't he turned her down? A right fool she made of herself over that one!

Surrendering to the inevitable, the redoubtable woman hoisted herself from the chair and proceeded to clean the windowsill. A few quick wipes brought her to a polished ebony table which Elsie detested, as just a speck or two of dust would stand out on the black sheen, potentially leading to her unquestionable work ethic being challenged.

As she dusted, a peculiarity arrested her attention… she was sure that funny looking dagger was there yesterday, how strange. She must remember to tell the master it was not in its cradle.

Elsie then surveyed the room and nodded in satisfaction. She decided it was time to clean the ground floor windows as was her routine.

Going downstairs and out the pantry door she limbered along the side of the house to the three study windows with a rag and bucket in one hand. Alexander Grimbourne was seated behind his great desk, his chin resting on his chest.

Elsie hoped that if he was stuck on a crossword clue, he would solve it before she went in to clean, otherwise she knew he would be in a foul mood.

After a few minutes, Elsie had finished wiping the middle of the three windows leaving the other two for when she was in the study, as the windows were barred, and the outer windows opened inward.

Twenty minutes later Elsie knocked softly on the study door having cleaned the kitchen window and dusted the halls. Receiving no response and thinking perhaps the master of Treefall Manor was still engrossed in his crossword puzzle Elsie rapped louder.

"Mr Grimbourne, sir…?"

Answered only by silence Elsie tried turning the door handle. Maybe her master had left the study a few minutes before? However, she found the door was locked and would not budge. Puzzling over the peculiarity of the situation Elsie decided to go around and look through the study windows. Pushing her inquisitive face close to the window bars it took her eyes a few seconds to adjust to the sight before her. Her mind computed the scene in the study and a screeching wail released itself from the depths of the cleaner's lungs which broke the stillness of the day and froze the blood of those who heard it.

Lying on the study floor was the body of Alexander Grimbourne. From his chest protruded the handle of the missing dagger.

✝

Superintendent Hill looked through the clear glass window of his second-floor office in Scotland Yard at a blue, raw morning. He sat in a high-backed chair, his cigarette slowly burning itself to the filter between his fingers, forgotten amidst a maelstrom of thoughts.

Fifteen minutes earlier, at precisely eleven o'clock he had answered the telephone that sat on his large desk. The switchboard operator had directed a call from the county headquarters of Rockinghamshire.

The voice on the other end of the line had belonged to an Inspector Young who had babbled excitedly before he was reassured that Scotland Yard would send help in solving what he described as a very strange mystery.

Superintendent Hill had promised to send two men to Swinbridge right away and had given the order for the crime scene to be untouched. He knew that not only the notoriety of the deceased but also the curious manner in which the crime had taken place would ensure great publicity. He had to send two officers who would crack the case quickly and cleanly.

Dying wisps of smoke fluttered and danced slowly, thinning towards the ceiling unnoticed by the man still staring out of the window. After a few more minutes of quiet contemplation Hill picked up the telephone receiver, "Get me Graves here at once."

†

Detective Inspector Graves walked slowly into the Superintendent's office. The two men had worked together for nearly forty years but, despite their friendship, Graves observed the formality of rank even when the two were alone.

"Good morning, sir. I didn't expect to see you today."

"Likewise, Graves, I drew the short straw to be senior officer this weekend. What's your excuse? You must have been in the station and not at home to get here as quickly as you have. I only rang for you ten minutes ago."

"Yes sir, catching up on some paperwork: the Higgins robbery from a few weeks ago."

"Ah yes. Well, I've got another one for you, what the press call 'high profile'.
A wealthy businessman and landowner knifed in Rockinghamshire. I'm told the body is untouched and no one has entered the room since the crime took place by all accounts. In fact, it's locked from the inside. This could be a special case Graves and, as such, will need to be handled delicately. That's why I have chosen you, I know I can rely on you."

"Yes sir."

"You can catch the one thirty train from Kings Cross, that should get you into Swinbridge for three o'clock to meet Inspector Young."

"Very good sir."

"There is one other thing Graves. You've needed a new

Detective Constable beside you since Burridge transferred out. I've got one for you. Clever, but a bit green. Needs someone to show him the ropes before he can pick up any bad habits."

"Name sir?"

"James Carver. Young, but was just old enough to serve for half of the war. He's come from off the beat in Cambridge. Felt he needed more of a challenge and the seniors up there agreed with him. He comes highly regarded. This looks to be a meaty sort of case to get his teeth stuck in to. I've got McKinley chasing him up now, he was meant to start with us on Monday and then be assigned to an Inspector but as this has come up it seems hand and glove. Providing Constable McKinley can find him at the address he gave us then Carver will meet you at Kings Cross."

"Very good sir."

"I believe there is an inn in the village, I'll get someone to ring up and get you a room."

"Book them all sir: don't give the press the chance to stay there in case the news does get out."

†

Inspector Graves left the Superintendent's office in precisely the same mood as when he entered. The call had been unscheduled but not unexpected. After nearly forty years as a policeman in one of the most bustling cities in the world, Graves had learnt never to be surprised by anything.

A trip to the countryside for a few days to solve a murder wasn't anything to get upset about. In fact, Graves was quite looking forward to getting some fresh air and to not hear the mechanical rumblings of motor cars which had invaded the city over the last ten years.

He walked down the familiar hallways of the police station, the walls were adorned with photographs and sketches of respected colleagues and cases.

The station was quiet that day, a few bobbies milled about the place fully at one with the relaxed atmosphere of the chilly autumnal morning. The muffled clicking of typewriters could be heard occasionally behind closed doors. Graves walked down a flight of stairs and along to his office, which he shared with two other inspectors. The room was empty as it had been all morning; Graves liked to complete his paperwork alone as he could work quicker with fewer distractions.

Without sitting down, he picked up the telephone receiver and put a call through to his wife, asking her to pack a bag for him with enough clothes for three days. He briefly explained to Mrs Graves about the business in Swinbridge and she received the news much like her husband had, not so much as a shrug of the shoulders.

Rita Graves had been married for thirty-five years and was the archetypal policeman's wife. Devoted, unassuming, and used to eating alone.

Inspector Graves straightened his tie in the mirror and took his hat from the stand beside the wastepaper bin. A few minutes later he was walking along Victoria Embankment.

The sky was empty save for lone pigeons seeking an easy snack. The cold air reverberated with the sound of engines and shouting. Graves walked along cobbled streets dodging children and their skipping ropes, thinking to himself how sweet their laughter sounded compared to the other city noises.

The detective walked for twenty minutes through the old centre of the city, crossing the ancient life-giving river at Waterloo Bridge. For a further five minutes he meandered through the throngs of people, never changing his pace until he reached a small, terraced house on Aquinas Street.

Mrs Graves opened the door before her husband reached it, having been alerted to his arrival by a bark from the little terrier who heard her master's familiar shoes on the cobbles.

After three and a half decades of marriage all that needed to be said was communicated through a smile and a kiss on the cheek and then the detective was off, case in hand and dog at heel, on his way to Kings Cross.

The clock tower above the main concourse of the train station showed the time to be one fifteen when the burly man with a straight back and border terrier beside him walked beneath it.

Graves had an image of James Carver in his mind based solely on the Superintendent's description of his non-physical attributes. The boss had alluded to this young man as being someone who had outgrown their current position. Of course, every policeman must cut their teeth on the beat, but Cambridge had plenty of detectives, why hadn't this Carver filled one of these positions? Why had he come all the way to London? Either, Graves decided, there were no detective positions available in Cambridge, in which case Carver couldn't be that promising, or a position would be made available as Graves knew from experience. *Or* this young chap was the real deal and his seniors at Cambridge had unselfishly let the bird fly the nest for his own good. Either way, he was young, probably tall, as Graves had noticed taller people seem to get on quicker in life, and thin, because most beat Bobbies are. He would undoubtedly be clean shaven around the cheeks and probably have a small, timid moustache.

Graves wondered if perhaps he was becoming more cynical in his advancing years, as though these young detective types could be mass produced all the same and picked out of a catalogue. Maybe, he thought, he was being too hard on the younger generation, after all he hadn't even met the chap yet and he was already stereotyping him. However, Graves was soon to discover the accuracy of his presumptions.

After stopping to buy a strong cup of tea, he made his way to platform five. The long runway was sparsely populated: a woman with a long shabby coat held one hand on a perambulator whilst using the other to wave a finger at a little boy in a worker's cap who had been crying loudly. An elderly couple who had known hard times and knew there were more to come stood midway along in silence, each preoccupied with their own thoughts.

Farthest along, standing closer to the train carriage than advised was a tall man in his late twenties.

The train conductor signalled that boarding could commence as Graves walked past him and the woman with children and the old couple gathered their things ready to depart. The young man did not move. He stood staring at his shoes, assessing the shine like a sergeant-major on a parade ground. Only when Graves was a few feet away did the young detective look up, and Graves could see that his imaginary vision of Carver was accurate.

Tall and slim, he had a handsome face and a closely cropped moustache. Intelligence shone behind young man's blue eyes which were kind and friendly.

"Detective Constable Carver, I presume?"

"Yes sir, you must be Inspector Graves. Pleased to meet you."

The two men shook hands and Graves made a point of breaking eye contact to look the man up and down from head to toe just so Carver could see him do it.

More flustered than a few seconds ago, Carver dropped to his knees and patted the dog who until that point had been craning her neck looking at what she perceived was going to be a new friend.

"This is Peggy," said Graves, answering the question that wasn't asked.

"She's a beauty," said Carver, as he scratched the border terrier behind her velvety ears.

"She is. Now, let's get on the train before it leaves us behind."

Both men were seated opposite one another in a wooden second-class compartment when the train dragged itself off.

The carriage was stuffy despite it being practically empty. Graves loosened his tie as Peggy sat panting on his lap, tired from her exertions across London. She looked at Carver with the expectancy typical of her species, that at any moment her head would be getting patted, or her wispy belly rubbed. Carver obliged the canine lady readily. He adored dogs and told both Graves and Peggy this. As the young man recounted his childhood dog stories, Graves wondered if he was talking through blind nervousness and what conversation Carver would have started if Peggy had not been brought along.

As he listened to the young man, he thought he certainly seemed amicable, which Graves liked, and Peggy had taken a shine to him which Mrs Graves would say is the real test of a man in her husband's book.

Yes, Graves thought, hopes are quite high with this one.

"So, this case sir," said Carver, getting down to business. "What is it all about?"

Graves recounted what Superintendent Hill had told him which, by his own admission, were scant details.

"We should find out a lot more when we get to the station. Inspector Young of the Rockinghamshire constabulary will meet us there. I believe he is at the manor house now. Tell me Carver, have you worked on a murder case before?"

"No sir. I once found a man dead beneath a streetlamp, but it was the cold that got him sir, too much liquor, passed out in the dead of winter. Poor beggar didn't stand a chance. Though as I say, sir, no foul play."

"Well, this could be a good one to start with. The victim is quite renowned by all accounts, sounds like the type of man to have more enemies than friends. Chances are it won't be an open and shut case, lad, so do yourself a favour and stick close by me, just follow my lead."

"Yes sir. How long have you been a detective, sir?"

"Too bloody long. Well, sometimes it feels that way, other times… well, it's in my bones you see."

Peggy looked at her master whenever he spoke, her head inquisitively tilted to one side. Graves continued his theme of police work and villainy in a matter-of-fact way, as though it were all incidental.

The train chugged on, past rolling hills and hamlets.

London, with its soot-stained heart was left behind and the only grey to be seen was the ancient stone walls which separate farmland.

The train stopped at remote little stations, where very few passengers alighted and even fewer got on. Carver thought that the great locomotive shattering the peaceful silence of these out of the way places must be the only noise to be heard for hours on end.
Graves checked his watch; they would shortly be drawing into Swinbridge.

Peggy, sensing their imminent arrival, hopped upon the carriage floor and stretched her little body for as long as she could before giving herself a shake. Graves, case in hand, was the first off the train.

The station of Swinbridge was the same as a hundred others scattered up and down the country: paint flaked on the wooden walls of the ticket office and waiting room. A kiosk serving tea and newspapers stood like a beach hut beside a large clock, which showed five past three when Graves passed it. He looked around the platform for Inspector Young and caught sight of a tall, awkward looking man next to the exit who was shuffling his feet either through nerves or holding in a call of nature.

"Good afternoon, you must be Inspector Young?" said Graves, holding out his hand.

"Inspector Graves, I am very happy you have arrived, it's quite a situation we've got on our hands."

"So, I believe. This is Detective Constable Carver."

"Pleased to meet you. I believe you're staying at the local pub. It's probably best to drop your belongings off before we go to the manor, the pub is on the way. I suppose this is your first time to Swinbridge? I thought so, we're a bit out of the way and not much of note tends to happen here in Rockinghamshire. This death will cause a great shock in the community, already word has got out."

"Yes, well, there are usually no secrets in rural areas."

"Quite. Especially with Elsie Barter around."

"Elsie Barter?" asked Carver who had plucked up the courage to speak as they strode toward a parked police car.

"One of the Grimbournes' cleaners and village gossip. It was her who found the body this morning. In a right state she was when I got there. She claims she was doing her rounds and went to Mr Grimbourne's study as she does the same time every morning. The door was locked, which is uncommon. Usually, she gives a knock and Grimbourne calls her in to do her dusting and what have you. Well, anyway, today she got no answer to her knocks and, becoming concerned, she went out through the back door and around to the window. There she saw Grimbourne lying with a knife sticking out of him and she screams blue murder so loud I'm surprised you didn't hear her in London."

Graves climbed into the front seat and Peggy leapt onto his lap.

"Tell me, who does the household consist of?"

"I'm not a Swinbridge man myself, I come from Rockingham, but the family is quite renowned in the county. Alexander Grimbourne is the patriarch, he has been a widower for some years, over twenty I should think. His wife died in a fire along with a family here in the village, it was a terrible tragedy. She left behind Alexander and their two children: John and Ruth. John is the elder by a couple of years, a pleasant chap, the apple fell miles from the tree, shall we say. Anyway, like I said, a nice fellow who doesn't seem too upset about his father's demise. He reckons he looks after the estate in some capacity or another, but from what the house staff tell me Alexander held the reins quite tight."

"How big is the estate?" interrupted Graves.

"A couple of hundred acres I would say."

"A substantial amount to inherit," said Carver who drew a glance over the shoulder from his superior.

"Oh yes indeed. A very large estate is Treefall. It's not open to the public, much to the chagrin of the local ramblers society. It was widely known Mr Grimbourne didn't want any outsiders on his land."

"You mentioned Ruth…" said Graves.

"Ah yes I digress, I do apologise, terrible habit."

"That's quite alright."

"Ruth, yes, as I was saying, a delightful girl by all accounts, seems very popular with the staff. The poor thing is meant to be married tomorrow. I can't imagine that going ahead now."

"Perhaps the celebration will be even bigger now," said Graves sardonically.

"Perhaps. The poor girl seemed in shock when I questioned her earlier. This is the pub here, the Blue Boar Inn." The three men had pulled up outside a thatched roofed building. A weathered sign hung above the door showing a faded blue coloured boar in a forest, it swayed slowly in the gentle breeze, creaking like a rubbed violin chord.

"Let us not go in yet, I'd like to hear about the rest of the household first. Who is Ruth to marry?" asked Graves.

"Lord Taylor, who lives on the adjoining estate. A good match I'd say, he's a charming man who I've met few times, sponsors the policeman's ball and that kind of thing."

"A good match from Grimbourne's point of view?"

"I would imagine so. Alexander Grimbourne was to some degree a self-made man, he inherited Treefall Estate but no title. The Grimbourne family are not noble in the true sense, their wealth has grown over the centuries, but the nature of their business has changed with the times. The old family wealth can be attributed to supplying wood for shipbuilding and the like but there is no demand for such things now. Alexander is a businessman, he owns, or owned I should now say, stocks and shares in various companies. He did very well I believe."

"Is there anyone else in the house?"

"There is an old cook who has been there years who lives in the village and a few cleaning girls who seem to take their orders from Mrs Barter. Only Hodgkins the butler, Jayne Brown, who is a maid, and Mr Campbell live in."

"Campbell? Who is he?"

"He is Mr Grimbourne's private secretary. He was quite distressed earlier, maybe he's worried that he will now be out of job."

"Carver, leave the cases in the inn quickly, we need to get to the manor as soon as possible."

"Yes sir, I'll only be a jiffy."

"There are two other houseguests staying who arrived yesterday. A Mr Osborn and a Miss Dunholme," added Young.

"Did they arrive together?"

"No. Separately I believe. They are both here for the wedding. Mr Osborn is some hotshot London barrister or other and Miss Dunholme is one of these socialites who spend an awful lot of money without too much thought about where it comes from."

True to his word Carver returned in a few minutes. Barely had the young man settled into his seat before Graves was instructing his cousin in rank to ease off the clutch and proceed to Treefall Manor.

Carver, plucked from his temporary bedsit in a new and exciting city just a few hours earlier was now about to embark upon the scene of his first murder case, one that he would never forget for the rest of his rather eventful life.

6. MURDER OR SUICIDE?

And lo, the knight was smitten:
A hand appeared and struck him to the bone

"The Man of Law's Tale"
The Canterbury Tales

The three men passed through wrought iron gates and snaked up the winding driveway at a speed not seen before on the ancient estate.

Inspector Young had left his deputy in charge at the manor, who was anxiously awaiting the return of his superior. Feeling enormously out of his depth having never had to contend with a violent death before, Constable Brent had shepherded the occupants of the house into the drawing room and waited as the minutes ticked by. After what seemed an eternity, the policeman heard the roar of an engine and knew he was delivered, like Noah at the sight of the dove. He straightened his tie and made bounding strides for the front door.

Graves left Peggy asleep on the passenger seat and marched up to Brent.

"Where are the family, Constable?"

"The family and the guests are in there, sir," nodded Brent at the room to his left. "I thought you may wish to see the staff separately, sir."

"Very Good."

"Do you want to interview them first or see the, well, you know...?" asked Young.

"No. Leave them where they are for now, we need to examine the body. I am going around to watch through the window, Young, please have your men force open the door."

The men of the Rockinghamshire constabulary had not wasted time preparing for this moment. Brent and another constable went to seize a battering ram which had been left in the driveway.

Graves stopped for a moment and made a routine inspection of the locked study door. The three detectives then followed the corridor around to the pantry and out through the back door.

As they walked towards the study window, Carver had to quickly lift his leg to avoid tripping on a large piece of stone which lay on the perimeter path.

The rear of the house was not as beautiful as the front, Carver thought as he looked around. The corridor that they had just traversed was lacking in windows for its length, just a couple of small ones to let in light. The largest windows Carver could see on the ground floor were that of the study which they were now approaching. The windowsill was level with Carver's belt; there were no plant pots or anything nearby which an intruder could use as a step. Even if someone could leap up, they still wouldn't be able to enter the room, the young detective decided. There were three windows: the middle one was fixed and the other two opened inwards. In front of all three were thin metal bars which stood an inch from touching the glass. Carver estimated the gap between each bar to be eight inches, hardly enough for a person to climb through, he thought to himself.

Looking further ahead now, Carver saw what Graves was looking at. In the middle of the room, twelve feet from the window lay the body of Alexander Grimbourne.

None of the men spoke, each processed the vision in their

own way, each was as still as the corpse upon which their gaze was fixed.

Graves, being the most experienced of the three, began looking at the area surrounding the body. The room was quite dark; little afternoon light penetrated through the barred window. A lamp in the corner by the desk splayed soft light around the room which was not luminous enough to enhance the crime scene.

The stillness was broken by a deep thud that shook the glass panes and made Inspector Young jump. Another thud followed a few seconds later followed by a crash as the third swing of the battering ram had the intended effect. The great door slammed against the wall and small splinters of wood exploded outwards like shrapnel onto the plush carpet.

Graves put his great fist between two of the bars and rapped urgently as a warning to the policemen not to enter the room. He then spun on his heels and retraced his steps along the perimeter with what Carver thought to be surprising speed. Determined not to be left behind the young detective chased after the older man and drew level at the pantry door.

"You only get to make one first impression, Carver, it's true of life and it's true of a crime scene too," said Graves as they neared the study. "Take your time, take it all in."

"Yes sir," replied Carver with a mixture and excitement and nervousness.

Brent and his colleague stood aside to let Graves and Carver through the doorway. Inspector Young stayed with his two officers giving the men from the Yard free rein over the crime scene.

Graves approached the body of Alexander slowly, carefully checking the carpet in front of his feet for anything he may consider evidence. Carver followed close behind, like a fawn to his mother.

Young watched as Graves circled the body, his leather shoes kissing the deep carpet with his little half steps. He saw the detective stand straight with head bent downwards and his hands thrust deep in his overcoat pockets.

"Tell me Carver, what do you see?" asked Graves. Carver, deep in thought took a minute to reply. He didn't want to rush his answer, he wanted to give a true interpretation of his thoughts.

"A well-built man in his sixties. Strong. No obvious signs of ill-health…"

"Besides the dagger sticking out of him."

"Yes… nicely cut suit, expensive watch, so… not a robbery. The dagger, as you mention, has a very intricately carved handle. Foreign made I should say, the hilt is bejewelled. There is blood on the left hand but not the right… ah, what's this…?" Carver dropped to his haunches next to Grimbourne's right arm. "A book clutched in his hand, sir. I can't see the title. He appears to have expired gripping it quite tight."

"Inspector Young, please be so kind as to write down all that Detective Constable Carver is saying," said Graves with authority. "Continue Carver."

"Perhaps we should wait until the doctor has examined the body before attempting to prise the book from the hand sir?"

"No, we'll get it in a minute. Continue."

"There is blood around the wound as would be expected, sir, but little anywhere else on the clothes, although the carpet beneath is sodden with it. I should say that the dagger has plugged the wound, stopping a great flow outward from point of insertion."

"From here it looks like the blood around the dagger has not run downwards much, if at all," said Young from the doorway.

"No, that's right," replied Carver, knitting his eyebrows in thought. "He must have hit the floor within a matter of seconds of the knife entering the body. Judging from the angle it would not surprise me if the dagger has struck the heart square on. The doctor will confirm, but I would guess death to be practically instantaneous. There is a coin beside his pocket where it has fallen out as he has hit the floor."

Graves watched his new man with an appraising eye. Inspector Young, emboldened by the excitement of the scene tiptoed unconsciously into the study.

None of the three men made a comment about the dead man's face but each had studied it intensely. The dead countenance spoke more of the man than the crime. The wide-open eyes were bulging with hate. The face was contorted, as if Alexander Grimbourne was letting out a silent scream of rage, audible only to the demons of the underworld.

"I think we can safely rule out suicide," murmured Graves.

"I agree it is not suicide, but we need some sort of proof. After all, the door was locked as well as the window," countered Young.

"When people kill themselves, they do it when they feel irretrievably lost or broken. This man had a fire in him, a burning anger. We can see it still. Men like that don't kill themselves."

"I'm not disagreeing with you, Graves, but a judge will not rule based on psychology, but on cold, hard facts."

"Very well Inspector," said Carver. "How about this, look at the man's desk. There, you see his pen is placed on the right-hand side of the desk. The same goes for his coffee cup and coaster. Therefore, I think it is safe to assume (and the family can corroborate) that the victim was right-handed. Yet, the victim's right hand is clutching a book meaning he would have to use his left hand to stab himself, a very unnatural thing to do."

"He could have stuck the knife in then taken the book from the bookcase..." protested Young, his words sounding feeble even to his own ears.

"Why would he? Besides, we have agreed that he must have died very quickly. Would he have time to do such a thing?"

"Hmm, no doubt you are correct, but people have been known to do and say unusual things in their dying moments," replied Young as he stared at the red patch around the blade.

"Indeed," agreed Graves. "People do *say* things with their last breath but in this old, solid room, who could hear? If you were attacked and knew you had little time left, what would you do?"

"Shout the name of my killer. Expose the man somehow," answered Carver.

"Exactly, but if you have the shock of a dagger being thrust into your chest the breath will go out of you quicker than your life. No, in that case you would have to find another way to reveal the name of your killer." Graves bent down and lifted the dead man's right arm. The book remained in the stiff grip of the corpse, wedged between the fingers and palm. Graves pulled on the cold, thick fingers with what Carver thought to be disrespectful force, prising the book free.

Graves stood up and straightened himself. Six eyes peered down in unity at the red hardback in the detective's hands.

"*The Canterbury Tales*," murmured Carver.

Graves exhaled a noise which sounded like "Hmmm."

"I wonder what it means?" uttered Young, speaking his thoughts aloud.

"If it means anything we will find out," said Graves, who was staring at the bookcase which the body was adjacent to. He could see a gap where a book was missing, and he pushed *The Canterbury Tales* into it where it fitted quite nicely. The experienced detective took a few minutes to look at the surrounding books. *The Decameron, The Divine Comedy, The Prince* all sat on the same shelf, books which Graves was familiar with. His fingertips softly grazed the spines of the volumes like a man caressing a lover.

Reading was a pastime for Graves. An escape from the brutality and rigour of his occupation, a way to forget through morphing to a different world. Acutely aware that his taste in literature did not align with his social standing or upbringing in the dirt of Victorian London, his reading was like a naughty secret which he enjoyed in his garden shed or by the coal fire. As a child he had strained his eyes by candlelight reading Dickens, the godfather of the working classes. His love of reading had blossomed as his teenage years passed into adulthood.

The world had changed and grown alongside him, sometimes against him.

When he was a youth, the world was so small it was four to a bed and hard work was measured in callouses, yet the years rolled on and the war had come. Motor cars became common, and horsepower had replaced horse power. These sad thoughts flooded the mind of the old detective and instinctively, almost without thinking, he looked on the bookcase for a copy of *David Copperfield,* but no Dickens was to be seen.

"I think perhaps we should let the doctor in now, the body has lain here for quite some time already," said Young, interrupting the thoughts of Graves.

"Fine. Let him in, we can look at the rest of the room before interviewing the family."

Carver looked around. The bookcase which he noticed had transfixed Graves took up nearly the entire wall, the splintered door filling the remaining space. The bottom shelf was filled with box files which one would expect to see in an accountant's office. The desk sat at the rear wall, right-angled to the bookcase and facing the barred window. The wall opposite the bookcase held a small fireplace and a mirror above, flanked by two large pictures depicting naval battles.

"Kiss me, Hardy."

"Beg your pardon sir?"

"Trafalgar. Nelson's last words," replied Graves, pointing to the picture left of the mirror. "You can see there where the artist has painted H.M.S Victory on the flagship."

"Quite right, sir."

"Look here, gentlemen," said Young who was standing midway between the body and the window. Graves and Carver turned to see the Inspector point at a white rectangle on the red carpet. Graves had seen it when he entered the room but had mastered his patience, knowing it would be examined in due course.

Young waited in vain for instruction from Graves to pick it up as Carver jumped the few short steps from his position and seized upon the paper like a ravenous animal. He unfolded the creased paper slowly, wary of ripping it.

"What is it?" asked Young.

"It's a piece of blotting paper by the looks of it. It is torn at the top where it has been ripped from a pad."

"Any writing on it?" asked Graves.

"No, it's blank. Oh… hang on, there are indentations on it. It appears to be from a letter, it must have been written on the previous page and the pressure from the pen has left traces of the text on this."

"Can you make any sense of it?"

"No, we will need stronger light and the paper has been folded quite a few times, so the creases interfere and blur with the writing. There are very small black specks on one side in two places but nothing else unusual."

"Very good. Put it in your pocket and say nothing about it when we question the household."

"Yes sir."

"Now, let us look at the window."

The three men walked the few steps, checking the carpet all the while for signs of blood or anything else unusual but found nothing.

Graves stood deep in thought with his hands still in his pockets.

The window had thin metal bars on the outside. The two windows either side of the fixed middle one were closed. Carver, who was thinking the same as Graves put his fingers between the glass of the middle window and the frame of the outers and pulled.

"They're closed sir."

"Open them."

Carver turned the handle and pulled. The window opened like a door. The handle on the inside did not move in unison with the one on the other side of the glass. Carver tugged on the outer handle when he had fully pulled the window into the room, but it did not budge.

"This handle has been painted over sir. It is not connected mechanically to the handle on the inside. I would bet the outer handle has not turned in many a year judging by the condition of the paint."

"So only the inner handle turns and opens?"

"Yes sir."

"What about the locking mechanism?"

"Typical spring-loaded latch, quite common nowadays, with the outer handle only for show it means the window could be pulled shut and the latch will snap shut and lock in place. No need for keys." The quiet, forensic examination was interrupted by a shriek of anger and bustle from the hallway. Constable Brent was attempting to restrain Miss Penelope Dunholme and was failing terribly.

"What are you doing? Move this instant or I'll have you stamping passports in some flea-bitten, backwater border town in Mesopotamia, you swine."

"Ahem, what is the problem, Miss?" asked Graves.

"The problem? You cannot be serious! We've been cooped up in the drawing room all day waiting to be questioned by some bigshot London detective and we've run dry of whisky and soda. There's your problem. And who the devil are you anyway?"

"I *am* said bigshot, madam," replied Graves curtly.

"Well, did you drop your manners in the Thames on the way here? Why have you not got on with interviewing us yet?"

Graves did not answer immediately, he was pondering why the lady had not so much as glanced at the corpse which lay a yard from her feet.

"Let me see, you must be Miss Dunholme?"

"Am I supposed to be impressed? Fifty-fifty chance."

"Go back to the drawing room, Miss. We shall be in to interview you all soon. We need to examine the crime scene first." Graves nodded towards the stiff form of Alexander Grimbourne but still Penelope did not break her gaze from the detective.

"Are the local police buffoons? Why have we had to wait all

day for you?"

"Go!" Graves pointed at the door; his patience finally worn thin.

Penelope let out a kind of "Harumph," and spun around on her heels, her red hair swishing like a flaming sword.

"What a woman," said Carver breathlessly when she was gone. Graves looked at his new man with raised eyebrows but did not reply.

Only the desk had yet to be examined. It was constructed of mahogany and was half the width of the room. Its surface gleamed. An electric lamp stood in the left corner, casting its light onto a typewriter in the centre and an iron key, which Carver took to the smashed door. He inserted the key in the lock where it fitted quite snugly, however the damage caused by the battering ram prevented him from turning it.

Graves rifled through the drawers without shame.

"Found anything interesting, sir?"

"Hard to say. There are some photographs of a woman beneath a fortnight-old copy of *The Times*. Is this Mrs Grimbourne do you know, Young?" asked Graves, holding up a picture of a smiling woman sitting on a beach. The Inspector nodded but said nothing.

"There's also an empty envelope, a few pens, an inkpot." Graves strained his eyes again on the photograph before continuing, "A few coins, some stamps, spare paper for the typewriter, a pair of spectacles, a thimble and a box of matches. Hmmph."

"Sir?"

"Nothing. As much as I do not want to look like I am placating Miss Dunholme, it is time we questioned the members of the household, but… something…" Graves shook his head and walked to the wall opposite to the bookcase. "Something isn't right," he continued.

Graves looked around the study. The crime scene was like any other: a room filled with blood and dead hate. Yet, something minute, a thing imperceptible confronted the detective. He felt a niggling feeling tugging at his sleeve, a force he called experience. He knew that trickery lay before his eyes. Before him was something wrong, something subtle, like warm gazpacho. "Aha! Very clever. Brent! Please ask the doctor to come here and examine the body, I've seen all I need to see," said Graves smiling, as he turned back to face the windows.

Once Constable Brent had left, Graves turned to Young. "Is there a room in which we can question the suspects individually?"

"Suspects? Well, err… yes, the dining room may be suitable, I don't believe it has been set since last night's festivities."

"Excellent. I will go to the drawing room and introduce myself to everyone then interview them one by one."

†

Entering the drawing room, anyone would have thought they were going into an empty room, such was the silence within. Instead, seven people occupied various seats and spaces, each with their own thoughts. Conversation had been spent throughout the course of the afternoon and a darkness hovered in the air.

Graves was followed in by Carver. Before entering, he had kindly asked Inspector Young to take his two constables and make a search of the grounds before the light faded into dusk.

"Ladies and gentlemen," started Graves, drawing the attention of the room. "This is Detective Constable Carver, and I am Detective Inspector Graves from Scotland Yard. You all know why we are here so I will cut to the chase. This morning someone attacked Mr Alexander Grimbourne in his study, killing him. I will need to interview each of you to establish the facts surrounding the events of today…"

"Excuse me Inspector, but I believe Mr Grimbourne was found in a locked room, how could he have been murdered?

Surely some terrible accident is more likely?"

"Excuse me, you are?"

"Roberts. Aldous Roberts. I am Mr Grimbourne's solicitor."

Graves saw a thin, bald man with a drooping moustache like a walrus. "Well Mr Roberts, the reasoning behind our deductions shall become clearer in due course, but, for the minute, let it suffice for us to say that Mr Grimbourne *was* murdered. We shall conduct our interviews in the dining room. Rest assured; we shall not keep you any longer than is necessary."

"I should hope not!" chimed in Penelope.

"I apologise on behalf of the Rockinghamshire constabulary, murders are not commonplace here, I believe. They may have been somewhat draconian in their bundling you all together in this room for much of the day, but I assure you that any more complaints about it will fall on deaf ears. Oh, Miss Dunholme? We shall interview you last. Please make yourself comfortable." Penelope's face matched the colour of her hair but to the surprise of Graves and those who knew her she kept silent.

"Mr John Grimbourne?" continued Graves, scanning the room until his eyes rested on a disfigured leg seated on a Chesterfield. "Would you be so kind as to proceed to the dining room?"

Graves followed John, as he didn't know where the dining room was. He watched him limp along, leaning heavily on his stick and wondered if this man was now master of Treefall Manor. He hoped Roberts had brought a copy of the will.

7. DISCUSSIONS IN THE DINING ROOM

Yet all the time they had not left the house
While being shown these sights so marvellous,
But sat within his study where there lay
His books about them; there were none but they.

"The Franklin's Tale"
The Canterbury Tales

The dining room had been cleared that morning by Jayne Brown; no trace of the previous evening's festivities remained. Graves gestured to where he wanted John to sit. Carver, who had been quiet but watchful since his comment about Penelope had escaped him, sat next to Graves opposite to their first interviewee.

"Mr Grimbourne…"

"Please, call me John. My father was the only Mr Grimbourne in this house."

"I'm sorry for your loss…" continued Graves.

"I'm not. I won't lie Inspector; I despised my father, and his death is not unwelcome. You think me heartless? You think I murdered my father?"

"I don't think anything. I watch and I listen, ideas form of their own accord and sometimes disappear in a puff of smoke in my head, but truth is like air: it is all around us. When it is pushed down like a balloon in a pool of water it fights to rise to the surface."

"I didn't kill my father."

"Tell me then, who did?"

"I don't know."

"But you suspect. You see, grief takes many forms and affects different people in different ways. My job as a detective is made harder by this fact, so instead of ascertaining how grief is affecting an individual person – which is fruitless and inaccurate – it is much better to simply recognise what is grief and what is not. Now let us take you for instance, John. You are ill at ease, perhaps in shock, but grieving? No. I don't think so. As you say, you hated your father. So, I ask myself, what is the cause of your visible strain? Is it guilt? Is your leg causing you pain? Maybe you are simply uncomfortable being interviewed by the police like this? It is, after all, an unusual and unpleasant experience. Or do you suspect someone of the crime and are worried that you will accidentally give them away? Someone close to you?"

Carver watched as sweat formed at the man's hairline. His hands shook and when the young detective looked at them John put them under the table.

He's hit a nerve, thought Carver.

"My damned leg has nothing to do with anything! Like anyone I am a man of a hundred virtues and fallibilities, and yet the first thing anyone ever notices is this useless leg! It does not define who I am!"

"You have a temper, John," said Graves.

"Everyone has a temper, it's what humanity has in common."

"Tell me, did your father have any enemies that you know of?"

"In truth, yes and no."

"Meaning?"

"What I mean is, he was reviled by most of those who knew him, including his own family, but he kept most of his business ventures to himself so if he had enemies in that sphere,

I couldn't name them."

"I see..."

"Of course, there was the odd business last night..."

"What business would that be?" asked Graves, who, without taking his eyes from his suspect, extracted his pocket watch and began swinging it slowly like a pendulum.

"Well, father was nearly killed, but we all thought it was some sort of accident..."

"How?! Did anyone tell Inspector Young of this?" asked Graves who was incredulous at this omission of important facts.

"Eh, not that I know of. At least I didn't mention it."

"Why the devil not?"

"Well, as I say, we all thought it some freak occurrence and then, with father's death and all, it quite slipped our minds."

"Tell me what happened."

John related the events of the night before. He spoke slowly, measuring each word, all the while staring at the swinging pocket watch which he found to be an irritating distraction.

"You do realise that the chances of this being unconnected to your father's murder are quite slim?"

"Inspector, I will co-operate as I am bound to morally and by law, but it would be a mistake on your part if you thought I have any desire to see a man hanged for ridding the world of my father."

"Tell me, why do you hate him so much?"

"My father never let me forget this," said John, pointing to his leg. "He viewed the family history as something to be proud of. Grimbourne after Grimbourne for hundreds of years, chiefs of Rockinghamshire. You've seen the grand house Inspector, the portraits lining the walls of our forefathers. Tell me, do I look like them? Do I look like one of those ruthless Grimbourne men who look down on you as you enter the house?"

"So, you take after your mother?" asked Carver.

"No actually, well, not in the sense that I inherited her familial looks, but I am more like her in other ways. No, mother was very tall and slim. Effortlessly elegant, she was. Father, as you have seen, was smaller but bull-like. I fall somewhere in the middle. No, father was like an ancient Spartan, no doubt when I was born, and he saw my withered leg he wanted to kill me there and then rather than have me as a son.

"But you asked me why I hated him and hating someone because they hate you is not a real reason. No, I hated my father because he controlled every aspect of my life. Through his design I relied on him for money, food, shelter, all the basic things a human needs. You have briefly seen George, tell me, why do you think my father employed a secretary when he had me here who could do the job? I'll tell you, because it's a job, it's experience, it's the first step towards a life away from here. Instead, he gets me to do menial tasks that anyone could do. Deliver eggs to the village shop, pick up guests from the train station, mend fences."

"If your father resented you so much, why did he keep you here?" asked Graves.

"I don't know. Maybe to punish me or simply to torture me by imprisoning me here."

"And now you are free…" Graves let the words hang in the air.

"I… I didn't murder my father!" John rapped the table with his stick as though to emphasise his point, all the while looking sternly at his interrogator and the swinging timepiece.

"Tell me, where were you this morning between nine-thirty and ten-thirty?"

"I was at the Granger's cottage, Inspector."

"Where exactly is that?"

"You go around the pond and carry on walking for fifteen minutes along the dirt path. Mr Granger was there, he will confirm my presence."

"One last question. Did your father usually lock his study door in the mornings?"

"Not usually, no."

✝

"Thoughts?" asked Graves when John left the room.

"Well, he certainly has a lot of anger directed towards his father, but if he's telling the truth about being at the Granger's cottage then that rules him out of it, no?"

"Don't get ahead of yourself, lad, we don't know the exact time of death yet."

"Why did you ask him where he was between nine-thirty and ten-thirty then?"

"To see how quickly he answered. Although, given what we know so far, that is the most likely timeframe in which the murder was committed."

"What do you make of this business with the falling stone sir?"

"Rum. Very rum…" At that moment Inspector Young appeared in the doorway.

"Ah Young, would you be so good as to fetch Miss Grimbourne here please?" asked Graves.

A few minutes later Ruth appeared, clutching a small purse with a pearl clasp.

"Please, Miss Grimbourne, take a seat," said Graves, indicating the dining chair vacated by John. "Let me start by saying, I am very sorry for your loss."

"Thank you. Such a shock."

Graves looked at the young lady who sat across from him. She was certainly beautiful despite the red, tear-stained eyes. The detective had interviewed many such products of Edwardian upbringing, girls whose reticence was instilled in them by nannies who themselves could never have been described as demure.

"Now Miss, I'm afraid I'm going to have to ask you a couple of questions. I know the pain and shock is still raw, but it is necessary that we get all the information we need so that we can apprehend whoever killed your father."

"I quite understand Inspector, please, ask me whatever you wish."

"Did you have a loving relationship with your father, Miss?"

"My father wasn't a very loving man, Inspector, except of course towards my mother."

"They were close?"

"Oh yes! He doted on her. You see, many people will tell you that my father was a cruel man, a vindictive man who lacked goodwill, maybe people already have. He had strong opinions and prejudices. But, you see, he wasn't always so horrible, at least, I don't believe so. When my mother died, my father changed. He darkened. I was only a little girl, but I remember. Please don't misunderstand me, I don't mean that while my mother lived my father was some sort of saint who handed out sweets to orphans, but I believe he was more content, less angry."

"I see. Your brother appears to have had quite a strained relationship with your father…?"

"Yes, poor John. He's so very sweet and sensitive, really, but father was always very hard on him. Nothing John could do was ever good enough. I was sent to an expensive boarding school whilst John was home schooled. He always thought father was ashamed of him on account of his leg and didn't want him seen in public. Of course, I always told John he was being silly but… well, maybe I was just trying to be kind to his feelings."

"Hmm. I understand you are due to be married tomorrow?"

"Yes, that's right, to Lord Taylor."

"Your father must have been pleased?"

"Yes, father was greatly attracted to the title," replied Ruth with some bitterness.

"And Lord Taylor? Was your father fond of him?"

"I have no reason not to think so. Father didn't exactly have any confidants. You would certainly know if he was displeased but not necessarily when he was pleased."

"And you, what are your feelings towards Lord Taylor?" asked Graves with a twinkle in his old eye.

"Excuse me, Inspector, but I fail to see the relevance of my personal feelings in this matter."

"Will the wedding go ahead tomorrow?"

"We haven't discussed it, but given the circumstances…"

"Hmmph. Miss Grimbourne, where were you between nine-thirty and ten-thirty this morning?"

"Oh… er, let me think. We had breakfast around eight o'clock, then Penelope said she was going to write a few letters for an hour or two before we were supposed to go into town. I saw father very briefly after breakfast in his study, then I lay down for an hour. I had a slight headache. Then Miss Barter's screams awoke me I think, or I might have already been awake, I'm not sure. It's all such a blur now."

"Of course. What did you see your father about?" asked Graves, now watching the light shine on his gold pocket watch.

"Wedding business. I couldn't find George and was wondering if father knew where he was."

"And did he?"

"He said he was collecting the flowers."

"I see. Tell me, Miss Grimbourne, how did your father seem when you saw him this morning?"

"In what way, Inspector?"

"In his behaviour Miss, his temperament."

"Oh, he was his usual self."

"He didn't seem nervous or excited in any way?"

"Not that I noticed." Ruth's hand went to her throat where it held a red ruby which dangled on a thin chain.

"Hmmph. Was the study door locked when you went to see him?"

"Yes, it was. I knocked and then tried it, but it was locked, and I had to wait a moment for father to open it."

"Was it quite common for your father to lock the door?"

"I'm not sure, Inspector. I have never given it much thought. I suppose he locked it depending on what he was working on. He was a very private man."

"Was your father working when you entered this morning?"

"I think he was taking a break from work. He was drinking coffee and there was a newspaper on the desk."

"Did your father have a safe, Miss?"

"Yes, there is a safe in his bedroom."

"Not in the study? Hidden in the wall perhaps?"

"No, I don't believe so. It would be news to me if there was."

"Thank you, Miss Grimbourne, that will be all for now. We will of course have to ask you more questions as our investigation progresses."

"Of course." Ruth gave a timid bow before fleeing the room.

"A safe sir? What gave you that idea?" asked Carver.

"The lady said that her father was typing when she entered. We have no reason to believe so far that Alexander Grimbourne left his study between his daughter visiting him and his death. So, either the letter is hidden away somewhere…"

"Or the murderer took it! Remember sir, there was an empty envelope on the desk."

"Don't start believing your theories yet, Carver, the empty envelope might have nothing to do with this matter. Alexander Grimbourne could have put the paper in one of the files we saw. Let us get all of the facts first."

"Yes sir."

"Who do you think we should see next Carver?" The young detective opened his mouth to answer then shut it abruptly as Inspector Young entered the room with a tall, handsome man.

"I thought you might like to see Mr Osborn next gentlemen"

"Of course," replied Graves politely.

Carver, who was about to summon George Campbell looked crestfallen.

"Please take a seat, Mr Osborn," offered Graves, as Young left the room.

"Call me Ed, I insist," smiled the barrister affably. Graves looked at the confident man who sat down and smiled. His dark head didn't have one hair out of place and his smile was given easily. Graves had dealt with his kind before, smooth and probably popular with the fairer sex. "Of course. Now, Ed, I believe you are a guest of Mr Grimbourne?"

"That's right. I'm here for his daughter's wedding, I'm an old friend of Lord Taylor's."

"But you are staying here at Treefall Manor? I would have thought you would be staying with Lord Taylor?" inquired Carver who was settling into his role.

"Well yes, but you see it was Mr Grimbourne who invited me. To be honest the whole wedding business came as rather a surprise."

"I see," said Graves, arching his eyebrows. "But Lord Taylor mentioned Miss Grimbourne, or perhaps you met her when you have visited previously?"

"Oh no, I mean the whole relationship came as a surprise. I've never actually visited here before. You see, Freddie and I were in the Army together, I'm now permanently planted in London, and we always catch up when he is down."

"When was the last time you saw Lord Taylor?"

"About two months ago, I should say. He has been spending little time in Westminster recently. I now guess Miss Grimbourne may have something to do with it," winked Ed.

"But you are close?"

"Oh, the best of friends, Freddie really is the most wonderful chap. He is very shy, but God never created a kinder fellow." At that moment, the subject of praise appeared at the door.

"Inspector I'm very sorry to interrupt, I'm Frederick

Taylor"

"Pleased to meet you Lord Taylor…"

"And you Inspector. As I say, awful rude of me to interrupt but it is getting late, and I have people coming for the wedding tomorrow… if you permit… I need to send them away… under the circumstances you see…"

"Of course, Lord Taylor, we're sorry for taking so long. Of course, you may attend to your business, and we can talk with you tomorrow."

"Thank you, Inspector."

"Just one question before you go, Lord Taylor…"

Freddie, who had already made to leave came back into view in the doorframe.

"Yes…?"

"Where were you between nine-thirty and ten-thirty this morning?"

"I was out walking on my estate."

"I see. Were you walking with anyone, milord?"

"Yes. I was with Ed here."

Graves looked at the handsome man opposite him who nodded in agreement.

"Very well, milord, we shall see you tomorrow."

✝

"I think we should speak to the secretary next," said Carver when Ed was down the corridor and safely out of earshot.

"I agree. Tell me Carver, why would Lord Taylor not tell his best friend he was getting married?"

"Maybe Lord Taylor is Ed's best friend, but Ed is not Lord Taylors?"

"You mean Lord Taylor does not like Ed but is too kind to hurt the man's feelings so instead of saying anything he lets the friendship fade out?"

"Exactly sir."

"But it was Alexander Grimbourne who invited Ed."

"The man had a cruel streak, sir. Maybe he took pleasure seeing Lord Taylor uncomfortable by Ed's presence."

"Maybe..."

✝

Carver watched George Campbell very carefully as he walked into the dining room. He entered with his back straight and his chin up as though he was sniffing the air, like a rabbit at dawn. His appearance was marked by the pallor of his face, and Carver was reminded of a soldier he had once seen walking towards the firing squad.

"Please, take a seat, Mr Campbell," said Graves gently. The secretary did so without uttering a sound. "We are trying to establish certain facts surrounding the murder of Mr Grimbourne..."

"I'm afraid I don't know anything."

"We haven't asked you anything yet Mr Campbell..."

"As I say, I don't know anything," repeated George, who folded his arms as though they could shield him from the questions about to be fired at him.

"Well, let's see. You know how long you worked for Mr Grimbourne, let's start with that."

"Of course. I'm terribly sorry Inspector, I hope I'm not coming across as rude, it's just... I've never been interviewed by the police before, it's quite unsettling. Such a shock, all of it. I cannot get my head around it. I didn't kill him, Inspector!"

"It's alright. Calm yourself my good man. No one has accused you of murder. We are merely trying to get an idea of the house, the family, of Mr Grimbourne. These are things that you know but we don't, so we need your help. Now, we'll go nice and slow... Brent!"

The petrified looking constable poked his head into the room.

"Get Mr Campbell here a glass of water, please. Now, as I was saying, how long were you in Mr Grimbourne's employ?"

"About... twelve years I should say."

"There we go lad, easy, isn't it? Now, how did you come to work for Mr Grimbourne?" asked Graves, tucking his pocket watch inside his waistcoat.

"I never knew my father sir, and my mother died of consumption when I was a boy. I had gone to live with an aunt, though I knew I wasn't wanted. Not that I can blame her, you understand. Another mouth to feed and her already having five children and a drunken husband. Well sir, I decided to get away as soon as I could. At school I was good at sums and writing, better than most kids, so as soon as I was old enough, I looked for a job. I've always had problems with my chest, sir, which limited the type of work I could do, you understand.

Well, one day I saw an advertisement in the newspaper. 'Position to be filled' it said. General duties, some accounts to look after. It was all rather vague, but beggars can't be choosers as they say, so I wrote and got a letter back a week later.

I came up to meet Mr Grimbourne. He seemed very strict, rather curt, but I was grateful for the opportunity, sir. Though there's not much to be said for the wages, I live in a nice house and get fed well. Not bad for an orphan."

"Indeed. Now, Mr Grimbourne: what was he like to work for?"

"As I say sir, I was incredibly grateful. Mr Grimbourne took me in and gave me a chance when I had nowhere to turn, and I'll always be thankful for that."

"Hmmph. Did he ever shout or beat you?"

"He had his ways, sir, as everyone does, but I'll not speak ill of the dead."

"Your loyalty is admirable, George, though some people have intimated that Mr Grimbourne had a cruel side to him..."

"As I say sir, he had his ways but there is good and bad in everyone is there not?"

"There certainly is George, there certainly is. How did Mr Grimbourne treat his children?"

"Well, I believe he was very fond of Ruth."

"And John?"

George stopped to take a sip of water, his eyes looked away from the two detectives who he knew were watching him keenly. "Mr Grimbourne was not the type of person… he…"

"Yes…?" encouraged Graves.

"I believe John feels his father was not fond of him. Whether that was the case or not I cannot say."

"I see…"

"John once told me that his father resented him for not being able to do his bit in the war, his leg…"

"Yes, I noticed," nodded Graves.

"Well, I believe that Mr Grimbourne ensured I wasn't conscripted due to my chest."

"What makes you think that?"

"Well, I got a letter from the War Office. I went for the tests and all that, then I got a letter saying I was to join the local regiment with a date and everything."

"And what happened?"

"Mr Grimbourne read the letter and told me not to worry about it, he said it must be a mistake and he would take care of it."

"And he did?"

"Yes. Well, at least, I got another letter a few weeks later saying there was some sort of mix-up and that I wasn't being called up after all."

"I see." Graves was pleased with how he had eased George into the conversation and had smiled when he observed the young man's shoulders slump slightly in relaxation.

"George, do you have any idea who could have killed Mr Grimbourne?" asked Carver.

"No sir."

"When did you last see Mr Grimbourne?" continued Carver.

"This morning sir, right before I left, so around eight-thirty. I had to get some letters from him which he wanted posting before collecting the flowers."

"Do you know what these letters were?"

"No sir. I guessed them to be payments for wedding expenses or something of that kind. I posted them in the box in the village."

"They will have been collected by now," murmured Carver, looking at his watch.

"When did you find out Mr Grimbourne had been killed?" asked Graves.

"When I got back here, sir, around midday. I came into the grand hallway sir and saw a policeman at the end of the corridor outside the study door. It was quite a shock I can tell you. Then Miss Dunholme came out from the drawing room smoking one of those thin cigarettes."

"What did she say?"

"She said, 'Where do you keep the good whisky? Oh, your boss is dead by the way.' Then she turned and went back in the drawing room. I followed her in. Everyone else was already there."

"Hmmph. What did you see when you entered? What did you notice about the people?"

"Well," said George, scratching his chin. "Ruth was sitting on the Chesterfield with her hands on her knees. She seemed frozen, as though in a daze. Miss Dunholme went and sat next to her and put her hand on Ruth's. Roberts was standing in the corner looking uncomfortable, as though he didn't wish to be there. The guest, what's his name, Ed, he was in the armchair by the window looking rather bored. John was pacing about. The only sound was his stick thumping the floor."

"What about Mrs Barter, where was she?"

"Elsie? Oh, I don't know, I believe Jayne and Betty took her wailing out of hearing distance, but where they took her to, I couldn't say."

"Are you aware of any ill-feeling directed towards Mr

Grimbourne by any of the other staff?"

"No sir. Old Hodgkins has been here donkey's years, Mr Grimbourne was always very respectful towards him. Mrs Barter comes in the mornings to clean. She is a blabbermouth but is harmless really, she has one hundred brats at home and likes a sip of gin. She has been working here thirty years, I should say. Old Betty works in the kitchen. Her husband was the gardener for many years, he died a few years ago. Betty still lives in their little cottage near the farms.

Other than that, there are a couple of maids, none ever stay long. They don't live in, except for Jayne, and they very much keep themselves to themselves. They report to Elsie in a very unofficial capacity."

"Jayne? Why does she live in, and the others don't?" asked Carver.

"No special reason, Constable, only she is not a local girl like the rest of them and, well, her wages are less for staying here so it is a good arrangement all round. She's a bit of a troublemaker though, forever gossiping to stir up trouble, more through malice than boredom I should say."

"Really? How so?" asked Graves, as he drummed the table with his fingers.

"Oh, petty stuff, you know. There was another girl here, another maid, who liked one of the local chaps. Well, by all accounts Jayne was sweet on him too, though I daresay neither girl's affections were returned by the young man. Anyway, one day there was a cry and a shout from Mrs Barter about some jewellery or other that had gone missing, and Jayne suggested checking this young maid's handbag. Well, lo and behold the article in question just happened to be exactly there. It was obvious that Jayne had put it there through spite, but Mr Grimbourne didn't concern himself with any squabbles he deemed petty. He sacked the poor girl immediately and that was that."

"I see. This business last night with the falling rock, what do you know about that?"

"There's nothing I can tell you sir other than the manor has needed repairs for many years although we didn't know the stonework was in such bad condition at the top."

"You didn't see what happened?" asked Carver.

"Afraid not. During dinner Mr Grimbourne asked me to see Hodgkins about taking the coffee to the drawing room. I'm afraid I felt a little queasy; I must have overindulged myself. Once I saw Hodgkins I retired to my room. I wasn't aware of any incident until this morning when John mentioned it at breakfast."

"What did he say?"

"He merely repeated what had happened. He said that Mr Grimbourne, Alexander Grimbourne I mean, thought that perhaps the stone was loosened on one of the towers a few years ago. Apparently, he remembered the tower being struck by lightning and this may have separated a piece of rock. "

"Do you believe that, Mr Campbell?" asked Graves, his voice layered with doubt.

"I don't know, I haven't had time to think about it."

"Hmmph. I don't think we'll keep you any longer. When you go back can you please ask Mr Roberts to come in."

"Yes, of course, Inspector. Good day."

†

George Campbell entered the drawing-room and walked to the fireplace where Roberts was standing alone, stroking his long moustache. After a few muffled words the solicitor walked out, being passed at the doorway by Jayne Brown, whose thin hips swung with the haughtiness of a peacock. In her hands was a heavy, crystal-cut ashtray which she wiped without care. Feigning surprise at the room full of sullen people, she exclaimed as she set the ash-tray on the table, "Oh my! What are you lot doing in here?"

"Good grief, who is this wretch?" said Penelope, who was sitting on a chaise longue with a tumbler of whisky in one hand and a thin cigarette in the other. She stared at Jayne from her greasy hair slowly down to her feet which were entombed in heavy black shoes and back up again finding furious eyes staring back at her. Penelope laughed at the reaction she had provoked and took a long drag on her cigarette.

Jayne looked at the figures scattered around the room. Only Ruth and Penelope sat close to one another. Ed stood by the window looking bored and disinterested in the girl who had interrupted their silence. George and John sat opposite each other, a low coffee table in the centre of the room separating them.

John, shifting uncomfortably at the awkwardness just produced decided to reply to Jayne's question. "The police have asked us to wait here for a little while. I imagine they may wish to speak to you as well."

"Oh, I see! All the suspects gathered in one room, is that it? Well, of course, not *all* the suspects," continued Jayne, her eyes resting on Ruth. "And such a respectable family too! Oh, I *do* hope the scandal isn't too great! Is it terribly upsetting for you? I can't imagine how you will sleep tonight." Jayne took her eyes from Ruth and stared at the coffee table before continuing. "I know what that's like. I couldn't sleep a wink last night. I was so restless I decided to get up and take a turn around the gardens. I do enjoy looking at the stars. Of course, there are plenty of other interesting things that you see in the early hours: unexpected things. Still, I expect I shall sleep soundly tonight, I wonder if the murderer will."

Jayne made slowly for the doorway, followed by a mixture of curious and angry stares.

✝

Aldous Roberts sat down quietly and waited for the detectives to begin their questioning.

"Mr Roberts, can you tell me why Alexander Grimbourne asked you here today?" asked Graves.

"Well gentlemen, as far as I am concerned confidentiality between my client and myself dies with him, therefore, I can tell you my client asked me here because he said he wished to change his will."

"I see, do you know if the terms of his will were common knowledge in the house?"

"I believe there were no secrets regarding the will my client had previously drawn."

"Could you please tell me what they were?" asked Graves patiently.

"Certainly. The main points, minus a few negligible sums to various institutions and staff, old and existing, were that the estate was to be bequeathed to John as oldest male heir. Ruth was to receive an annual pension which was a considerable sum based on dividends of various investments. There was also a separate bulk of capital which was to be divided between the two siblings."

"Hmmph. And what, pray, was the new will to consist of?"

"The new will was to be much the same as the old one, the only notable difference being a much-improved legacy for Mr George Campbell at the expense of Miss Ruth Grimbourne."

"How much improved?"

"A pension the same size as that which Ruth would have got."

"Did Mr Grimbourne state any reason as to why he wished to make this change?"

"No, not explicitly, however I believe the fact that Miss Grimbourne is due to marry a very wealthy man and will not need her father's inheritance may give indication to my client's state of mind."

"Hmmph. Did Mr Grimbourne mention to you whether or

not he had informed anyone else of this new arrangement?"

"He did not say either way sir and it wasn't my place to ask."

"I understand."

"There was to be one other change Inspector."

"Yes…"

"My client expressed the wish that the local church was not to be entitled to any money as was stated in the original will. A small legacy sir."

"I see. Did your client elaborate on the matter?"

"He did not."

"I see. Do you handle all of Mr Grimbourne's business matters?"

"From a legal standpoint, yes," continued Roberts, twirling his whiskers.

"Would you be so kind as to send me a portfolio of his business interests?"

"Of course."

"Thank you. Unless there is any other light you believe you can shed on this matter, we shan't detain you any longer."

"I wish I could be more help sir."

"Oh, just one other thing actually, Mr Roberts?"

"Yes Inspector?"

"Where were you this morning between nine-thirty and ten-thirty?"

"I would have been motoring down Inspector. I spent last night in London, you see. I was at a meeting of the Law Society and stayed at Judge Barrett's house. I left rather late this morning. The judge will be able to corroborate this."

"Thank you."

Roberts exited as silently and as calmly as he had entered.

"Let's walk back to the inn. I could do with some fresh air. We can interview Hodgkins and the other staff tomorrow."

"Aren't you forgetting Miss Dunholme?" asked Carver.

"I see you're not," replied Graves, with a twinkle in his eye. Carver turned a deep shade of scarlet.

Miss Penelope Dunholme entered after being summoned by Constable Brent. She pouted as she sat, taking a long drag of her thin cigarette, which she then blew across the table towards Graves. If the lady was surprised to see the small smile curl on the Inspector's lips, she did not show it.

"I think perhaps, Carver, I'll let you take this one on your own. When you are done come and find me." With that, Graves rose and left without another word being spoken in his presence.

Carver, feeling a mixture of trepidation and excitement at being left to interview the suspect alone adjusted himself in his seat and looked down at his blank notepad. He felt those cool eyes looking through him and could feel the heat radiate from his cheeks. Mustering the courage to raise his head he saw Penelope sitting with her legs crossed, staring at him with impatience. Her red hair glowed in the soft light of the dining room and her emerald eyes shone like a cat's.

"Well?" she asked, as though speaking to a child.

"Yes. Ahem. You are Miss...?"

"Penelope Dunholme, as you already know."

"Er, yes. Quite. Can you please tell me, Miss Dunholme, the nature of your visit to Treefall Manor?"

"The nature of my visit? I'm here for the wedding."

"Of course, yes. How long had you known the deceased, Miss?"

"I wouldn't say I knew him. When Ruth and I were at school together I'd visit for a few days during the summer holidays. We'd see him for dinner and that was about it."

"And after you left school? Did you visit much then?"

"I'd still visit every year. Ruth and I write to each other very much, it's rare for her to visit London but if she did, she would let me know in her letters and we would meet."

"Why would Miss Grimbourne visit London?"

"Why wouldn't she? The parties are fabulous, there are handsome men with bulging wallets and of course her gorgeous best friend lives there. It gets her away from this prison too. I mean, half of the villagers belong in a zoo. I don't know how she continues to live here."

"I see," replied Carver, writing as he spoke.

"She also has an old aunt who lives there who she visits when she's down. Well, it's her mother's aunt, but Ruth and John call her Auntie Nell. Ruth tells the prison warden she's going to visit her, then we have our fun."

"I see..."

"Look, this is all terribly boring, and you've clearly not done this questioning lark before. Why don't you ask me if I killed the old bastard?"

"Oh... er, well..."

"Go on then!"

"Miss Dunholme, did you murder Alexander Grimbourne?"

"Don't be so stupid! What reason could I possibly have to kill him. Really! The police come out with the most offensive and insulting questions!"

"Oh... I'm very sorry Miss Dunholme"

"I think I'll ponder your apology over a whisky and soda. Heaven help you if I decide to make a complaint. Goodbye." Carver had barely gulped down his breath when Penelope had reached the door.

"Wait!"

Surprised at the aggression in the plea, Penelope turned in expectation.

"What?"

"Where were you between nine-thirty and ten-thirty this morning?"

8. THE EIGHT POINTS

*They saw great difficulties in the case,
Reasoning thus (to make their feelings plain)
That there were such discrepancies to face*

"The Man of Law's Tale"
The Canterbury Tales

Carver sat for a few minutes absorbed in the stillness of the now empty room. His mind raced, trying to foresee the questions Graves would ask him about his interview with Penelope Dunholme. It had not, Carver reflected, been a success. In fact, he had found out next to nothing about Penelope herself other than when she was a child she went to school, which could hardly be deemed a ground-breaking discovery. He also doubted whether Graves would be impressed that he had found out Ruth had a great aunt who lived in London.

A sense of panic set in. He could feel his chest tighten as he recalled the interview. How had she done it? She had totally taken control and dictated their discussion. What would Graves say? So far that day, Carver had seen his new boss be rude to Penelope yet kind to George. He was tolerant of the men of the Rockinghamshire constabulary when their dithering and behaviours may have been grating to a man of Graves's experience. He seemed, thought Carver, to approach others based on their individual merits and sensibilities. Was this a deliberate method obtained through years of policing? Or was it part of the senior detective's inherent nature? Either way it gave Carver no clue as to how he himself would be treated by Graves as he had no idea what the Inspector thought of him. He put his head in his hands.

Constable Brent walked past the door without looking in, bringing Carver back from his trance. He pocketed his notepad, which was ashamedly sparse of ink, and lifted his overcoat from the back of his chair.

Carver was surprised to find that Graves was not in the drawing room, which was now deserted. Looking around the room he saw empty tumblers on tables and trays. The smell of Penelope's cigarette smoke hung in the air causing him to shiver as their interview flashed once again through his mind. Escaping as fast as he could, he decided the murder scene was the most likely place to find Graves, although again he was wrong.

Constable Brent stood guard by the door as Carver passed with a nod. This room was also empty, the body having been examined and removed while the detectives were carrying out their questioning.

"Ah Carver. There you are!" cried a voice over his shoulder. Turning, he saw Graves standing beside the statuesque Brent whose shoes were being sniffed by Peggy.

"Yes sir, here I am," replied Carver, smiling towards the dog.

"The new master of the house always wanted a pet, he said, but was never permitted one, so he is happy for Peggy to have the run of the place while we're about. Jolly good of him don't you think? Ah, Peggy, no!" admonished Graves, seeing the dog had progressed from sniffing to chewing laces.

"You saw John again then?" Carver wondered what Graves had been doing in his absence.

"Only briefly. Let's walk to the village."

"I could take you in the car, sir, if you wish?" said Brent eagerly.

"No, thank you, Constable. It's a fresh night, perfect for a stroll; cleans out the lungs. Besides, you have more to do here, remember? Come, Carver."

As the two men walked out of the house, they saw none of its inhabitants. Carver pondered how long it would be before his superior officer probed him about the devilish Miss Dunholme. Much to his surprise, however, Graves did not mention the interview or the case at all as they walked to the inn.

"I say Carver, it may dip to freezing tonight."

"I daresay, sir." The sky was opaque, the black ceiling of night. The stars twinkled in defiance against the darkness.

"Beautiful, isn't it?" said Graves, craning his neck to admire the celestial beauty above him.

"Terrifying would be my adjective sir."

"Oh? Why's that?"

"Well, it's just so huge, isn't it? It makes one feel so small, so insignificant."

"Significance is objective lad."

"How so sir?"

"Well, a pound is significant to someone living in the slums but not to someone on Wall Street. You see what I mean?"

"I suppose, sir," replied Carver doubtfully.

"Why does that vast expanse above us make you feel insignificant, lad?"

"I'm not sure, sir. I suppose it's, as you say, vast, whereas I'm so small in comparison."

"We are vessels lad. Nothing more. Your spirit or soul could fill that void for all you know. Not everything is material."

"You surprise me, sir."

"Why? A detective thinks about what he does not know and tries to work it out. A detective must also acknowledge when he does not know something, whether it be a scientific fact, historical fact, whatever, even if it's only to himself and no other. Conviction and doubt must walk the same path lad, though never hand in hand."

Flanked by mighty trees on both sides, the two men walked at a leisurely pace down the long driveway of Treefall

Manor. When they reached the gate, which earlier in the day they had flown past, they turned right to traverse the short road which led into the village.

The night was quiet, though the tinkling of the brook, which followed the direction of the main road, could be heard.

White cottages looked ghostly, glowing through the darkness.

"You wouldn't think the murder of a notorious person had just been committed would you, sir? The village is so quiet, all of the lights are out," said Carver, as they approached the inn.

"And why do you think that is, lad?"

"Sir?" asked Carver, his face sculpted by confusion. Graves pushed open the heavy oak door of the pub. A cacophony of noise flooded out and drowned the detectives. Graves turned to Carver with a knowing smile.

"Everyone is in here, lad."

The two men and Peggy entered. The noise, which a few moments before had been fearsome, died quicker than Alexander Grimbourne had. All heads turned towards the strangers, inquisitive faces showing excitement and curiosity.

"Good evening," said Graves, addressing the entire room in a booming voice. The reply he received was short nods and a few coughs. The people stood in large packs, such was the excitement the murder had caused. Although the public bar was teeming with people, few seats at tables were occupied as though being stationary would mean missing out on juicy gossip by being unable to flit between different groups. By the time the two detectives had squeezed their way through to the bar the noise levels had risen again, their presence becoming a new topic of conversation for the excited villagers.

"What will you have, Carver?"

"That's very kind of you sir, I'll have a pint of bitter please."

"Don't mention it lad, it's your first day. Besides, you'll be buying the rest. Take Peggy and grab that table over by the fire. Mind she doesn't get trampled on."

"Yes sir."

Behind the bar worked two men, sweat glistened their brows despite the season. Samuel Mason, whose red cheeks glowed, lumbered around the younger man to serve Graves.

"Good evening, you must be the Inspector?"

"Good evening."

"Yeah, your young feller nipped in with your cases this afternoon. My William here took them up to your rooms for you," said Samuel, nodding at the other barman who Graves could see was trying to look like he wasn't listening to their conversation.

"Your son?"

"My nephew. Though I raised him as a son. Took him in when my sister died you see. He was only a nipper."

"Ah. You must be Samuel Mason?"

"I am. How do you know that then?" asked the landlord in a jolly fashion.

"I'm a detective... and your name is above the door. Licensee."

"Aha, very good, sir. Samuel Mason, at your service, this 'ere is William Hopkirk. William! Come o'er here and meet Mr..."

"Inspector Graves."

"Inspector Graves!"

William topped off the pint he was pouring and slowly walked the few feet to join his uncle. Graves watched him as he did so. Tall, athletic, with a shock of black hair. He was quite dissimilar to his uncle, Graves thought.

"Evening," said William rather curtly.

"Good evening."

"I hope you haven't come here to get any clues out of this lot," indicating the drinking villagers with a flick of his eyes.

"Oh, no? Why's that?" asked Graves affably.

"Well, half of them probably couldn't name you the Prime Minister never mind tell you who killed Grimbourne. If you listen to old Morgan over there, it was the ghost of the man's wife, come back and killed him for taking a new lover. Then there's Agnes over there, soaked in sherry. She reckons the butcher done it because old Grimbourne was going to shut him down for selling rotten meat. Reckons she got leftover tripe that made her fluffy little Jingles sick. 'And of course, who has more knives than a butcher,' she says." William laughed recounting what he had overheard. "So, you see Inspector, you'd get more sense at the lunatic asylum over at Broad Hill than you will in here."

"Thanks for the advice, lad."

"What drinks can I get you, Inspector?" asked Samuel hurriedly, "I've a lovely stout on, fresh today!"

"I'll have two pints of bitter please landlord," replied Graves, though he was still eyeing William as he said it.

"Right you are, Sir! Coming up!"

"Who is your money on, William?"

"Beg your pardon, Inspector?"

"Well, if it wasn't Mrs Grimbourne's ghost and it wasn't the butcher, who do you think murdered Alexander Grimbourne?"

"I say, I don't know sir, could have been a vagrant passing through, like. Could be anyone."

"Vagrants don't kill people, lad."

"Course they do, see it all the time in the papers."

"Don't believe what you read in the papers, lad, believe what I tell you," said Graves firmly.

"Well, as I say, could be anyone. He wasn't a popular man. If you do catch whoever it was, vagrant or not, don't expect much thanks from folk around here."

"What I think my nephew means Inspector, well... Mr Grimbourne has upset a few people over the years."

"How so?" asked Graves.

"Well, there's been many a folk who's worked up at the house, you know, maids and the like. Well, there's been a few times where people have taken exception to how Mr Grimbourne would speak to them, like. Course, people would throw up the head and walk out or be fired, no one would resort to murder."

William walked away to serve a thirsty old man with a

dirty beard.

"Tell me Samuel, who was the last person to leave Mr Grimbourne's employment?"

Samuel Mason scratched his jowls, "Er, right enough my memory ain't what it used to be, sir. There's been so many come and go it's hard to keep up. Anyway, here's your pints."

"Thank you."

✝

Peggy lifted her head for her ears to be scratched when her master returned as the new man hadn't taken the hint of her longing gaze. She was lying beneath the table, directly in front of the fire. Graves reached into his pocket, pulling something out that Carver could not see and gave it to Peggy whose jaws set to work instantly, then he satisfied her itch.

"What did Miss Dunholme have to say for herself?" asked Graves nonchalantly.

Carver, mid-gulp of his nutty brown pint, was blindsided by the question resulting in ale being expelled through his nostrils.

"Good Lord, man, what's the matter with you?"

"Sorry, sir, thought I was about to sneeze," fibbed Carver. "Erm... Miss Dunholme?"

"Yes Miss Dunholme, you know, the redhead you were quivering over."

"Oh, I don't think I was, I mean... she... Ruth has a great aunt who lives in London."

"She tied you in knots, didn't she?"

"Oh, sir! I don't know what happened! I swear!" cried Carver.

"I do!" Much to the young man's surprise, Graves chuckled. "Don't look so worried lad, I knew you weren't pleased with how the interview went."

"How sir?"

"Because, if it went well or you found out anything of interest you would have told me straight away. Instead, you were very sheepish. Don't be too hard on yourself, lad, it was cruel of me to leave you with her. If it is any consolation, I am sure you would have been fine interviewing any of the others alone. Miss Dunholme, however, is a tricky customer. At first glance she appears to be an attractive woman from the upper class and, typically, women like that can be coy and quiet. But always remember, don't judge a book by its cover."

"Thank you, sir. You are right too; she was tricky. She twisted the conversation to act affronted, it brought the interview to a close, but it also made me suspicious of her."

"Perhaps she likes a bit of drama in her life. I've met her type before, they act guilty when they are innocent because it excites them."

"That sounds a dangerous game to play, sir."

"It is. That's why it excites them. Unfortunately, they also tend to withhold information which can be useful to us. They like the power and control they feel," mused Graves. "Murder can be a game to some people."

"Do you think the killer is playing a game sir? If it's not Miss Dunholme, of course."

"I don't know. Certainly, there are curious aspects to this case. What was Miss Dunholme's alibi anyway?"

"She said she was writing letters, then she disappeared up the hallway before I could ask anything further."

"Well, that ties in with what Ruth told us. Remember? She said Miss Dunholme was spending the morning writing letters and she lay down during that time. By the way, I gave that piece of paper we found to Young, he'll have it back to us tomorrow. If there is anything legible written on it, we'll get it. Another pint?" said Graves, wiping his frothy lips.

"Yes sir, same again?"

"Yes, thank you, and a half for Peggy. She's quite partial to a drop of the good stuff. Oh, and see if Mr Mason is still serving any grub, I'm starving."

THE MYSTERY OF TREEFALL MANOR

The contented canine opened one eye at the hearing of her name being spoken but thought better of lifting her head.

On his way to the bar, pushing gently through the throngs of people, Carver passed a bare headed Constable Brent, who enquired where the Inspector was. Carver indicated with a flick of his head. When he returned with the drinks, using a dog bowl as a tray, he found Graves alone reading from a single sheet of paper.

"Sir?"

"Coroner's report," answered Graves without looking up. His eyes worked their way slowly down the page. "Hmmph. Well, no surprises, I suppose." Graves handed the sheet to Carver and continued speaking. "It seems we were correct in our estimation regarding the time of death. Coroners are notorious for spurting out ambiguities and cautious statements but this one has the time of the murder placed between nine-thirty and ten-thirty with ten o'clock being the most likely time."

"How do they work it out, sir?"

"You don't want to know lad. Thermometers and dark places is all I'll say. Anyway, ten o'clock doesn't help us any regarding alibis."

"No sir, though don't forget we still have Elsie Barter to speak to and the rest of the staff."

"True. Maybe they can shine some light on the matter. Have a read of that," said Graves handing over the coroner's report. "Notice anything interesting?"

Carver held the sheet close to his face, reading furiously, knowing he was being tested. "Well, there is one curious point, sir," he said unconvincingly.

"Go on…"

"The dagger, sir. When we looked it was buried up to the hilt. It says here 'the dagger has a blade almost nine inches long', surely only a man could generate the force required the penetrate that deep into a man's body?"

"Excellent Carver, I noticed the same. However, the report does also say that the dagger has a thin blade which would assist the killer in driving the dagger in deep. Still, an interesting point nonetheless."

"So, we are looking for a man?"

"Steady. There have been cases in the past where women have found almost superhuman strength within themselves when in a fit of rage. Unusual, but bear it in mind. *'Hell hath no fury'* and all that. Like Mrs Graves when I don't leave my muddy boots by the door," joked Graves.

"How long have you been married, sir?"

"Thirty-five years give or take a few months. Rita, my wife is called. She is one in a million. It takes a special kind of woman to be married to a policeman what with one thing or another. Sometimes I am away on a case for days on end or late home and then dinner is cold. You can imagine how it is."

"Have you any children, sir? Ah, speaking of dinner..." said Carver.

Samuel Mason appeared at the table with two steaming plates in his hands.

"Here you are, sirs, two steak and kidney pies straight from Mr Lee's farm shop with some lovely potato and peas to go with and a basket of bread."

"Thank you very much, Mr Mason," said Graves, deciding not to answer Carver's familial question.

"Would you care for more drinks?" asked the proprietor, eyeing the half empty pint pots.

"A wonderful idea," cried Graves enthusiastically. "The renown of your hospitality should be heard all over the county."

"Oh, I don't know about that, Inspector, but anything you need while you're here, anything at all, just give old Sam a holler."

"Your words seem to have pleased him greatly, sir," said Carver when Samuel Mason was safely out of earshot.

"Hmmph. Mr Mason is a little *too* hospitable lad."

"Sir?"

"Look at the man, Carver. He knows we are policemen so his behaviour towards and around us is bound to be somewhat affected by the fact. But there is something else. He is overly kind, overly helpful. A big ruddy, rough fellow like that with hands the size of bear paws doesn't usually kowtow to anyone, especially not in his own establishment where regulars can see him. No, Mr Mason is nervous."

"About what, do you think, sir?"

"I don't know but I do know one thing."

"What's that?"

"He didn't answer my question."

"Question sir?"

"I asked him at the bar who was the last person to leave Mr Grimbourne's employment. He pretended that he couldn't remember who, but he knows. He knows rightly. The local landlord knows more in a village than anyone else, including the postman. Don't forget that, Carver."

"I won't, sir."

"Good lad. Now, tuck in."

"But what about the Mrs Barters of the world, sir?" continued Carver, his train of thought not slowed.

"How do you mean?" asked Graves, taking a mouthful of hot pie.

"Well, by all accounts she's a bit of a busybody about the village. Would she not be a source of gossip?"

"Yes lad: gossip. The Mrs Barters of this world (though, bear in mind I haven't yet met the woman and don't want to be too assuming, nor cast aspersions), are a source of gossip, not facts. Besides, they are just as likely to be the ones making up the information that they spread around whereas the Samuel Masons of this world will hear variations of the same thread of story from different people and thus be able to pluck fact from fiction. As well, of course, as be able to distinguish the merits of each individual piece of information based on the source from which they come."

"You mean that if Lord Taylor strides in here and whispers in Mr Mason's ear that old Betty the cook is having an affair with Mr Grimbourne, he is more likely to believe it than if Mrs Barter hobbles in and says the same thing?"

"Hmm, yes I suppose. You see, if Mrs Barter walks in and tells Mr Mason what you say he might raise his eyebrows and mutter something or other about how Mrs Barter is an oracle or such like but really, he would be very dubious because he knows the woman too well. It's like the horses lad: you study the form. That's what the Samuel Masons of this world do, they don't put five shillings on a sixty-six to one shot because Mrs Barter heard from sherry-soaked Agnes it's going to win. But if Lord Taylor or whoever walks in and gives the same tip and has previously given solid information and knows the trainer, then the prudent landlord will give more weight to this statement."

"I see! That is why you took the approach you did with George Campbell!"

"Precisely. Besides the fact that the man was quite obviously ill at ease, he holds quite a unique position in the household. If anyone were to give us an accurate depiction of what it is like to live at Treefall Manor and to the character of Alexander Grimbourne it is Mr George Campbell. He is not a blood relative so his loyalty should not be as strong than if he were. He worked closer to Alexander Grimbourne than any of the other staff, and in a position of trust..."

"But what we found was the opposite! Out of all the people we interviewed George Campbell was the one least willing to say anything bad about Mr Grimbourne."

"Perhaps we should have interviewed Roberts first."

"You mean maybe George knew about Alexander planning to change the will and he felt a sense of loyalty knowing his boss intended to leave him all that money?"

"It's possible. After all, if anyone were to know it would be the secretary."

"Of course, if Ruth knew about the will..."

"Hmmph." Graves used a chunk of bread to mop the last of the gravy from his empty plate and leaned to feed Peggy the juicy scrap. The little dog took it gently from between her master's fingers then took a long slurp of her ale before resuming her previous position in front of the fire. Carver threw a few logs on the fire from a basket next to his chair. The glowing coals embraced the wood lustfully. Flames rose, shadows danced on the walls as the large gathering of people seemed to sway as though standing on a ship's deck in a rolling sea.

"Of course," pondered Carver. "There are two mysteries in this case."

"You mean the who and the how?"

"Precisely. I wonder if the how will lead us to the who or vice versa."

"It's possible, lad."

"As far as I can work out sir there are several important aspects which we can't ignore about the murder."

"Go on lad, let's hear it," said Graves appraisingly.

"One. The murder was committed right before Roberts arrived and the will was to be changed.

"Two. The murderer took a tremendous risk committing the murder in daylight when others could be in the vicinity.

"Three. Alexander Grimbourne locked his study door this morning, perhaps he knew he was in danger.

"Four. The incident last night with the falling rock which may explain point number three.

"Five. The force needed to inflict the wound, as we have discussed.

"Six. The book found in Grimbourne's hand.

"Finally, Seven. The piece of paper found on the floor which shows writing from a previous letter. I believe if we can answer or elaborate on these points, we can solve the case, sir."

"I think you can add another point, lad."

"Sir?"

"Why did Alexander want to cut the church out of his will?"

"By all accounts Christian ethics weren't firmly entrenched in the man."

"Still… I'd like to satisfy myself on the point."

"About the book sir…"

"*The Canterbury Tales*?"

"Yes. Have you read it?"

"Many years ago, yes. Though I must say I don't remember much of it, just the premise really: a group of pilgrims are travelling to Canterbury, each must relate two tales there and two on the way back. Why do you ask?"

"I was just thinking. Maybe Alexander was leaving us a clue."

"Go on lad, talk freely," replied Graves, hearing the lack of conviction in the young man's voice.

"Well sir, picture this. The murderer stabs Alexander who knows he has only a few seconds left to live. What does he do? He tries to reveal the identity of the person who has killed him. His eyes scan around him and he sees a book on the bookshelf, what if he takes a book whose author's initials are the same as the killer's?"

"Geoffrey Chaucer…"

"George Campbell."

"It's possible, though Grimbourne would have to have tremendous clarity of thought to do something like that in such a short space of time. Besides, once Grimbourne expired after a few seconds would the killer not just pick up the book and put it back?"

"Yes, I suppose he would. I guess we are just going to have to figure out how the killer got in and out to know all of the answers, sir."

"Not we, you."

"Beg your pardon sir?"

"*You* will have to figure out how the murder was done."

"Ah, I see sir," smiled Carver. "It's a test for the new man. Work out how a murder was committed to prove my worth type of thing, yes?"

"No. I already know *how* the murder was committed, let us see if you can draw the same conclusion."

"Sir?! You know how someone killed Grimbourne inside a locked room?"

"Yes. There's just one thing I need to check tomorrow to be sure. Although I must say I don't yet know *who* the killer is. Anyway, I'll think I'll call it a night."

"But... sir?" said Carver incredulously.

"I'll tell you what," said Graves, rising to his feet. "I'll give you a clue."

"Thank you, sir," gasped Carver.

Graves reached into his overcoat pocket and brought out an object which he tossed on the table with a thud. Carver looked down wide-eyed at *The Canterbury Tales*. When he looked up Graves was walking to the back stairs of the inn, Peggy following, though she was reluctant to leave the fireside.

†

Graves found his case next to a rickety wooden writing desk under which Peggy lay. He hung his overcoat on the back of the door. The only sound to be heard was the low rumble of people in the bar downstairs, like a distant train lumbering through the night.

The Inspector sat at the desk and sighed deeply. From one of his many pockets, he took a hipflask and set it next to the inkwell. He then opened his case and rifled through the few items of clothing until he found what he was looking for. He took the picture and placed it gently next to the metal flask. Looking back at him was a handsome, square-shouldered boy in a soldier's uniform. He was smiling into the camera, his rifle held tight by his side. Graves unscrewed the cap from his flask. An owl hooted somewhere close by.

†

Carver tiptoed up the old wooden stairs, eager not to disturb

Graves whose room was next door. As he passed, he stopped to listen momentarily, but no sound escaped from within. He entered his own room silently and let his overcoat fall over the back of the chair. Lying on the hard bed, he studied the book that was in his hands, illuminated by a small lamp on the bedside table. Unlike Graves, he was unfamiliar with the medieval work and knew nothing of the tales within. He felt the weight of the book and closed his eyes to shut out any distractions so that his senses could focus on the problem at hand. How had Graves figured out how the murder was committed and what had this book to do with it?

Ideas formed, floated, and dissipated, lost in a haze of brown ale. How long would it take to read the book he wondered. Is the answer in the book and that is how Graves had worked it out so quickly? Because he had read it? Surely not. After all, he had read it so long ago. He flicked through the pages, hoping words or a phrase would catch his eye but all that happened was he felt the disturbed air waft on his face like a hovering fairy blowing on his nose. He was about to set the book aside when he remembered he hadn't looked inside the front cover. Turning the dust jacket, he saw a dedication written in spirally handwriting.

Dearest Enid,

I hope you enjoy the book. May it take you on a pilgrimage of your own to a happy path.

Yours sincerely,

Malcolm

P.S. Happy Christmas 1894

Carver read the inscription three times. Presumably, Enid was Alexander's wife but who was Malcolm?

9. CURIOUS, THE THINGS PEOPLE DO

That none may have the impudence to irk
Or hinder me in Christ's most holy work.
Then I tell stories, as occasion calls,

"The Pardoner's Tale"
The Canterbury Tales

The sky looked like it had been coloured in by a child who had only a grey pencil to hand when Carver drew the curtains. The clock on the wall told seven o'clock. A cautious rap at the door helped focus his mind to the present. For a second, he thought he imagined the sound, so softly had it penetrated the beer-induced fog which lay on his brain. "Come in."

"Beg your pardon, sir," cried Samuel Mason. "The Inspector asked for breakfast to be sent up for you both."

The proprietor had opened the door with one hand and on the other balanced a tray filled with tea, bacon, eggs, and bread. He walked slowly to the table as Carver switched on the lamp to help him on his way. After a few pleasantries between the two and the landlord inquiring how the young detective had slept, Samuel left Carver to his breakfast. The young detective had in fact slept well, though his slumber was fraught with dreams of ancient tales of knights on journeys and songs mingled with flagons of ale.

He lifted his little teapot to find a folded piece of paper beneath.

Meet outside at 8 sharp. G.

The aroma of the bacon had awakened his stomach and, being alone, Carver tore into the meal in front of him like an animal half-starved. The thick slices of bread were lathered in butter; the bacon was crisp. He pierced the sunny yolk; the yellow vitellus ran slowly over the bread like lava across arid plains. The strongly brewed tea warmed him, its steam clouding the cold windowpane.

He gave a satisfied yawn as he stretched before the now empty plate and figured he had a leisurely forty minutes until he was to be outside. He spent the time doing his ablutions and dressing. When he went downstairs, he found the back door open, his attention being alerted to it by a cold draught which whispered on his neck.

Stepping tentatively into the public bar he saw the chairs on the tables and wooden shutters upright on the bar top. Stale smoke from the previous night violated his nostrils, the sickly-sweet smell filled the air. There was no one to be seen and he assumed the front door to be locked.

Turning back, he followed the fresh air to the rear of the inn. Droplets of moisture clung to the grass. Logs and bits of wood were strewn around a battered old shelter which covered crates of beer bottles. Turning to his left he walked around the inn and there sitting on a bench beneath a window sat Graves, slowly puffing on a pipe. He didn't appear to hear Carver as he approached, his eyes were fixed on Peggy as she sniffed a pile of raked leaves.

"Good morning, sir."

"Morning Carver," came the reply after a few moments of puffing.

"Did I disturb you, sir?"

"No, lad. I was just thinking."

"I see. I didn't know you smoked, sir."

"I'm fond of an occasional pipe. It gets the old noggin ticking," replied Graves, tapping the stem against his temple whilst maintaining his watch on Peggy.

"Maybe I should try it, sir."

"Ha, no luck with your conundrum then?"

"Not yet, sir, but I'm sure I'll crack it."

"I'm sure you will too, lad. Peggy! Come here."

The sky was full of clouds that hid the sun, giving off a grey sheen so that one squinted despite the dullness. "I spoke briefly with Mason this morning when I gave him that note to put under your teapot. He says Elsie Barter will be working at Treefall Manor until noon today, then she will clean the pub."

"I would have thought there wouldn't be a requirement for Mrs Barter to be at the house today considering there was supposed to be a wedding and now there has been a murder."

"Perhaps there isn't, but that's where she'll be. Say, it's a bit early to go straight up, they're probably still at their breakfast. What say we take a stroll around the village?"

"Excellent, sir."

As the two men ambled through the rough roads seemingly without any particular destination in mind, they saw no sign of life. Carver commented on how many of the cottages still had their curtains drawn despite country living folk being famous early risers. Graves took his time in making a reply, he searched hard for the right word, for though he was sure the curtains being closed was a sign that the villagers had enjoyed too much drink the previous night he was reluctant to associate the words 'celebration' or 'festivities' with the murder.

"I think maybe a few around here may have overdone it, lad. The death of Grimbourne will have come as a shock, people naturally gravitate to the village inn at such times and drink more than they're accustomed to." The cottages they were looking at were of rough granite with matching garden walls topped with slate, which Carver found to be quite hideous. He admired the thatch, and the colourful little gardens, which were at odds with the dark clouds overhead. He took a deep breath of the sour air and felt a momentary calm as though all his troubles were expelled through his lungs. The sudden feeling of relaxation in his joints and brain posed a question to him which brought back a level of anxiety. What were his troubles? That he didn't know how Grimbourne had been murdered? He didn't have time to think; he could sense a sideways glance from Graves.

After walking through little lanes set back from the main road, they soon found themselves looking at a spire. As they made their way in the direction of the church, Carver wondered to himself if this had been the intended destination of Graves all along. "What say we take a walk in the graveyard? I quite like a walk among the headstones, morbid as it may sound," said the older detective.

The village cemetery was like any other in the country. Uneven rows of gravestones made crooked by the shifting earth like a bad set of teeth. In each graveyard generations of families will be found resting for eternity within arm's reach of each other. The remnants of tragic infant lives cut short by disease or illness lie with the bones of men and women aged by many winters and happy struggles. Sad is the sight, Graves often thought, of a headstone whose inscription has all but been washed away by centuries of rain: a life erased from the memory of the world.

"Good morning!" came an exclamation from behind a weathered looking stone cross.

The two detectives turned to an old white-haired man wearing gardening gloves with a handful of weeds.

"Ah! Good morning! Is it vicar, reverend or father?"

"Ha ho! It's vicar!"

"I've never known the difference between a vicar and a reverend, and I wouldn't want to cause offence by asking," said Graves, eyeing the white collar and black cloak.

"There would be no offence, I'm sure. I can assume, then,

that you are not here for my service. You are rather early if you are."

"I'm afraid you have guessed correctly vicar. You see, we are—"

"Detectives! London's finest, I believe."

"I see word travels fast in Swinbridge."

"In the whole of Rockinghamshire, I think you'll find. Although I wouldn't have to be Father Brown to work out that two suited strangers in this tiny village the day after a murder was committed are here to investigate the matter."

"Quite... I'm Inspector Graves, this is Constable Carver."

"If I can be of any assistance, gentlemen, I am happy to help. After all, are the work of the church and the work of the police force not aligned somewhat? I try to prevent people from falling into sin and when I fail you try to prevent them from sinning further by restricting their liberties." The old man smiled.

"That's very kind, vicar. Tell me, were you acquainted with Alexander Grimbourne?"

"Oh yes! Everyone in the village was acquainted with Mr Grimbourne in some fashion or other, even if only through reputation. I suppose you could say I was better acquainted than most."

"One of your flock?" enquired Graves.

"Not quite. He wasn't a regular attendee of my services you understand..."

"No?"

"Well, he didn't attend at all in fact, at least not for many years."

"Did Mr Grimbourne lose his faith do you think?"

"If he had faith to lose then yes, but..."

"When would you say this occurred?"

"Well, I should say when his wife died. She was very devout, you see."

"I see. Is she buried in this graveyard?" interposed Carver.

"Yes, just over there." The three men walked with the

slow solemnity fitting of the circumstance. They passed a dozen headstones of different shapes and sizes before stopping in front of a smooth grey slab.

Here lies in eternal grace
Enid Helen Grimbourne

b. 16th July 1869

d. 17th March 1906

"A tragedy when one passes so young," stated the clergyman, staring at the cold stone.

"Indeed. How did she die?"

"In a fire. Five died that night. It'll haunt me my whole life."

"Where?"

"At the Broon's farm. A mile or so outside of the village."

"I see. Why was Mrs Grimbourne there"

"She grew up on a farm, was very good with the animals. It was lambing season, there was an ewe in distress, Enid was there giving a helping hand. The whole family were in the barn, Desmond, his wife Laura, their son Des junior and little Aimee. There was an upper level in the barn accessed by a ramp where the lambing was done. Anyway, there they were when a fire broke out. The police reckon a gaslight hanging on the door caught some straw. Soon enough the door was on fire and the dry straw and wood caught in no time. There was no way out. That's the Broon grave over there, all buried together. Poor little Aimee was such a sweet child, only six years old. Such a tragedy, and little Des only a few years older." The old man gave a vague wave of his arm and a weary sigh, his cheerful demeanour had changed with the telling of his story.

"You seem to have known Mrs Grimbourne well…"

"She was very devout, as I say."

"And the children?"

"Ah, the children, poor things. To be left motherless at

such a young age.... And such a trying time for Alexander."

"It must have been very difficult..."

"It was. Enid was very fond of bringing the children here to tea, we'd sit in the vestry, the four of us and the children would draw pictures or sing whilst Enid and I would plan our little events. You know, village fêtes, Christmas carolling and that type of thing. Nearly every afternoon they would come, and then..." the gravelly voice of the vicar trailed off, fading like his memories.

"Do the children still come to see you?"

"Yes, though they can't be called children anymore. John pops in now and again for a talk when he does his little errands. Ruth, such a sweet girl, so like her mother, she comes to see me from time to time. It really is a wonder what joy youth can bring to an old man. Do you have children?"

"Do John or Ruth not attend your services? I would have thought in a small village like this it would cause quite a stir if they didn't," asked Graves ignoring the vicar's question.

"Oh yes, at times, though not frequently. It is as you say. Our village is small and firmly held in Christ's loving embrace, I believe, though the people who are not regular churchgoers are somewhat outcasts, I'm afraid. I'm pleased to say the number is few however."

"Perhaps it is amongst those few where we should seek to find our killer," said Carver. "Tell me, do you know of any reason why someone would wish to murder Alexander Grimbourne?"

"Gentlemen, I don't know of your experiences with clergymen, and I don't wish to presume, but I can tell you that in the community we are quite unique. You look apprehensive, let me explain what I mean. You see, we vicars are in a position of trust. We are not dependent on others in the community, like landlords and factory owners for example, for income. We move at a slower pace, have more time for thought and are central to the community, especially in a small village like this. This white collar around my neck is very small, yet it is the first thing people see when they encounter me. A vicar is unimaginable in 'civilian' clothes and because we wear the same outfit every day, we are a constant in the lives of our parishioners. The weather will change, circumstances will change, people, attitudes, marriages will all change, yet we vicars remain the constant at the centre. So, you see gentlemen, what I am describing is a very curious aspect of human psychology. People, whether they are good or bad, familiar, or unfamiliar, treat the vicars of this world differently. No one gets lied to more than the man with the collar who tells the truth, and the reason for that and for why we get treated differently is a blind sort of kindness. If I walk into the pub, the place will go quiet because the patrons will not wish to accidentally offend me with their curse words or blasphemies. Young people will avoid us because they think we know nothing of sex, or carnal sin, that we are delicate, and so they figure my knowledge of the world and people cannot be complete and that the vicar's wisdom is built upon niceties and naiveties. So, to get back to your question young man, I can tell you that Alexander Grimbourne could be a very unpleasant man who made a lot of enemies. He was, I believe, a ruthless businessman but I know nothing more specific than that and I can promise you that I do not know who killed him."

"Did Mr Grimbourne treat you differently to other people because you are a vicar?" asked Graves.

The old man creased his brow in thought. "No," came the reply. "He was kinder to me, not because I am a vicar but because of my friendship with Enid, I believe. Sometimes, very occasionally, you understand, he would visit me, and we would sit in my little cottage there behind the church. I would drink tea and he would drink whisky."

"What would you speak of?"

"Quite often nothing. Sometimes we would play chess, other times we'd talk about something that had been in the newspaper that day or some event or other in the village."

"Did you ever speak of Enid?"

"Never. It was like she was there, and it would be rude to talk about her in her presence. I can only assume the reason for his visits was that Enid spoke highly of our friendship and that Alexander felt a kindness towards me for it. I hope that doesn't sound too conceited?"

"Not at all."

"He never stayed for long. Curious, the things people do; one wouldn't expect it of him."

As they walked away Graves dug his hands deep into his coat pockets and nuzzled tight against his chest, a sight Carver would come to know to be his boss deep in thought. Peggy, who throughout the verbal exchange had stayed on the pebble-strewn path, joined the men once again.

Cracks appeared in the grey sky, the land on the horizon seeming brighter and less oppressed. As they passed from the uneven church path to the main road of the village Carver glanced over his shoulder. Behind the low wall was the church sign.

Parish of Rockinghamshire
Church of our Lord God, St Peter's of Swinbridge
The Reverend Malcolm Thorpe

†

Ed had had a restless night. He had always struggled to get a good night's sleep when not in his own bed, and now he had spent two nights in two different beds. He had felt rotten of course. John had been so polite and hospitable, but Freddie had insisted he stay with him. After all, he was Freddie's friend and what with this murder business and all, was it really appropriate to stay at Treefall Manor? Of course, John had been polite and protested at him leaving, but surely deep down he must have been glad. Ed didn't like to think of himself as a burden but given the circumstances...

Having tossed and turned for hours on end he had given

it up as a bad job and finally dragged himself out of bed before dawn. Because, he admitted to himself, it was not only an unfamiliar mattress that had kept him awake. Hell, he had slept soundly in trenches with rats crawling over him. No, he had other concerns.

He breathed in the cool morning air. As he walked along towards the village, he replayed his interview with the police over and over again in his mind. Shame and embarrassment fought each other for supremacy in his self-conscience. He was supposed to be one of London's most promising and gifted lawyers and yet when he was interviewed by the police, he had completely forgotten to mention the events of the day of his arrival! Dear Lord! If it ever got in the papers! Imagine if the gentlemen at the club found out! Not only was he an unreliable witness, at a trial he could be seen to be perverting the course of justice!

Was it too late? Could he go to see the detectives and tell them what he had overheard in the shed? Would they believe him? Should he mention the man he saw lurking in the woods?

These thoughts were tossing around in his head like a raft on a stormy sea when he looked up and saw Graves and Carver coming towards him, the little dog at their heels. They were still some way off on the main road but if they had seen him, they would surely wish to speak to him. His mind was now in turmoil, should he admit what he knew? The gap between them was shrinking, he had to make a decision.

"Good morning!"

"Good morning, Inspector, good morning, constable."

"Off to church to confess your sins?" asked Carver jocularly. Graves watched with interest as Ed reddened then gave a little laugh at these benign words.

"I ate beef on Friday. There, all done, ha. Off to the Manor again, are we?"

"Yes," replied Graves. "We have a few more questions to ask."

"I understand. A terrible business to find oneself in the

middle of. Truly awful."

"Yes. Tell me, how did the family seem to you last night after we left? We didn't upset anyone too badly, did we?" asked Graves coyly.

"Oh, I don't think so. We had a cold supper that the cook cobbled together, it was quite reasonable, actually. Then we all sort of gravitated to the drawing room for some reason. I was just following everyone else, you understand."

"Of course."

"The old butler glided around with a tray of drinks, it was all a bit glum really, though Miss Dunholme livened things up a bit, telling a few jokes and singing some songs. Quite saucy really, and funny. She's quite a girl."

"Isn't she just," replied Graves dryly.

"Then at around eleven o'clock I thought it time for bed, but as I mounted the stairs I looked up and saw Freddie and George descending them from the top. Freddie had come back to fetch me. He had managed to shoo away any expected visitors and he insisted I stay with him, which is what I did. Luckily, I brought a small case and hadn't unpacked much."

"I see."

Ed found Graves's short replies to be somewhat awkward. He knew from his line of work that the detective was deliberately saying little to create this feeling in Ed in the hope that he would carry on talking. He was surprised that despite knowing the police tactics they were working on him, for his mind was racing for something else to say. Should he mention what he had overheard or the stranger in the woods? The eyes of both detectives were cutting through him, he felt clammy despite the cold.

"Say, if you are in a hurry to the Manor there is a path that leads you there through the woods called Poacher's Lane, it's up there on the left. Freddie showed it to me yesterday."

"Ed, there is something on your mind."

"No, I don't think so."

"I wasn't asking. There is something on your mind and I

suggest you tell us what it is. A problem shared is a problem halved after all."

"Oh Lord. I'm sorry, Inspector, you're right, but you must understand my position. I don't want to be embroiled in any of this and I don't want to cause any trouble to anyone. My career could be ruined!"

"Whatever you say will be treated with confidence, I assure you. Now, what is it you know?"

"I overheard something, but it may be nothing important."

"What did you hear?"

"Well, I was walking in the gardens on the afternoon I arrived. I heard two voices near me, and the tone of their voices told me that it was very much a private conversation, so I hid myself in the shed."

"What did they say?" persisted Graves, his hands thrust deep into his pockets.

"I heard a woman's voice say something along the lines of *'My father must die'* or was it, *'I won't be free until my father is dead'*, yes, I think that was it."

"Did you see the people speaking?"

"No, but the lady was talking to a man. I'm sorry, Inspector, I should have told you sooner."

"You should, but no harm done. Is there anything else?"

"Well, actually Inspector, there was one other thing though I'm sure it is of little importance."

"Go on."

"When I arrived, I saw someone from the bedroom window, prowling around the trees. I took them to be a poacher. I didn't get a good look at them at all, I'm afraid. Then, the night before the murder I awoke and heard someone creeping about the house. They may have been trying to be quiet so as not to wake anyone."

"Undoubtedly. Do you know who or where they went?"

"No, I swear."

"What time was this at?"

"It was four o'clock exactly. Though like I say, probably nothing important."

When the detectives had gone on their way Ed stood staring at the sky clenching his teeth in self anger. *'I hope I've done the right thing,'* he said to himself.

10. ELSIE TELLS HER TALE

His master, then, gave Peterkin the sack
With curses, and forbade him to come back

"The Cook's Tale"
The Canterbury Tales

Twigs snapped underfoot, breaking the silence of the woods as Graves and Carver followed the path. It was darker here, hemmed in by the canopy of blackish green. Invisible creatures scattered as they approached, their presence known only by the shaking of a scrub or branch.

Carver imagined the poachers who gave the path its name. Men who, in the dead of night, stalked their quarry with skill and guile. He thought of Alexander Grimbourne, the type of man he was. It would take a determined poacher to hunt on Treefall Estate in modern times.

"I suppose sir, certain criminals should be respected too?"

"What brought you to that thought, lad?"

"Well, only that it must take a brave man to poach off Alexander Grimbourne. From what we understand, he would probably shoot anyone he caught. Still, as a police officer the thought doesn't quite sit right. Respecting a criminal, I mean."

"Think of it another way, lad. You are respecting a man

who is hunting, just like we are hunting a murderer. The word criminal is a label applied by the courts, it doesn't sum up a person's whole world or everything he stands for, or even the reasons why he does what he does. There are good men who are criminals and there are bad men who aren't."

The path came to an abrupt end, like the conversation. Carver wondered about Graves. Was he philosophical or reflecting his experiences? Was he a more complex mystery than the murder they were trying to solve? Undoubtedly he was working class and no stranger to a scrap in his younger days, Carver thought as he eyed the man's broad shoulders and gnarly hands. Yet, he spoke with a thoughtfulness, and spoke as if what he said was fact in a confident, nonchalant kind of way. Was that wisdom or experience?

The daylight around them had grown perceptibly and the bald earth that was the path showed patches of green grass which led to a clearing. A few trees stood in their way to the open space.

"A hunter would not need to come any further than this," said Graves. "Look, there is the manor house on ahead, you can just see it between those trees." Sure enough, having squeezed through the small gap of two great trunks, the two men stood looking at Treefall Manor which was one hundred yards away. Peggy, catching sight of an unsuspecting rabbit, gave fruitless chase before tiring and returning to her master.

"That's the side of the house, is it not sir?" asked Carver who like Graves was seeing the house from this distance in daylight for the first time.

"I think so, with the front door around to the left. Let's go the longer way, around to the right." The two men walked over the still wet grass. They initially made a beeline for the house but after a minute veered to the right.

"Do you think what Ed told us is of much importance, sir?"

"Well lad, it wouldn't be uncommon for a daughter to say she wanted her father dead when in a fit of anger. The important piece of Ed's story may be who Ruth was talking to."

The two men approached the rear of the house.

"I can't see where that piece of masonry fell from, can you sir?"

"No. Let's see if it is still where it landed."

They reached the rear corner of the house and passed the window of Alexander's study. A few yards on, where the perimeter path met the grass verge lay the slab of stone.

The two men spent a few minutes inspecting it. Carver lifted it without much difficulty.

"Not as heavy as it looks, but still a hefty lump. It would certainly put a dent in one's head."

"Hmmph. Let's carry on." Putting the stone back where he had taken it from, Carver followed Graves's lead. Peggy followed her nose, excited by this undiscovered land. The three of them passed the little back door and the kitchen.

"That must be the door which leads to the wine cellar," said Graves, with a point of his hand. Peggy, uninterested in dusty old bottles, ignored the underground entrance and sniffed the ground all the way past the little shed to the clump of rhododendron bushes. The two detectives followed her, seemingly in little hurry to make their way around the house to the front door.

"I say, what fabulous gardens," cried Graves. "They are completely obscured by the rhododendrons and those Judas trees. Though those flower beds could do with a bit of weeding I should say." For ten minutes, Graves strolled through the rows of flora, seemingly oblivious to Carver and to the objective which had brought them there. He retraced his steps inspecting all before him again and for a few minutes Carver lost sight of him behind the rhododendron bushes before the older detective emerged. After passing the same bed of crocuses for perhaps the fifth time Graves approached the younger man with a broad smile.

"Now then Carver, should we continue?" Graves gave a shrill whistle to summon Peggy and then another when she didn't appear. "Where can she have got to? Peggy!"

After several minutes their calls were answered by muffled barks which came from behind the Judas trees in the direction of the forest. The two men approached and saw Peggy at the treeline, still barking. When they got near to her, she bounded off into the woods, disappearing into the undergrowth.

"She wants us to follow her lad, which means she's found something."

Several yards from the treeline, the detectives found Peggy standing on guard beside a still, lifeless figure. Graves crouched and patted the head of the canine before turning to look at the bloodied face of Jayne Brown. The girl's hair was matted with dried blood, her eyes were closed. She lay on her back, a few dead leaves had fallen from the trees above her and rested on her apron.

"Look sir." Carver pointed to a rock which lay next to the maid's left arm. "There is blood on that rock, it must be what the killer used to bash her head with."

"We shall need to get the police doctor to establish time of death, but I should say she was killed earlier this morning."

"Why not last night, sir?"

"Because the animals haven't got to her yet. This is a nasty business, Carver." Graves drew out his pocket-watch which dangled on the golden chain and looked at the face. "I'm expecting Constable Brent to arrive at the manor in fifteen minutes time. Unfortunately, we must leave the poor girl alone here until he arrives."

"But sir! We can't leave her out here with no one to mind her, it's not decent."

"Murder isn't decent, Carver, and I don't like leaving her any more than you do but time may be of the essence. If she was killed this morning her absence may not have been noticed yet. We still have to interview Hodgkins and Mrs Barter about Alexander Grimbourne's murder and I don't want them to know of this when we talk to them."

"Why, sir?" asked Carver, his gaze fixated on the dead girl.

"Because, if one of them is the killer they may answer

my questions differently if they know we are aware of a second victim. Playing dumb can have its advantages at times. And, more importantly, if we tell Mrs Barter that Jayne is dead, we are by all accounts likely to get an episode of hysterics and no sensible answers out of her!"

"So, you believe both victims were killed by the same person?"

"I do, lad, and there is no mystery about how this killing was done. No locked room trickery here. This was cold-blooded, desperate murder. The killer lured their victim here or arranged a meeting, either way it seems Jayne didn't suspect danger. The murderer then picks up that rock and the deed is done. Blast it, Carver, I should have spoken to the girl last night. She walked past myself and John when you were interviewing Miss Dunholme, but I had more pressing matters on my mind, fool that I am!"

†

The front door was opened after a few minutes by Hodgkins, who looked as ghostly as the day before. "The young master is out on one of his walks sirs."

"Perhaps we could trouble you for a few minutes of your time instead then?" asked Graves. The old butler answered by raising his eyebrows and by giving a customary bow.

"Would you like to conduct your questioning in the dining room as before, sirs?"

"Oh, nothing so formal as that," intervened Carver. "Is there perhaps a library?"

"Of course, it is on the first floor. Let me show you. Would you like coffee?"

"Wonderful!"

"You are quite the gardener then, sir?" asked Carver in the

library when Hodgkins had gone to get the coffee.

"Oh, I like to potter about. Of course, my garden at home is very modest, there's not much room for them in London. Perhaps when I retire, we can move out a bit and have a bigger patch in the countryside."

"This is where the murder weapon was taken from, sir," said Carver, who was bent over the ebony table looking at the empty cradle.

"I know," replied Graves who was staring at the bookshelves. "This is where I came last night while you were interviewing the delightful Miss Dunholme."

"You know it's rude to speak of a lady when she's not present," came a purring voice from the doorway.

"But you *are* present, Miss Dunholme," responded Graves without taking his eyes from the books. "I heard your heels clicking closer from down the hallway."

"Very good, Inspector"

"Tell me, do you always wear those things? I imagine they are very uncomfortable."

"They may look uncomfortable to you, but women are made of sterner stuff than men despite the rumours. The only discomfort we notice is that which we cause." Penelope smiled at Carver as she said this, resulting in him looking like he was being choked. Graves suppressed a grin.

"Is Miss Dunholme staying for coffee too?" asked Hodgkins, who appeared next to the lady's elbow carrying a tray.

"N-no she is not!" stammered Carver.

"Bye boys!" laughed Penelope, as she disappeared down the hallway.

"How can I be of assistance, sir?" asked the old butler when the sound of clicking heels had faded into silence.

"How long have you been employed here at Treefall Manor, Hodgkins?"

"Over forty years I should say, Inspector, though they may be more than I can count sir."

"I see." The next few minutes were filled with questions

and answers which floated back and forth like a tennis ball in a warmup rally. Hodgkins told how he had been taken on as a young man by Alexander's father who, he, said was much like his only son. The old butler confirmed the personality of the murdered master yet told the detectives with a touch of pride that he himself had never given cause for serious admonishment. He spoke with regret at the passing of Mrs Grimbourne and told how a change came over Alexander shortly after that tragic event.

"Tell me, where were you at the time of the murder?"

"I was having a cup of tea with Betty, as is our habit."

"I see. Did you see or hear of anything you thought suspicious yesterday morning?"

"No sir was just like any other day. Breakfast was over, I had cleared the morning room of the plates and things. Jayne was washing them clean as myself and Betty had a cup of tea in the kitchen as we always do."

"The kitchen is down the hall from the study. You are sure you didn't hear a scream or an argument of any kind?"

"No sir. It is an old house sir, the walls are thick. Besides, the kitchen is down a few steps, kind of half on the ground floor and half below. You never hear anything down there."

"Do you and Betty always have tea at that time?"

"Every day for forty odd years."

"I suppose members of the household would know your daily routine?"

"Yes sir, I suppose they would."

"Tell me, how was the murder brought to your attention? Presumably, you didn't hear Mrs Barter's screams like the rest of the house?"

"Oh, I did, sir. She burst through the back door wailing like a banshee. I nearly spilled my tea over my lap. Screaming she was, about how there was a knife in him. That's what she kept on repeating. *'there's a knife in him, there's a knife in him'*. I believe Betty had to put a tot of whisky in her tea to help calm her nerves."

"Is Mrs Barter here today? Would you please ask her to come here?"

"Of course, sir. I believe she is looking for Jayne." The two detectives were left alone as the old man went on his errand. Graves sipped his coffee while Carver rubbed Peggy behind the ears.

"That seems to rule out Hodgkins and Betty," said Graves over his cup. "And now we also know Jayne was in the kitchen when Alexander was murdered."

"You didn't seriously suspect them did you, sir?"

"I suspect everyone and no one, Carver, but you're right, it was always unlikely to be them."

"No motive as far as I can see, sir."

"Exactly."

"Mrs Barter, as requested," announced Hodgkins from the doorway.

"Thank you, that will be all, Hodgkins."

The woman in question stood timidly in the doorway clutching a handkerchief. The shock and excitement of the previous day had left her looking somewhat bedraggled. Her hair was an unkempt mass and her relentless tears had burnt her cheeks red as though they were composed of acid. Graves looked and summed up the woman in his mind, deciding on the best approach to take. "Please come in Mrs Barter, take a seat," soothed the older detective in his sweetest voice. "How awful this must be for you. Please, don't distress yourself, Mrs Barter. Really I am surprised to find you here at all given what you have been through."

"There's so much to be done, really I am needed, Inspector! And I can't think where Jayne has got to!"

"But Mrs Barter, you should rest after the horrible time you have had."

"It *was* 'orrible sir! It was! Seeing the master lying there like that with a knife poking out of him! 'Orrible it was!"

"Indeed, Mrs Barter, indeed," continued Graves in his honeyed voice. "I'm sure the family could make do without your services for a few days. It must be terribly traumatic being in the house after what's happened."

'Wild horses couldn't drag her away from all this juicy commotion,' thought Carver looking on.

"Terrible traumatic as you say, Inspector! But I'm needed as I say! I couldn't leave the family at a time like this! Who would Ruth turn to if I'm not here?!"

"Well… her friend is here, isn't she? What's her name, Poppy, Polly…"

"Penelope, Inspector. Penelope Dunholme. A piece of work if you ask me, walking around the place in those dresses as though she were in some seedy nightclub in Paris. And those shoes! How girls walk in them heels I don't know!"

"Times have changed, more's the pity Mrs Barter…"

"How right you are, Inspector! When I was a girl, my mother would blush if you could see my ankles and nor do I blame her. Decency, Inspector! Where's it gone I'd like to know!"

"Indeed, Mrs Barter…" sighed Graves sympathetically.

"I said! I said to Betty, 'You mark my words, Betty Inglethorpe, no good will come of having a girl dressed like that stay in the house, you mark my words!' and here we are, *murder!*"

"How right you were, Mrs Barter."

"Every year she's been coming to visit Ruth and every year when she leaves, I breathe a sigh of relief that God hasn't punished us by tearing the place down around us like Gomorrah! I'm sure the boys in the village have never seen the like!"

"Well, that piece of masonry that fell…"

"Lor' almighty Inspector, you're right! I never thought of it! It was a sign! A sign of what was to come! Send her away, Inspector, take the harlot away from this house I beg you! Poor Ruth doesn't need friends like that, such a sweet, lovely girl is Ruth. Looked after her I have, since her poor mother died, dear girl."

"You must be like part of the family, Mrs Barter…"

"Oh, I wouldn't presume to say that, Inspector, though the family might, I'm sure."

"You are too modest, Mrs Barter! No doubt as a trusted confidant of the family you know all that goes on here ..."

"Well... as you say, I am trusted... really I couldn't break faith..."

"Oh, good gracious no, Mrs Barter! I know you would never speak out of turn. But this is a devilish business Mrs Barter..."

"It is Inspector! Devilish!" cried Elsie, twisting her handkerchief in her hands.

"Indeed, and you see I would hate for us to get wrong information... you know how unreliable young maids can be..."

"Oh yes indeed, Inspector! Young'uns these days don't know their heads are screwed on. Look at Jayne! Disappears off whenever she fancies and at a time like this too! And she's been slacking recently, not doing her jobs properly! Thinks she's too good for work all of a sudden: it's called honest work for a reason I likes to remind her! Got money coming her way she reckons, pfft, where would she get money from? Head full of hot air is all she's got! Girls these days Inspector, I don't know!"

"Exactly Mrs Barter! And men, pfft, men don't pay attention to anything, Mr Campbell for example..."

"Oh, how right you are sir! Men wouldn't know what day of the week it was if you didn't tell them. And that Mr Campbell! Well, calls himself a secretary, I daresay. He can't be that good at his job otherwise Mr Grimbourne wouldn't have to tell him off so much would he?"

"Really?"

"Oh yes sir! Always having a go was Mr Grimbourne. God rest his poor soul! Mr Campbell was always making mistakes. I'm not surprised; sickly looking man."

"Was Mr Campbell upset when Mr Grimbourne had to tell him off?"

"Oh, I couldn't say, sir, you don't know what goes on in a man's head, neither do they half the time. I'm forever having to remind my husband to do this and that. One time I said to him, I said Harold Percival Barter you promised—"

"Mr Campbell…"

"Oh yes, where was I? Oh yes, Mr Campbell is meek as a anything though, wouldn't say boo to a goose, except that time…"

"Yes… which time was that?"

"Oh, I don't like telling tales Inspector."

"Oh no of course not, but you see—"

"Well, it was a few weeks ago," interrupted Elsie hastily. "I was doing a bit of dusting not far from the study door. Such a commotion I heard, I said to myself, 'Elspeth Barter there's trouble brewing here,' anyway, I couldn't make out what was being said but there were two voices shouting at each other. I figured one must be Mr Grimbourne because it is his study, but I couldn't for the life of me imagine who would dare argue back to Mr Grimbourne. You can imagine my surprise when the door flew open and out stormed none other than George Campbell!" Elsie looked at the two men with an air of triumph.

"And you didn't hear anything that was said?" asked Graves.

"Well… not really. I definitely heard Mr Campbell say, '*I won't do it!*' and Mr Grimbourne might have said something about him being ungrateful, which of course he is. After all Mr Grimbourne has done for him, God rest his soul! I said afterwards to Betty, I said 'Betty Inglethorpe let m—'"

"And this was uncommon you say?" cut in Graves quickly.

"What was? Oh, you mean, oh yes! No one would dare argue with Mr Grimbourne, except maybe John on the odd occasion…"

"John?"

"Well, I don't like to say but he sometimes can be a bit fiery, though who can blame him what with his leg and all."

"What does John get fiery about?"

"Oh, I don't know, Inspector, it's nothing to do with me."

"Of course, maybe Betty might kno—"

"You'll get no sense out of Betty Inglethorpe Inspector! All rumours and gossip that one! Where was I? Oh yes, poor John, he does get angry sometimes. Feels like a prisoner, he says. I heard him tell Lord Taylor to expect things to be different when he is master of Treefall Manor."

"He said that?"

"He did."

"Does Lord Taylor visit often?"

"No, not too often. As a matter of fact, we barely saw him until a few weeks ago. A very private man is Lord Taylor with an Indian as a servant no less!" said Elsie wide-eyed as though she were surprised.

"A few weeks ago? Is that when he started courting Miss Ruth?"

"Indeed, it is sir, one day I was dusting near the study door, and I hears Mr Grimbourne on the telephone... 'Lord Taylor, I will be visiting you at seven tonight,' he says, then he says, 'I don't care if you have plans, you're going to want to hear what I have to say!' And that was that, we started seeing more of Lord Taylor after that. I am glad Inspector I have to say..."

"Yes?"

"Oh yes, such a lovely girl is Ruth, Lord only knows what kind of men that trollop Miss Dunholme introduces her to when she goes to London to visit. I mean, begging your pardon, sir, but why would a young lady want to go to a filthy place like London? Murders and arsoners and all sorts on every street corner no doubt! Lor' I don't know!"

"Are there no other young men in the village who have their eye on Miss Grimbourne?"

"Well Inspector, I'm not likely to know but they'd be mad not to. Such a lovely girl. Besides, I don't pay any attention to some of the gossip I hear in the village, I keep myself to myself thank you very much!"

The two detectives exchanged glances.

"Mrs Barter," began Carver. "Can you tell us how it was you came to find the body?"

Elsie looked at Carver as though noticing him for the first time then burst into renewed lamentations for the dead and the horrors of the previous day.

"Lor' o' mercy! It was terrible! Lying there he was! There was a knife in him. Never in my born days did I think I'd ever see the like..."

"Yes, Mrs Barter, don't distress yourself, it's over now..." soothed Graves.

"Over...? How do you know that sir? Have you caught the devil? How do you know the madman won't come back and murder us all in our beds at night? Lor' have mercy!"

"Really Mrs Barter, with your help I'm sure we'll catch him in no time." Graves and Carver exchanged a glance, the body of Jayne lying in the woods still fresh in their minds.

"My help? But what can I do Inspector?"

"Well, you can tell us how you came to find the body as Constable Carver here suggests. It might not seem like that can help us to catch the killer Mrs Barter but believe me it can. All information is important and it's reliable witnesses like yourself who more often than not are the difference between justice being served and a guilty man roaming free, believe me, Mrs Barter."

"Oh, I do Inspector; I do!"

"Well then, just you take your time and tell us what happened."

"Thank you, sir," replied Elsie with a sniffle. "Well, you see I have my routine. Every day I come up to the house and I set the girls their tasks. Once that's done, I have a piece of toast and a cup of tea while Betty starts preparing the breakfast."

"Very good, Mrs Barter," said Graves encouragingly.

"Then I start the cleaning, see. I do the dining room so it's ready for breakfast then I come here and do the library as John will sometimes like to come here in the mornings. Then I do some of the ground floor windows and the halls, then finally Mr Grimbourne's study. Jayne does most of everything else."

"Is Mr Grimbourne usually in his study when you go to clean it?" asked Graves.

"Nearly always, sir. He doesn't mind me cleaning while

he's there, he's used to it. I do my work very quietly so as not to disturb him."

"And the study door, is it usually locked when you go to clean it?"

"Oh no sir! Sometimes if Mr Grimbourne has someone in there like Mr Campbell the door will be closed but not locked. Very rare for that to happen sir."

"I understand. And yesterday..."

"Yesterday it was locked! I was *very* surprised I was sir. I knocked softly and got no answer, so I tried knocking harder. Eventually after a few minutes I got concerned and I went out the back door and around to the window..."

"Excuse me, did you see Mr Grimbourne alive yesterday, Mrs Barter?"

"Oh yes sir."

"When exactly?"

"When I cleaned the window, the middle one that doesn't open. I clean the other two from inside the study as they open inwards. It's easy what with them security bars on them all. But the middle one I have to clean from the outside."

"And you saw Alexander Grimbourne when you cleaned the window?"

"Oh! I did sir. He was sitting at his desk. He didn't look up, but quite often he doesn't."

"Was he typing on his typewriter?"

"No sir, he was just sitting there quite still, looking down. I thought he might've been reading something."

"Tell me, were the two windows on either side of the middle one closed?"

"Yes sir, I didn't make a point of checking, but they didn't seem open a crack sir. And nor would they be what with it being a cold day and all. Mr Grimbourne was terrible against the cold, Inspector. He wouldn't stand to have the windows open."

"I see. Please continue."

"Well, as I was saying, I went out the back door and around as Lor', what do I see but Mr Grimbourne lying on the floor with a knife in him." Elsie burst into fresh sobs at the memory etched on her brain.

"There there, Mrs Barter. Tell me, how long would you say it was between seeing Mr Grimbourne sitting at his desk while you cleaned the window and seeing him dead on the floor?" Elsie whose face was buried in her hankie, paused, and said, "Oh, only about twenty minutes or so."

"Do you know what time you cleaned the windows?"

"Not exactly, probably around a quarter to ten."

"Thank you, Mrs Barter you are helping us enormously."

"I'll always do my bit for the right side of the law, Inspector," said Elsie righteously.

"I'm sure you would. Now, can you remember yesterday when you cleaned this room?"

"I can, sir."

"Excellent. Did you dust that ebony table by the window?"

"I did, sir."

"And was the dagger in its cradle or missing like it is now?"

"It wasn't there, sir. I'm sure of it because I remember thinking how odd it was that it was gone. I was going to tell Mr Grimbourne when I saw him, but then…" Elsie broke off again, her voice strained by emotion.

"I see, it's alright Mrs Barter, there was nothing you could have done. You have been an enormous help, really you have. We won't distress you any longer, you go have a rest."

"Thank you, Inspector." Elsie Barter slowly got to her feet and dragged herself to the door. She was just about to cross into the hall when the sweet voice of Inspector Graves stopped her. "Oh, Mrs Barter, I'm sorry, there was one last question I wanted to ask you. I know that *you* will know the answer and since you are so keen to help us you won't mind telling us."

"Y-yes Inspector?"

"Who was the last person to leave Mr Grimbourne's employment here at Treefall Manor?" Graves watched as Elsie hesitated for a moment, the handkerchief in her hands turning like the cogs in her brain.

"Well, er, I…"

"Come now Mrs Barter you *must* remember…"

"Well, oh yes, I remember now. It was the gardener a few months back."

"And what was the gardener's name?"

"William."

"William…?"

"William Hopkirk."

11. THE LETTER AND THE WILL

And thrust this letter down with subtle skill
Under his pillow, read it if he will.

"The Merchant's Tale"
The Canterbury Tales

"Do you believe her sir?"

"About what, lad?" replied Graves.

"About not knowing why William Hopkirk got sacked"

"I do as a matter of fact. You could see that she was reluctant to tell us he had been sacked but also how irritated she was when she said she didn't know why. Yes, I believe she doesn't know but would dearly love to."

The two detectives were still in the library. Mrs Elsie Barter had left them a few minutes before. Hodgkins appeared with more coffee. "Thank you Hodgkins. Can you tell me if Miss Grimbourne is still in the house?" asked Graves.

"I believe she is, sir. She is due to go out with Miss Dunholme, although they have not left yet I think. Would you like me to ask her to come to you?"

"If you would, thank you."

"Yes sir, although on my way up I saw a police car through the window, it was coming up the driveway…"

"Ah, that will be Brent. Please don't disturb Miss Grimbourne until he has left."

"Yes sir, very good sir. I shall show the policeman up."

"Good morning, Brent," said Graves when the constable entered the library.

"Good morning, sir."

"What's that you carry under your arm?"

"A few reports sir, would you like the headlines?"

"No thanks, lad, I'll read it myself." Graves took the reports and placed them on his lap. "Say, is Young not with you?"

"No sir, the Inspector is dealing with a small local matter. However, he wished for me to relate to you that Mr Roberts's alibi checks out."

"Ah, very good! Shame he is not here though. I'm afraid I have an urgent task for you and not a pleasant one." Graves told Brent the circumstances surrounding the discovery of Jayne's body and instructed him to discreetly ring up the police doctor with as much haste as he could muster before quickly getting himself out to the woods. Carver eyed the folder of papers hungrily, wondering what information they contained.

"You suspect Roberts?" asked the young man when Brent had left.

"No more than anyone else, though his alibi should have been easily proved. I gave Brent a few instructions to relay to Young last night when he came to the pub. Now, what have we here?" said Graves, picking up the reports. For a few minutes he was silent as his eyes scoured the pages, picking out words and phrases which caught his attention.

"Hmmph."

"Anything of interest, sir?" asked Carver who was fidgeting restlessly in his chair.

"It appears there are two sets of fingerprints on the murder weapon. One set belonged to Alexander Grimbourne."

"And the other?"

"To our high-flying lawyer."

"Ed?!"

"Indeed."

"He did seem rather excited when we saw him this morning, at least I thought there was something off in his manner."

"Yes, I noticed it too. Nervous demeanour; unusual in a lawyer. Well, we shall have to question him again before we make any assumptions."

"Anything else there, sir?"

"Alexander Grimbourne's business dealings, Mr Roberts sent them over to Young first thing, they will take a bit more reading though. Ah, and that piece of paper we found on the study floor has been analysed and the wording deciphered."

"Good morning, Inspector, good morning, Constable, Hodgkins said you wished to see me?"

Graves stood and gave a little bow to Ruth, who stood in the doorway wearing a long dark green dress. Her hair was fashionably tied, and her cheeks had dabs of make-up applied beneath a birdcage veil. "Good morning, Miss Grimbourne, please take a seat. I'm afraid there are certain things which we either don't know or half know, and I was hoping you could help us with some information."

"I am happy to help you, Inspector."

"Thank you. Firstly, can you tell me the substance of your father's will?"

"Can't Mr Roberts tell you that?"

"He could, but I don't know when I will get hold of him. You know how solicitors are, Miss, busy people, or at least pretend to be, especially when the police wish to talk to them." Graves gave a reassuring smile to counter the reluctance he observed in the young lady's manner.

"Well, I'm afraid I don't know the exact content. I believe the gist of it is that the estate will go to John and there will be some money for me. Really, I've never thought about it. Father was such a robust man, he never had any health complaints, why should I think about his will?"

"Hmmph."

"Is there anything else Inspector? Penelope is waiting for me."

"Is John in the house, do you know?"

"I believe he has gone to the lake. He sometimes does."

"Oh?"

"Yes, he likes to write poems and clear his head there."

"I see. How do we get to the lake?" Graves watched as Ruth's hand reached up to play with her necklace, as she had when being interviewed before, only to see that the necklace was not there. Ruth quickly placed her hand in her lap.

"Go through the gardens, through the farthest Judas trees, turn left before you get to the woods and keep walking for five minutes or so."

"Thank you. The gardens are very lovely, aren't they? We were admiring them before we came in."

"Yes, they are wonderful."

"Unfortunately," began Graves. "As we were there, we came across the body of Jayne Brown…"

"Good Lord!" gasped Ruth. "In the garden?"

"In the woods just beyond."

Ruth held her hand to her heart and Graves readied himself to lunge forward, fearing that the young lady might fall out of her chair. "How… how did she die Inspector?" said Ruth trembling.

"I'm afraid she was murdered. Struck with a rock over the head. It appears death would have been quite instantaneous. Tell me, can you think of any reason why someone would wish to hurt Miss Brown?"

"No Inspector, I–I can't."

Graves cursed the veil obscuring the face of Ruth. He wanted to see the effect his questions had on her, though he did not miss the whiteness of her knuckles as she clung to arm of her chair. "Miss Grimbourne, what were your movements this morning?"

"I had breakfast with John around eight o'clock then did some sewing in my bedroom until now."

"I see. Tell me, why did your father sack William Hopkirk?" asked Graves. Carver watched as Ruth tensed into stone.

"Oh, it was such a long time ago…"

"It was only a few months ago was it not?" continued Graves.

"Yes, but so much has happened since then. No doubt he displeased father in some trivial way. Father was often hard on the staff."

"So, you're telling us you don't know why William was dismissed?" Ruth paused for a moment before answering.

"No. I don't."

"She's lying," said Carver through gritted teeth once enough time had elapsed for Ruth to make her way down the stairs.

"Yes, she is certainly lying about William Hopkirk. Though I am not so sure she knew the provisions of her father's will. Perhaps she never gave it much thought, as she says."

"What does the piece of paper from the study floor say? Miss Grimbourne interrupted us."

"We'll discuss that where we can be sure there are no ears nearby."

"Are we going to see John now?"

"Not quite yet. We need to look in Jayne's room first."

A few subtle and hushed words with Hodgkins gave the detectives the necessary information needed to locate the maid's room which was on the uppermost floor of the manor. Peggy followed enthusiastically, seemingly unperturbed by her grisly discovery less than an hour before. When they arrived at their destination Carver turned the doorknob, but the sturdy oak door did not budge. "It's locked, sir," he said, frowning.

"Not to worry lad, it's hardly the Bank of England we're trying to get in to." Graves dug into a pocket and extracted a small pouch which looked like an eyeglasses case. He opened it to reveal an assortment of pins and keys before bending down to peer at the keyhole. "Hmmph. I don't think a key will do it, a pin it is then!"

"Sir?" enquired Carver, his curiosity mingled with confusion as he watched Graves insert a thin metal rod into the keyhole.

"Well, lad, you'll find that a good skeleton key will fit into a good many locks but usually for things like wardrobes or sheds or the like, things that don't often contain items of value. But this is an old door with an old lock, not too dissimilar to the study where Alexander was murdered. You'll find that the only key that opens this door is probably on the body of the poor girl in the woods. So, what I must do is pick the lock. Easy."

"Could someone have picked the lock to Alexander's study do you think?"

"Not a chance lad. Firstly, Alexander would have heard them scratching at the keyhole and undoubtedly would have investigated. And secondly, the study lock would be an incredibly difficult lock to pick. It is quite an intricate design." Graves stood back allowing Carver to twist the doorknob for the second time. The door swung inward into a small room whose darkness exuded a musty odour which seeped into the hallway and into the nostrils of the detectives. "Let's have a look, shall we?" said Graves to Carver as the younger man wafted his hand before his face.

The two men stepped in, Peggy close at their heels. The room was dominated by a small metal-framed bed which lay in the middle of the room directly in front of the door. Graves looked to his left but only a blank magnolia papered wall met his eyes. To the right was a small desk beneath a window. Only a flimsy looking wardrobe and a wooden chair, the type you might find in a Sunday school, exposed themselves to the view of the visitors.

Carver took a step forward. "There doesn't seem to be much to speak of, sir."

"Hmm, seemingly not. However, that door was locked for a reason, or so I would guess. You look in the wardrobe, I'll check the bed."

Carver opened the double doors and looked at a sad arrangement of aprons and cotton day dresses. A maid's cap hung on the back of one of the doors. A cream-coloured pinafore was the only indication that leisure might have existed outside the thick walls of Treefall Manor. "There doesn't appear to be any personal effects, sir," said Carver as he rummaged through the pockets of the dresses. "The poor girl must have had rather a sad existence, don't you think? No letters from family or friends here, one day off a fortnight or whatever it is, working from dawn until dusk. Aha, what's this?" Carver fingertips brushed a cold stone. He pinched his fingers together and pulled from the dress he was handling a jewel on a golden chain. Graves, who at that moment had found a lump in the pillowcase he was holding, turned to Carver and exclaimed, "What you have there, lad, is Ruth Grimbourne's red ruby necklace! Hmmph!"

"What have you found, sir?!

"I'm not sure, let's have a look." Graves turned the pillow in his hand and shook it violently. Onto the bed fell banknotes, fluttering down like the spinning seeds of a sycamore tree.

"Look! There must be one hundred pounds there!" cried Carver. "Where did she get money like that from, do you think?"

Graves looked at the scattered money lying on the bed then looked at the glinting red ruby dangling from Carver's hand.

†

The two men and Peggy made their way down the left-hand flank of the grand staircase. Generations of strong Grimbourne men glared at them from their picture frames as they descended.

"Sir, that trick with the lock. Where did you learn to open doors like that?" asked Carver.

"It wasn't a trick lad. It could in fact be called

workmanship if it wasn't often associated with nefarious motives. My father was a magician, he taught me. He used to do card tricks, mind reading and the like. Any escapologist knows how to pick a lock. It's not difficult, though some locks are harder to pick than others."

The carpet underfoot ensured they moved noiselessly into the grand hall and along the corridor which led them to the door of the study where they saw Alexander Grimbourne's secretary loitering.

"You need this to open it," exclaimed Graves, holding a key, as he watched George Campbell turn the door handle, though the door itself stayed firmly in its place.

"Oh, Inspector, I didn't see you there."

"Evidently," replied Graves drily.

"I was just… I think I left my attaché case in here."

"You didn't, there was no case in there when I left here last night. I asked Constable Brent to apply a temporary lock to the door. He gave me the key at the inn along with a few other things of interest…" said Graves, lingeringly.

"I see… ah, yes, I remember now. It's upstairs beneath my bed, how forgetful of me."

"Indeed," replied Graves, staring coldly at the secretary.

"You wished to see me?"

"Yes, Mr Campbell, there was just a thing or two we wanted to pick your brains over."

"Of course, shall we go to the drawing room? I think the fire has been set, it's quite chilly today."

The fire was in its infancy, it crackled with new life. Peggy hurried to claim her space in front of it as if there might soon be a stampede of heat seeking creatures.

"What did you wish to see me about?" asked George when the three men were seated.

Carver, who thought he could see the train of thought Graves was following took the initiative. "Do you happen to know the contents of Mr Grimbourne's will?"

"The old one or the new one? Proposed new one, I suppose

I should say."

"Both," replied Carver.

"Well, no is the short answer I'm afraid, gentlemen. Mr Grimbourne did not talk of such things, though I could guess that the estate would likely be left to John as first-born son and there would be provisions made for Ruth."

"Would it surprise you Mr Campbell, to learn that in the will which Mr Grimbourne planned to make yesterday he was intending to leave *you* a substantial sum?" asked Graves.

"A substantial sum?" asked George in a trembling voice.

"Very substantial, in fact."

"Oh, gracious. I had no idea Inspector," replied George, quickly breaking eye contact with the detective.

"Are you quite sure about that?" asked Graves, who was eyeing the man keenly.

"Yes Inspector, *quite* sure."

"Hmmph. Tell me Mr Campbell, has William Hopkirk been at Treefall Manor since he was dismissed for stealing?"

"Stealing? He wasn't sacked for stealing."

"No? What was he sacked for then?"

George, feeling he had been tricked gave a wry smile. "Mr Grimbourne did not want him employed here any longer. Such things were not uncommon. With regards to Mr Hopkirk in particular, I can't tell you why he left but I can say for certain it wasn't for stealing and I don't believe he has been back, Inspector. Leastways, I haven't seen him around."

"How can you be certain he wasn't dismissed for stealing if you don't know the real reason?" asked Carver.

"Because Constable, if he were stealing, Mr Grimbourne would have informed me as the inventory of whatever he was pinching would have fallen under my accounts. Besides, there is very little to steal except of course the family silver and the paintings. I would certainly notice if any of them had disappeared."

"Quite..."

The echo of footsteps could be faintly heard down the

hallway. They grew louder as the men listening to them fell silent. Expectantly, the three of them looked to the door. Penelope entered abruptly and did not slow or show surprise when she saw the six eyes watching her. She was used to men becoming silent and looking at her when she entered a room. "Still here, are we? Lucky us."

"Yes Miss Dunholme, still here," answered Graves.

"I say, I've lost my lighter, have any of you seen it? I thought I may have left it in here." Penelope started digging around cushions seemingly oblivious to the comforts of the gentlemen sitting on them. Graves watched her with bemused eyes.

"Where could I have left it?" she continued as she made for the table by the window, it must be here somewhere."

"Perhaps in the library?" offered Carver.

"No. I checked there. I see you get correctly questioned, George."

"Miss?" enquired the frowning secretary.

"Well, I got interrogated earlier on in the cold, draughty library. You, on the other hand sit in front of the fire, the only thing missing is a swirling glass of brandy. Sexism, that's the word." Graves, not taking the bait merely smiled. His compatriot's inexperience however trumped his judgement.

"Miss, may I remind you that it was you who came into the library? You were not sent for!"

"Sent for?! Sent for?! Constable Carter!" wailed Penelope. "Who might you be to send for me, might I ask? A vicious policeman who enjoys frightening defenceless women? Sent for indeed! I am not a dog, Mr Carter!"

Peggy watched this tirade with one eye open and blinked curiously at the word 'dog'.

"It's Carver, actually! Lord, give me strength, I've never met a woman as intolerable as you!"

"Steady on, my good man!" cried George chivalrously.

"I will not steady on, thank you very much. Defenceless! Ha! Don't make me laugh."

"Everyone! Settle down," commanded Graves sternly. He looked each person in the eye and conveyed a warning message before continuing. "Now, Miss Dunholme, it appears that your lighter is not here in this room, I would appreciate it if you weren't either."

"Well! I never! I only—"

"Out!" bellowed Graves.

Carver marvelled that Graves didn't turn to stone such was the gorgonian glare shot at him by Penelope. The lady continued to complain loudly to herself at the insolence of men as she made her furious exit.

"Dear me, I've forgotten what we were discussing," said George when silence had again filled the air.

"We were discussing Mr William Hopkirk," replied Graves. "Though there seems little point, as everyone who speaks to me lies." George reddened at this outburst yet did not speak either to confirm or deny the accusation. "If you won't speak to me about the gardener perhaps you will speak to me about the maid…"

"Which maid?"

"The one who is lying cold and dead in those woods out there!" Graves flung his arm towards the window in anger. He watched the secretary's face contort in confusion before quickly turning to horror.

"You mean… there has been another murder?"

"Yes. Jayne Brown was murdered this morning. What can you tell me?"

"Nothing, Inspector! I don't know why anyone would wish to kill Jayne! Good grief! I suppose you want to know where I was. I arose early and drove over to Lord Taylor's house. I hadn't been back here five minutes before you saw me at the study."

"What was your business with Lord Taylor?" asked Graves, barely containing the anger in his voice.

"He asked me to bring him all the receipts and things for the wedding. He didn't want Ruth to be troubled with anything, you understand, what with the circumstances so I helped him sort through things. Mr Singh saw me arrive and leave. He can vouch for me."

"I see. I think that will be all Mr Campbell. Unless there is anything else you wish to tell us?" George stood up, his arms rigid to his sides. He looked at Graves who eyed him curiously. He saw the secretary's lip quiver, the bead of sweat at his hairline, the angst in his eyes.

Slowly, somewhat unsure of himself George replied, "No, nothing," in a defeated tone.

"Well," said Carver when he and Graves were the only two men in the room. "He certainly knows a great deal more than he is letting on, I should say."

"So would I, lad. Mr Campbell is a man bearing a great burden unless I'm mistaken and moreover, I think he was close to getting it all off his chest before deciding against it. We were close Carver, we were very close. Oh, and bloody hell lad, do yourself a favour and mind your temper."

"Yes sir. Sorry, sir."

"I mean the woman might be an arrogant pain in the you know where, but don't let her rile you up; her nor anyone else for that matter. You don't want too many complaints going in your file, especially at your age."

"Yes, sir," replied Carver meekly.

"Alright, good lad, I won't labour the point. Now, shall we see if we can hunt down the new master of the manor?"

†

The change in temperature caused Carver to shiver a little. They had just left a warm firelit room and now plunged into the fresh air, which, though not deeply cold, was certainly a change to the south on a thermometer.

Graves looked at the sky, or rather at the clouds blocking it. Heavy mountainous masses which looked as though they must be being held from above, such was the gravity defying weight of water contained within.

"Should've brought an umbrella."

"Right, you are sir. Now about that letter…"

"Ah yes. Not much chance of being overheard out here, I suppose." Graves took from his pocket a crisp piece of paper folded in two places and handed it to Carver who opened it. The words were typewritten and had clearly been transposed as accurately as possible. Words, sentences which were incomplete were copied with sometimes long, sometimes short spaces between them, showing Carver where indecipherable words must have been on the original. He read the scant information carefully.

Dearest one,

Oh, how I wish for us to be together. I hate Alexander **with all of my being and long for the day when we** *can live side by side without that tyrant towering over us! Oh, what folly am I speaking! I am* **trapped here in this prison. There** *is no way out!*
The old man must die for us to be free, *there is no other way. If only he died* **before the wedding** *all our troubles would be solved! An accident, a sudden illness, anything* **to free us from his grip! But how** *selfish of me to even dream.* **This is not only** *about us, there is poor Ruth to also consider. No doubt she longs for the day she can marry you and she has been so sweet to me I have her good***will to think about.** *Yes, it is not just us under the yoke of Alexander Grimbourne!*

All   my love

"Penny for them?" asked Graves.

"Well, it certainly appears to be a love letter of some sort and the death of the old man is mentioned, which we must assume is Alexander Grimbourne. I just wish we had the complete letter."

"Yes. A dangerous game trying to fill in the blanks through

guesswork. Any thoughts on the author?"

"Well... Ruth would be my guess, although I have a few doubts in my mind."

"Such as?" asked Graves.

"Let's say Ruth did write it. When did she write it? Clearly in the last few weeks, as the wedding is mentioned, but if that is so, who is the letter written to? Marrying Lord Taylor is Ruth's ticket out of here so why then does the letter say, 'the old man must die for us to be free'?"

"Very good Carver, anything else?"

"Yes," continued the detective, warming to the evolution of his thoughts. "What if the letter is a fake? What if the murderer wrote it out then destroyed the letter? He then tore out the piece of blotting paper beneath for us to find to make us think Ruth had written the letter."

"Hmmph. Not bad," said Graves, as he navigated his way through the gardens on the way towards the woods.

"If the letter is a fake, sir, and it is designed for us to suspect Ruth then the question has to be who would want to frame Ruth and why?"

"If Ruth is hanged for murder, I guess the estate and all of the money would then go to John."

"I suppose so, sir, and look, it says here 'will to think about' which means whoever wrote this whether it is fake or not knew about the will and possibly it was to be changed. Someone has been lying to us sir!"

"Hmmph. I doubt there are many people here who haven't been lying to us lad. This must be where we turn left, let's follow the treeline around." The two men stood near the spot where they had heard Peggy's barks earlier in the day. They veered left as Ruth had instructed in their search for the lake. The water was not yet visible, though the two men felt the cold air around them become fresher still, indicating to them that they were not far from their destination. The cracking of twigs sounded off to their right and Peggy, eager to investigate ran off into the forest only to return a few seconds later jumping at the heels of Ed.

"Ah! Mr Osborn! We meet again!"

"Indeed, we do Inspector, though I must say I believe you are going the wrong way. Those clouds look rather ominous, and I have no intention of being caught outside when they burst."

"You are heading back to Lord Taylor's house then?" asked Graves.

"I am. That's enough walking for one day!"

"Did you happen to see John as you were coming past the lake? We are looking for him."

"No, I'm afraid not, Inspector. I cut through the trees for a few minutes, perhaps I just missed him. I saw one of your police chaps though, he was beating branches and bushes like he was searching for something."

"Ah yes, routine search. I'm afraid I must inform you that the body of Jayne Brown was found in the woods this morning. She was murdered."

"Good grief. I'm sorry, but who is Jayne Brown?" asked Ed.

"She was a maid at the manor."

"Ah yes, a rather plain looking girl? Yes, I remember."

"Could you please tell me your movements this morning sir?"

"Well, I woke early as I said before, then I went for a walk to the village where I met your good selves."

"Did you see anyone on your walk?"

"No sir, you were the first person I saw all morning, I think. Oh, hang about, I saw Mr Campbell driving towards Freddie's estate a few minutes after I left."

"I see. What time would that have been?"

"Around seven-thirty, perhaps."

"Very well, we shan't keep you any longer. Oh, one other thing. Do you remember seeing Miss Brown at all yesterday?"

"Only last night. As you were interviewing Mr Roberts, she came into the drawing room to replace an ashtray."

"How was her manner? Was she excited in any way?" asked Graves with half an eye on Peggy who was curiously sniffing a toadstool.

"Well, I'm afraid Miss Dunholme may have made an unkind comment which did seem to rile the girl somewhat. She was only in the room for a short time but most of what she said seemed to be directed at Ruth. You know the type of thing, Inspector, sarcastic condolences, and hints of scandal, that type of thing. An unpleasant attitude to take towards a bereaved family, I thought."

When the lawyer had continued on his way and Graves had managed to nudge Peggy away from what looked to be a particularly poisonous mushroom, Carver asked a question he had struggled to contain within himself.

"But sir! Why didn't you ask him how his fingerprints got onto the dagger?"

"I will lad, don't worry, I will. But first I want to know if any fingerprints were discovered on the rock used to kill Miss Brown."

A few minutes' walk brought them to the local policeman Ed had passed a short time before. He told the two detectives that no fingerprints had been found on the stone and that the police doctor had indicated time of death to be between six-thirty and eight-thirty that morning, though the timeframe may be narrowed after further analysis.

The dark clouds continued to threaten their downpour, without unleashing their arsenal. The lake, seen now by the human and canine triumvirate looked menacing; the darkness of the clouds mirrored on its surface hinted at murky depths where earthly goodness could not tread.

"Hello there!" called Graves, espying John, who was sitting on a tree stump with a notebook in hand. John gave a timid wave but did not rise to greet the trio. Peggy ran forward and was soon getting rubbed behind her ears and on her belly which seemed to please her very much.

"Writing your confession?" asked Graves jocularly whilst looking at the notepad.

"N-no," stammered John who the detectives could see was embarrassed. "I like to write a few lines. I find it very soothing."

"I know, don't fret yourself, I was only joking."

"I'm sorry for not getting up, my damned leg has been giving me grief all morning. As you can see, I have no seats to offer you. What was is you wish to see me about?"

"Oh, nothing in particular, we were just taking a walk, looking for a bit of creative inspiration, like yourself I imagine. We went down to the village this morning and had a chat with your vicar…"

"Ah yes, Malcolm is an old family friend. He can be a bit eccentric at times, mind."

"Your father was on good terms with him?" asked Graves.

"Better than most people, Inspector. My father would occasionally pop in to see Malcolm, though he didn't attend his services, if you were wondering."

"Do you know what they discussed together?"

"Nothing of importance, I should imagine. I've never really given it much thought, Inspector. Tell me, how is the investigation progressing?"

"Quite nicely, I should say," replied Graves. "There are just one or two points which require clearing up."

"Like the identity of the murderer?"

A smile played on John's lips.

"Exactly."

Carver wondered at the exchange. He thought he could detect false confidence on the part of Graves, knowing what he did about the case, though John's attitude struck him as odd. The heir to Treefall estate smiled like a bookmaker who has fixed a race. Was his attitude based on the fact he knew he was innocent of murder and the realisation of his inheritance had dawned on him, or was John's hatred of his father so intense he was enjoying watching the police struggle to catch his killer?

"You are a very wealthy man, John. Tell me, how wealthy would you be if your father died today instead of yesterday?" asked Graves.

"You mean if Roberts had managed to complete his appointment and father had managed to change his will?"

"Precisely."

"I should say around the same. Am I wrong? Was father going to cut me out?"

John tapped his thumb on his walking stick and, to a casual observer, may have appeared disinterested.

"A large amount of money would have passed to Mr Campbell had the new will been made," said Graves, not answering the question head on.

"I see. How strange..."

"Strange? Why's that?" asked Carver quickly, seeing doubt dispel the man's confidence.

"As I've told you, Constable, my father was not a nice person and certainly not what anyone would call generous. If he were to reward anyone for their service, I would have imagined Hodgkins or Betty would top the list, though of course George worked alongside my father on many matters. Still...I find it odd."

Carver thought of the long service of the butler and cook and nodded unconsciously.

"Inspector," continued John, turning to the grey-haired man, "there was one other thing which I feel I should tell you about."

"Oh, yes?"

"Yes. It concerns the night before my father's death. I'm afraid the incident slipped my mind due to the later events: genuinely, Inspector." John continued to stroke Peggy as he spoke, craning his neck towards the detectives.

"That's quite alright. It's perfectly normal to not recall something after a traumatic event, just tell us what it is now and that will be fine," said Graves.

"Well, it may be nothing. In fact, I barely thought anything of it at the time. I was woken up by some noises which sounded as though they were coming from downstairs."

"What kind of noises?"

"Well, nothing too sinister, just someone going around the place, but you know when someone is trying to be quiet but sort of fumbling? Well, it was like that, someone tiptoeing about the place. At the time I assumed someone must be hungry and going to fetch a snack or glass of water or something."

"But now you don't think so?" replied Graves, turning towards the water.

"I think the sounds were coming from my father's study, Inspector, though as I say I thought little of it at the time."

"I see. Do you remember when this occurred?"

"Yes, I do. I recall looking at my bedside clock. It was two o'clock."

"You're sure on that?" replied Graves, watching a duck bob up and down on the lake.

"Absolutely, Inspector."

"Hmmph. Mr Grimbourne, this might not come as a surprise to you, but Jayne Brown was found murdered this morning just a few hundred yards from here."

John reeled in shock. "What? How?! And what do you mean it may not be a surprise Inspector? Are you accusing me of killing her?"

"Not at all, my good man," said Graves innocently. "I merely thought you may have met a policeman on your way here like we did and enquired as to what they were doing. It is *your* land now after all, you have a right to know what is going on."

"Well, I can tell you I met no one, Inspector! This morning I breakfasted with Ruth at my usual time before setting out for my walk. My time has been quite uninterrupted by anyone until now."

"I see. Was Miss Brown fulfilling her duties to an acceptable standard?"

"As a matter of fact, she was not. She was certainly capable, but her attitude was atrocious at times. In fact, just this morning at breakfast I suggested to Ruth that we should let her go. Sack her I mean. Though of course her death is a tragedy," added John quickly, looking at his shoes in shame.

"I see, and was Miss Grimbourne in favour of letting her go?"

"Actually, no. She talked me out of it. I was surprised knowing Ruth's feelings towards her, but she was quite insistent that the girl should stay. Then again, maybe I shouldn't be too surprised, Ruth has always had a kind soul."

12. LYING AND TIGERS

My tongue will be a dagger; no escape
For him from slandering falsehood shall there be,

"The Pardoner's Tale"
The Canterbury Tales

"Poor Malcolm! I wonder what the matter with him was!" Ruth looked in the wing mirror to see if the clergyman was still visible in the churchyard, but, as she did so, Penelope tugged gently on the steering wheel to manoeuvre a corner causing Ruth's vision of the receding village to blur.

"Oh, Ruth darling, I shouldn't worry too much, he may have been fine, he said he was after all."

"Oh Penny, you can't really believe that! You saw him! He was white and shaking!" replied Ruth earnestly.

"He's a priest, I thought they couldn't lie."

"He's a *vicar* and they *shouldn't* lie, it's not quite the same thing!"

"Still, I don't see why you are so worried, he's bound to be nearly one hundred, I'm sure it's perfectly natural for people that are so near to death to be so pale and cadaverous looking."

"Oh Penny, you really are absurd at times! Malcolm is barely over seventy and he's fit as a fiddle. *You* are probably nearer to death with the amount you drink and smoke!"

"Oh, my dearest Ruth! Now who is being absurd? Stress is

what kills people, and I don't have a care in the world!" Penelope took a long drag of a thin Russian cigarette as she said this and slowly blew the resulting smoke through the gap in the car window. She was an accomplished driver and could handle the shiny Triumph quite easily with one hand. She took great satisfaction in driving and even more in telling uptight old men at parties about her motoring skills, seeing their eyebrows rise at the thought of a woman behind the wheel filled her with rage and pleasure in equal measure.

The two young women had left Treefall Manor and driven along the much-trodden main road adjacent with the stream and past the pub. When they approached the church, Ruth had asked Penelope to slow the car, having seen the Reverend Thorpe standing stock still, like a scarecrow beside the entrance gate.

"Well, if stress kills people, then I worry about Malcolm," continued Ruth, the image immovable from her mind. "He looked right through me when we pulled up and it was a full minute before he was enough of himself to even know who I was!"

"Yes dear, but then he said all the right things, didn't he? 'Poor dear', 'so sorry for your loss', 'despicable crime' et cetera, et cetera, all the things one expects when one's father is murdered."

"Dear Penny, if I didn't know you as well as I do, I would think you to be heartless. Luckily, I know there to be a soft centre beneath that hard shell."

"Oh rubbish!" retorted Penelope as she clunked the gear lever forcefully.

"Really, you are sweet for getting me away from home for the day, although a better lie might have been suitable. The police aren't stupid, if you say we are going shopping in Rockingham they are very definitely aware there are no shops open on a Sunday. I really don't know why you couldn't tell them the truth and say we are going for a drive to get away from it all."

"Because that sounds weak, darling. Besides, it's fun lying to the police. You are wrong too, that younger policeman is stupid, at least he might be, I'm not quite sure."

"The older one isn't: Inspector Graves."

"No, quite right, he says more with his eyes than he does with his mouth. I don't know what thoughts go on in his head, but I would bet they aren't stupid. It was probably those two that spooked your friend the reverend, he did say he had spoken to the police today after all."

"Hmm maybe," replied Ruth. "Although, oh I don't know, he seemed afraid, though I can't think why."

"Maybe he murdered your father, and the police are on to him," said Penelope bluntly.

"Penny! Don't be ridiculous! Malcolm would never do such a thing." Ruth, feeling the weight of the suggestion reached her hand to her bare throat and bit her lip gently.

"Well, who do you think is the guilty party?"

"I told you, I don't know…"

Penelope took her eyes off the road and looked at her friend for what many a passenger would consider a dangerously long time.

"Ruth, what is it you are not telling me?"

"What? Nothing."

"Ruth, you are a terrible liar, and I am your best friend. You are hiding something from me, I know it! Now tell me what it is."

"Oh Penny, please don't go on!"

"See, you wouldn't be getting upset if you weren't hiding something! Is it to do with the wedding? Because if you tell me you are upset that it is off, I will know you are lying!"

"Oh, Penny it's terrible," cried Ruth, bursting into sobs. "I'm.. I'm in love."

"Well, that does sound terrible, but most fools would think that's a good reason to be getting married."

"Oh, if only it were that simple. It's not Freddie whom I love!"

"Who is it and why didn't you tell me more importantly?!"

"It's… it's William."

"Who?"

"William Hopkirk."

Penelope's face was contorted in confusion. "William Hopkirk… the gardener?!"

"Yes. Father dismissed him when he found out. He said Jayne told him about our relationship. I'm worried the police will suspect him. They'll probably think it was some sort of revenge killing."

"Well, I daresay they might. Do they know any of this?"

"I'm not sure what they know. They asked me about William getting sacked, but I lied and said I was oblivious to the reason. One of father's whims, I said."

"Hmm… does Elsie Barter know about this love affair?"

"No. At least I don't believe so."

"Well then you might be alright. Does Freddie know?"

"No. Only father knew, I think. When he found out he insisted I marry Freddie. Though how he got Freddie to agree I don't know."

"I do. Ruth you are the most beautiful woman in the county, everyone knows it! I bet the good Lord Taylor thought Christmas had come early when your father made the suggestion."

"Penny you are too sweet. To me, at least. But really, what am I to do?"

"What is there to do? It seems to me things have fallen in your lap somewhat. Your father was making you marry a man that you don't love and preventing you from being with the man you do love. Your father, I may remind you is no longer an obstacle in that particular road. If you want my advice, you will ride out this little storm that is the police investigation and wait for all the hubbub to die down. Then, in a few months' time subtly let it be known that relations between yourself and the good Lord Taylor have broken down, all the while carrying on with your mucky gardener. It's simple really, dear."

"What if father's murderer is not caught? People will think it was William or the two of us together and I shall be trapped as much by suspicion as I was by my father. It's all so intolerable. Besides, that's not all," continued Ruth, wiping away a tear.

"Lord! What else is there?" asked Penelope incredulously.

"The police told me this morning that they found Jayne's body in the woods. She was murdered! What if – what if…" Ruth broke out into continued sobs.

Penelope, feeling her arms should be around her friend and not resting on the steering wheel brought the car to a screeching halt next to a field full of ruminating cows.

"That horrid little wench is dead?! Who on earth would risk their neck to kill her? Oh! darling Ruth! Are you afraid William killed the girl for spilling the beans about you two?"

"It can't be, but…oh, I feel such shame for doubting him."

"Really Ruth, why didn't you tell me you were suffering so much?"

"Because my fears and anxieties are pierced with moments of joy when I am with William."

"Lord! You really have fallen for the boy, haven't you!"

†

William Hopkirk swung the heavy-headed axe skilfully, bringing its sharpened edge down sweetly in the middle of the last log which cracked cleanly in two. A pile lay at his feet, the fruits of his morning's labour. His back ached and arms shivered with the heat of the rushing blood within. The handsome young man closed his eyes and flung his head back to face the grey sky. He saw summer in his mind, his favourite season. In summer there was no need to swing an axe, no dark, heavy sky to dull his senses. In summer he could throw his head back as he did now and feel the sun's rays wash over his face. He could watch the butterflies float from one flower to another, watching them rise and swoop through the heavy air like a conductor's wand. The sunlight in his mind. Dreams of different days, past and future. The golden sun. Ruth's golden hair. He could see her walking around the gardens, glowing. She moved lightly around the flowerbeds, stopping to smell what he had grown for her. That was how they came to talk. Always, his eyes closed, his thoughts drifted back to Ruth. Ruth ...

"William!"

His eyes opened, all was dark and glum again. "William!" called the familiar voice again.

"Yes, uncle?" he called back, sounding more resentful at being disturbed than he really was. Samuel Mason came around the corner of the pub, his red cheeks puffing as if he was trying to blow up a balloon but had forgotten the balloon.

"Are you alright, uncle? You seem terribly out of breath."

"I'm alright laddie, just been taking down the chairs from the tables ready for opening. You're done I see. Good work." The breathless landlord eyed his nephew closely between puffs. "You must've been up bright and early, Will, I didn't even hear you this morning."

"Yes, I had trouble sleeping, I got up before dawn. Went to bag a few rabbits, though I had no joy I'm afraid."

"I see. I hope those two policemen didn't see you with a gun. They'll be looking to you for the murder!" exclaimed Samuel seriously.

"Grimbourne was stabbed uncle, not shot."

"Was he now? I wouldn't put it past them police folk to lie to people, tell them he was stabbed when really he was shot then try to trick the person who did it by getting them to show his hand as it were."

"Well, Grimbourne was definitely stabbed. Where are them two anyway?"

"Left this morning not long after they had breakfast. Went up to the big house, I think. Asking about where to find Elsie Barter, they was. I hope they find her there and not here. The less around here they are sticking their noses in places it's not wanted the better."

"Why would they start poking around here? The murder was committed at the manor."

"Because, William, coppers are naturally nosey beggars and if they take a dislike to you, they will think it fun to upset you."

"What are you trying to say, uncle?"

"Last night your manner was offish. You were short with the older detective, and he eyed you funny for it. I didn't like it. Try to play nice and not be a smart Alec with the police. We don't want them poking around here and least of all not in the shed down the back. D'ya understand?"

"Yes, uncle."

"Listen, William. Whoever stuck a knife in Grimbourne did us both a favour, we just have to hope the police arrest some chump and leave us well alone."

✝

Malcolm Thorpe set down his fountain pen and gave a deep sigh as though he were trying to expel any badness within him. He folded the piece of paper he had been writing on and tucked it into an envelope. He was sitting in his small, cramped vestry. Coloured light, like a rainbow, shone in through a single stained-glass window. The only other illumination was provided by a few candles on the table at which he sat. The room was untidy, vestments were piled on a chair by the old wooden door. Parchments were scattered around old books whose titles were often indiscernible due to age and neglect. Only one of the four walls was plastered and painted, the rest being of rough stone quarried and set by hands laid to rest many centuries before. Even the section of painted wall was messy; a child had drawn unevenly upon it. To an observer it appeared a depiction of hell with sinners cast amongst flames, though the crayon had faded somewhat over the years.

Into this sacristy very few people came, the Reverend

Thorpe preferring to give host to guests in his little cottage which he kept tidier than the vestry for such purposes. Sometimes, however, he was caught unawares, and polite protocol demanded he give counsel or condolence here in the little room. When Malcolm heard the timid little rap on the door, he knew that this would be such an occasion. Rising from his little wooden chair the elderly vicar shuffled the short distance to welcome his visitor. Standing before him was George Campbell who looked in such a state of despair the reverend took him by the arm and gently ushered him into the seat he himself had just vacated. "Goodness, Mr Campbell, are you quite alright?"

"N-no, not really, vicar."

"What's the matter man?"

"I can't take it anymore," sobbed George. "It's all such a burden."

"What is?"

George lifted his head and looked at the vicar for the first time since arriving. Even in his semi-lucid state he was shocked by the sight he saw. To his eyes Malcolm Thorpe had aged twenty years since he had last seen him a few days previously. The white hair was all the whiter yet lacked the soft vitality of snow. The lines on the old man's face were longer and the eyes sat heavy in a sunken head.

"What is such a burden?" repeated Malcolm.

"I am afraid, and I have done wrong, so much wrong. I deserve what is coming to me."

"George, I don't understand, are you referring in any way to the recent events at Treefall Manor?"

"Yes... amongst other things."

"I see. You know, George, we all sin to varying degrees, myself included. What we must do is ask God's forgiveness and try not to sin again."

"What if trying is not enough? What if we can't stop?"

"My dear boy, I wish I had the power of absolution, but that is reserved for the Almighty himself. All I can say is pray my boy, pray. God will hear you."

"Can God forgive me if I can't forgive myself?"

"Yes, because he can see how great your contrition is. Tell me plainly George, what have you done?"

†

"Your manservant is a fine chap, Freddie," said Ed cheerfully. "He managed to get some shoe polish out of my trouser leg. I have no idea how he managed it." The young man looked at the now unblemished spot on his leg which was crossed over his other in wonder.

The armchair in which Ed sat was so upright that it almost felt to the occupant as though it were tipping them out of it. In fact, this chair had been bought and placed there some years before for the single purpose of providing a suitable seat for the late Lord Taylor to pose for a portrait and had been left there by the new Lord much unthought of. The piece, by a revered artist of the time was directly, above Ed, though he would have had to crane his neck unnaturally to see it.

The sitting room was luxuriously decorated, as was to be expected by such esteemed ownership. Paintings adorned all four of the walls, though none as large or expertly painted as the picture of Freddie's father who sat proudly in dark and red robes. Silk ties made the appearance of holding the heavy curtains in place though the expensive silk covered fine metal chains, such was the height and weight of the drapes. Curios and ornaments from around the world filled the vast, high-ceilinged room, each with a story to tell, not yet told, for the room was hardly ever used and often lay like a treasure-filled cave, lost under a sea of sand.

"Yes," said Freddie, following on from his friend. "Singhy is a marvel."

"How did you come to find him? Presumably your father

came across him in India?"

"Yes, father was out there in the eighties. Of course he had no need to go, the family being what it was, but I think my father felt the title and history of our ancestry somewhat of a burden. He wanted to escape it all and go where no one would know him."

"So, he took a commission?"

"Indeed. They say young men crave danger and adventure and undoubtedly people would say that about us, but it doesn't feel like that when it's yourself sometimes. Motive can be strong but not what others expect at times. Though of course my father was looking for adventure, I do think he was running away, to a certain degree. Anyway, I digress. My father was stationed in India. Well, one day he went on a tiger hunting expedition, though as a rule he didn't agree with hunting big game, he went out of curiosity and the experience. He told me once that the only animal that can be shot justifiably was man.

"Well, on this particular day, unbeknownst to my father, the party was being hunted by a large male Bengal tiger. It was stalking them along a river. Father was at the back of the group and stopped to collect some water alone, a foolish thing to do as he later admitted. Anyway, as he was crouching, filling his canteen, he looked behind him and saw the beast staring at him with bared teeth. He was a man of few words, my father, and generally private with his thoughts, but he told me the effect the sight had on him, and I can tell you it was profound. Unarmed and alone, it seemed that he stood little chance of surviving the next few moments. He thought of screaming but the sound he tried to let escape was so large it stuck in his throat like a blocked pipe. Just as the tiger crouched and dug its hind legs lower into the dusty sand ready to pounce, a rock landed between the cat's eyes. Then another in quick succession. Beast and man saw the miraculous intervener at the same time. Standing only a few yards away was a native not much older than a boy with a long, sharpened stick in one hand and a rock in the other. He shimmied sideways and forced himself between the animal and my father, his stick pointing at the snarling mouth and black eyes. Then, with the suddenness and unexpectedness with which it appeared, the animal turned and fled into the undergrowth.

"Father was by no means superstitious, but he regarded the lad as a lucky charm and wanted him as a servant. Communicating wasn't easy to begin with but it was soon established that the boy was an orphan who lived in a village nearby and gladly accepted the offer to start a new life with a Britisher. After that, Sukhbir Singh himself joined the regiment and was my father's batman. In fact, my father threatened to resign his commission when the army tried to give him a different batman. Their loyalty was to each other and nearly forty years of friendship grew from that day when a tiger went hunting."

"It must have been a great loss to him when your father died."

"It was. They went through much together. They fought side by side in the Boer War and, to his dying day father, was angry at the treatment he perceived towards Singhy."

"How so?"

"Towards the end of the conflict my father's battalion held a hill and having the higher ground must have bred some complacency, for the Boers crept up at night undetected and gave a surprise attack at dawn. Father was cut off from his troop and was in serious danger of being killed or taken prisoner, when Singhy, who was not at his side, for he had gone to fetch breakfast, appeared, and fought off a group of the Boers by himself. Father said he killed four with his knife and the rest fled. After that he put him in for a medal, but the recommendation was denied. No reason was given so father assumed it was because of his colour. Once the war had ended, father left the Army and came back here, bringing Singhy with him. I sometimes wonder, now that father is gone, whether he would like to return to India. It was after all my father and not myself that Singhy swore to serve."

"Why don't you ask him? Good old Gunga Din."

"Oh, I could never do that. I would fluff my lines terribly and there would likely be an awful misunderstanding. The last thing I would want is for Singhy to think that I wanted him to go. I would wish to convey that if his heart desired a return to his homeland, he would be free to go with my blessing and a considerable sum for his years of service. Of course, I should be quite distraught if he did wish to leave. However, one thing that I am sure of is that one must listen to one's heart."

"Speaking of hearts, how do you think Ruth will take the news that you don't wish to proceed with the wedding?"

"Oh, I think she will be just fine. In truth it was always somewhat a marriage of convenience. Living so close to each other and being of a certain age and of good family and all that. It seemed to Alexander to make much sense. When he suggested it, I was surprised but soon found myself agreeing…"

"Yes, well if she is upset, she will have her friend Penelope there to comfort her. Say, what do you make of her?"

"Penelope? She's certainly a bit of a livewire. Has a bit of a reputation around some of the London establishments as being a bit of trouble."

"Really? How so?" asked Ed, taking a sip of whisky and soda.

"Nothing too bad. All I mean is that she has considerable financial means and is very free minded. She says what she thinks and doesn't hold back. I'm surprised you haven't been acquainted with her, you run in similar circles as far as I can tell."

"Yes, well I've been damned busy with the cases I have. She is very attractive though, isn't she? What are you laughing at?"

"I am laughing at you. I saw the way you were looking at her at dinner the other night. I hope you conceal your thoughts better in the courtroom."

"Ha! Alright, I admit I may have been a little captivated by what I saw but I was just a little stunned to find such a woman in such an out of character place."

"Yes, Penelope does dress very, er, London shall we say."

"I think modern is a more judicious term. The villagers here seem to be stuck in the eighteen fifties," said Ed looking towards the window as though the village would be visible, but all he saw was a wall of trees, the tops of which were swaying in the stiff afternoon breeze.

"Penelope does certainly stand out, though I think you may have a rival for her affections."

"Oh? Who?"

"John."

"John?" replied Ed with obvious surprise.

"Yes, John."

"Well, I had no idea. Is there any sort of history there?"

"I'm not too sure, truth be told. Though I can tell you he looks at her in the same way you do. Although…"

"Yes…?"

"Well, poor old John doesn't share your confidence, does he? I guess on account of his leg. He mumbles and fumbles a great deal when Miss Dunholme is in his presence from what I've observed."

"Ah well, unfortunately for poor old John, I would estimate that this would give myself the upper hand in this affair of the heart."

"Oh?"

"Yes. You see, vivacious women like Penelope act up in order to draw out a strong man who can control them. Women like a firm hand, you see. I'm afraid poor old John doesn't quite fit that bill now, does he?" explained Ed with a smile, swirling his glass all the while.

"You know, Ed, one day your views will be considered old fashioned and wholly unacceptable. Hopefully that day is not too far off."

†

John had decided to walk through the forest before making his way back to the lake. He walked slowly, not because his leg was causing him discomfort but because his mind was so convoluted with thoughts competing for dominance that his energies were focussed on them.

He was in the woods. *His* woods. Could it be true? Could his father be dead, and the heir was now the owner? It seemed like a dream: the tyrant who had ruled over him his whole life was gone in the blink of an eye. It did not seem real. Was it grotesque to feel happiness? What should he feel? If he was not sad that his father was dead, should he pretend he was out of societal decency, or was it more indecent to lie in such a way? And what of Jayne?

The first spits of rain brought him back. He judged it would rain steadily but not heavily and decided to continue his walk to the lake. The moisture made the air fresher and John breathed it in deeply, like a man who has accomplished some great task of endurance.

He reflected as he rambled through the forest. He had completely lost his line of thought in the composition of his poem and had given up when the detectives had left him by the lake.

The ground changed underfoot as the trees cleared and the lake came into view once again. A marshy softness preceded the muddy banks. Aiming for his favourite stump, he trundled along when a dark mass in the lake caught his eye.

John stopped still more due to the unnaturalness of the scene rather than any sinister foreboding. His eyes adjusted to see George Campbell walking slowly into water. He was thirty yards away and the water was nearing his shoulders by the time

John had recovered from his shock to call out.

Dazed and confused, John stood wondering why his shout had been ignored when the reality of the situation dawned on him. Throwing his stick to the ground John scrambled as fast as his crippled leg would allow him to reach the shore where George had entered the lake. He flung off his overcoat to reduce his weight and waded into the water. He gasped desperately for breath as the shock of the freezing lake sucked the air from his lungs. He tried to continue his wild cries to George as he watched the secretary's head submerge in front of him. Flailing like a hooked fish, John swam the distance to where he thought George had gone under. He took a deep lungful of rainy air and plunged his head beneath the surface. His eyes stung but before him through the murky brown fog he saw the outline of George. Pushing and pulling his arms with all his might he grabbed the man's coat and tugged. It felt to John like he was an imposter trying to pull Excalibur from its stone, such was the futility of his attempts. John kicked to the surface to take in more air and with the rush of oxygen came the clarity of thought he needed to solve his problem. If George was attempting to kill himself, he must surely have weighed down the pockets of his coat. Armed with this logical deduction, John dove again and immediately began clawing the coat from the drowning man's back, pulling the arms free of their sleeves. After a few lung-bursting seconds, John had resurfaced and, on his chest, rested the head of George Campbell. The last of John's energy was spent swimming back to the shore where he collapsed exhausted with George semi-conscious beside him.

13. RAIN AND FIRE

His face was very pale, I dare maintain.
The bitter frosts, the driving sleet and rain
Had killed the gardens; greens had disappeared.
Now Janus by the fire with double beard,
His bugle-horn in hand, sits drinking wine;
Before him stands a brawn of tusky swine

"The Franklin's Tale"
The Canterbury Tales

The rain had started falling as Graves and Carver made their way along Poacher's Lane, back towards the village. Peggy, knowing the destination, set the pace. She hurried to the warm fireside of the inn and the malty smelling air and wondered why the humans were so slow. So, when her master led her and the new man up the stairs to the cold bedroom, she looked at him with her head tilted to one side and let out a pathetic little yelp. "I thought you wanted a pint by the fireside, sir?" asked Carver, equally put out.

"I do lad, but first of all we need to discuss something which the good landlord cannot be allowed to overhear." Graves whispered his reply and Peggy gave him a more conspiratorial, understanding look. Graves then took a match from his pocket and lit the bedside candle while Carver stood impatiently waiting to hear more of what the Inspector had to say. "Amongst the files given to me this morning by Brent was a report that caught my eye. Here lad, have a look." Carver took the paper and sat at the writing table. After a few minutes of frantic reading, he raised his head and his eyebrows.

"That's right, lad," said Graves watching him. "Alexander Grimbourne was going to buy the inn. At a knockdown price too."

"That's an understatement sir if you don't mind me saying! Samuel Mason is practically giving it away! Surely the Blue Boar Inn has got to be worth more than this?" Carver flicked the paper he was holding with his index finger; the sound was like a log cracking in a fire.

"It is. Amongst the other reports in the file are the financial statements associated with the Inn and they say quite clearly that the Blue Boar Inn is worth four times as much as what Alexander Grimbourne was going to pay for it."

"So, what happens now that Grimbourne is dead?"

"The deal died with him. It was signed in principle. The ownership wasn't due to change until tomorrow."

"So, what you're saying is Alexander died just in time for the deal to be stopped?"

"Yes, lad."

"But I don't understand, sir, why would Samuel Mason sign this deal in the first place? It's terrible for him."

"That, my good man, is what we need to find out. Time for a pint."

Much to the delight of Peggy, the table by the fire was unoccupied. The only other table in use was in the far corner where an old man sat slowly smoking a clay pipe. At his feet lay an ancient mongrel who slept like the dead.

William Hopkirk stood polishing glasses with a rag behind the bar. When he saw the detectives enter, he gave a curt nod. Graves watched the young man closely as Carver fetched the drinks. He watched the stiff movements of his limbs, the clenched jaw which betrayed his anger and emotions.

"He doesn't like us," said Graves when Carver returned with two brimming pint pots.

"He was very frosty serving me, sir," replied Carver between sips.

"He sees us as a threat," continued the experienced man who hadn't taken his eyes from the barman. "He looks at us as two aliens landed uninvited into his world and he's angry because he's fearful. And why do you think that is, lad? It's because people fear the unknown and, in his case, *we* are the unknown. Our power, our aims, our thoughts, even our motives, all of this makes that young man afraid. And because he is young, he is proud and he is vain, and his own fears scare him. He knows he must protect that which is dear to him, but he doubts himself, which fuels his fears, which fuels his anger, which leads to him glaring at me like he is now. Fear is what makes smart people do stupid things."

Carver leant in so as not to be heard. They were several yards from William, but the bar was as quiet as a grave, the only sounds were the flames licking the logs in the fireplace and Peggy's gentle snores. "Do you think him capable of murder sir?"

"He has the passion, I believe."

At this moment, Samuel walked into the bar from the door which led to the back of the pub.

"Ah Mr Mason," cried Graves jovially. "Won't you join us for a drink?"

"Oh, hello Inspector, er, yes, of course. William, bring me a pint of bitter over please, there's a good lad." Carver pulled a chair from a nearby table onto which plumped the landlord.

"I say, Samuel, are you alright? You look like you have been boiling in a pot in the kitchen," said Graves.

Samuel mopped his forehead with a handkerchief. He was panting though trying not to and his great barrel-like chest heaved up and down. "I was just chopping some logs out back; not as young as I used to be, Inspector."

"None of us are my good man, though I didn't hear any wood being chopped I must say…"

"Oh, well, the doors here are good and thick. Keep all sorts of sounds out. Say, did you manage to see Mrs Barter up at the big house? She left here not half an hour ago. I hope you didn't miss her?"

Graves decided to ignore the fact that Samuel had hastily changed the topic of conversation away from his own afternoons actions and answered the man courteously. "Yes, thank you, we did. A delightful woman wouldn't you agree, Carver?"

"Oh yes, sir! Delightful …"

"Yes, a very informative woman is Mrs Elsie Barter." Graves looked again at William who was setting down his uncle's pint on the table. "Tell me, why were you dismissed from your employment at Treefall Manor, Mr Hopkirk?"

Graves could feel Samuel tense beside him as he unleashed his words. William however seemed quite unperturbed. "The old devil never gave a reason, he just called me to his study one day and told me not to come to the manor again."

"Lies."

"If you don't believe me, Inspector, why don't you ask Mr Grimbourne? Oh! Wait! That's right, you can't." William smirked as he walked away but, much to the surprise of Carver and Samuel, so did Graves.

"Sorry about him, Inspector, you know what young folk are like these days."

"There's no need for you to apologise Mr Mason," replied Graves, still grinning. "Now tell me one thing that I'm dying to know…"

Samuel Mason looked like a man walking to the gallows at these words but replied dutifully. "Yes sir?"

"How did the Blue Boar come to get its name? Carver, get a fresh round of drinks in before the good landlord commences his story, there's a good lad."

"Well," started Samuel once the ale had been delivered, "you see long, long ago, before the village was properly established this whole area was deep forest. Much of it still is, but back then the only feature which would have been recognisable in the dense woodland would have been the stream which survives still.

Anyways, folk back then were a superstitious bunch and there were a fair few mystics and hermits around by all accounts. Well, the legend goes that the people of the forest were beset by a series of tragedies, but before each of these catastrophes occurred a blue boar was seen. It would appear and be gone in a flash and of course the people thought that there was a curse on them, and that the boar was a sign of some impending doom."

"What kind of tragedies occurred?" interrupted Carver.

"Well, the story goes that there was a little girl, no more than five years old, who was standing staring at a blue boar when out of nowhere she was dragged off into the woods by a wolf and never seen again. Another thing that happened was there was an old man fetching water from the stream and, as he bent down to collect the water, the stream rose rapidly into a great flood and washed the man away before settling as quick as it had risen. There was no trace of him, but on the other side of the stream stood a blue boar with steam coming out of its nostrils. Well, things of this nature occurred for many years until the people of the forest were at their wits end. They had been hunting the boar for years but every time one was killed or trapped it was found to be a normal grey boar without a hint of blue. So, eventually the leader of the people of the forest travelled for two days deep into the wooded country to seek an old woman who lived in a hermitage inside a great oak tree. The woman was said to possess great power and wisdom and had lived an unnaturally long life on accounts of sucking on the roots of the ancient trees. It was thought their longevity was transferred to her in this way and when she walked in the forest all the animals disappeared at the sight of her. Even the wolves scattered before the old hag.

"Well, as I was saying, the leader of the people whose name has been forgotten by time went to see this sorceress and she told him that she knew of the boar and of the disasters which had befell his people. She said that to rid themselves of the boar they must offer a sacrifice to the king of the forest. The leader was confused by this because there was no king of the forest, but the old woman would say no more.

"For two days the leader travelled back to his people, mulling over the problem in his mind, when on his way he came across a little girl dressed in rags and leaves. This little girl was talking to herself and laughing, or so it seemed, for when the leader asked her if she was not afraid to be alone in the deep, dark woods, she replied that she was not. She said that the king of the forest would protect her. 'Who is the king of the forest?' asked the leader. 'The king of the forest is the one to whom I am speaking,' replied the little girl. 'I see,' replied the leader, not seeing at all. 'And where is the king of the forest?' he asked. The little girl pointed to a mighty oak tree beside which they were standing. It was the greatest and most ancient tree in the land and the girl said, 'This be the king of the forest.' 'Tell me, little one,' said the leader, 'what gift should I bestow to this great king?' 'The king desires that which is dearest to you,' replied the mysterious child.

"The leader thanked her and continued his journey home. When he eventually got there, he found his people in a state of panic. 'What is wrong?' he cried. His tearful wife then ran up to him and told how their only daughter had ventured into the deep forest following tracks made by a boar and had not returned. 'Where? Show me,' said the leader. And so, the leader and a band of men followed the tracks left by the boar and it took them back to where the great tree: the king of the forest stood. Only… the tree was gone and so was the little girl who had been talking to it. It was then the leader realised that the little girl was in fact his daughter, who was the thing most precious to him, and that the king of the forest had taken her forever. Never again after that has the blue boar been seen in the woods."

"What a sad story," said Carver.

"Aye, folk still say that at night if you walk into the forest, you can hear a little girl talking and laughing. Don't believe it myself mind. Another pint?"

"Yes," replied Graves. "This really is a delicious drop, I don't think I've had it before."

"Eh, no, eh, it's a local drop Inspector. I don't think it has made it to London yet," said Samuel, picking up the empty glasses.

"A pity, it really is wonderful. Tell me Samuel, how long have you been landlord?"

"Oh well sir, the inn has been in the family for two centuries. I inherited when my father passed away thirty year ago it would be now, though time flies."

"Two hundred years! Blimey! There must have been a lot of stories told and songs sang here in that time!"

"Oh yes sir! And pints drank and all!" laughed Samuel.

"I must say, it has a wonderful, homely feel to it, this inn." Graves looked around the room. A few more customers had entered whilst Samuel had been telling his story. William had lit candles on all the tables to conquer the invading darkness from the windows. The uneven, rough stone walls produced their own dancing shadows flamed by the flickering fire.

"Aye, we don't like to change much around here. Tradition is important, you know."

"It is Samuel, I agree, which is why I am surprised that you planned to sell the inn to Alexander Grimbourne. It is something I just can't fathom, can you shed some light on it?"

Carver watched the landlord and momentarily worried he was suffering from apoplexy, such was the contortion of his face.

"Who... who said?"

"We have the legal documents in our possession, please don't deny it."

"I won't deny it," replied Samuel indignantly.

"Then tell me, why were you going to sell the pub?" persisted Graves.

"Business hasn't been too steady since the war, and William's a good lad, but he wants other things in life. I have no son of my own to leave it to. Grimbourne came in with an offer and it made me think is all. I'm getting no younger as I said before Inspector. I can't afford to take on help, but I can't be lugging beer barrels around for the rest of my days neither!"

"Alexander Grimbourne came to you with a terrible offer, any fool could see that."

"Well then call me a fool! An offer is an offer and beggars can't be choosers as they say,"

"I don't believe you, Mr Mason," retorted Graves.

"Believe what you like!" shouted Samuel loud enough for the rest of the drinkers to turn their heads.

The detective and the landlord stared at one another for a minute before Samuel got up and walked out of the back door. The bar was deathly quiet until Graves eyed each silent drinker who in turn resumed their conversations in hushed voices.

"Does it feel like we are getting somewhere, sir?" asked Carver.

"Yes, lad, it does."

The two men sat drinking and talking for some time. The quarrel with Samuel was not mentioned and slowly the noise levels in the bar grew higher as more people entered for the evening. Graves assessed each soaking wet person who entered. He wanted to get a feel for the village, for its life and its people. The story of the boar had sparked his imagination and, as he looked around at the ruddy faces, he pictured these people as progenies of the forest people in the story. He could well imagine how mysticism could seep into the fabric of such a small rural community.

"How are you getting on with solving how the murder was committed, lad?" said Graves, seeing Carver was looking at him as he stared into the village's past and character.

"Well, sir, I have been thinking about it as you can imagine but I must say I am still having difficulty putting the pieces together."

"Stick at it, you'll get there in the end," consoled Graves who took a long sup of his pint. Carver smiled half-heartedly. The gentle faith from Graves, whilst assuring in nature, added to the pressure he had put on himself to solve how someone could stab a man in a locked room. This was certainly not the type of case he expected to be sent on to begin his detecting career, he reflected. "Do you think we'll solve the case, sir?" said Carver doubtfully.

"I do, lad. You'll never solve every case that you set upon but this one I have a good feeling about."

"Why, sir?"

"Well, first let us consider the murder of Alexander. We have a finite number of suspects. Yes, a stranger *could* have roamed through and committed the crime, as young Mr Hopkirk has suggested, but really the chance of that happening is nigh on impossible. The striking aspect of the case is who had the *opportunity* to kill the victim. Forget the locked room aspect for a second. Whoever murdered Alexander Grimbourne must have known where the other occupants of the house were going to be at the time they struck. Either that, or the murderer was so desperate to kill the victim they regarded the chance of being caught as a risk worth taking. So that leaves us a pool of suspects, and out of that pool there is one person that I think we can definitely rule out."

"There is?"

"Yes, lad, but no names yet. The other reason why a stranger did not commit the crime is that the weapon used was not kept in the room that the murder was committed. A potential burglar would not go to the library on the first floor, pick up a valuable curio then go to a locked room downstairs and use it to murder the master of the house. No, it would not happen. And don't forget, there were only two sets of fingerprints on the dagger."

"Grimbourne's and Ed's"

"Exactly."

"So, you think Ed did it?"

"Not so fast, lad. I certainly want to know how his fingerprints ended up on the murder weapon, but there may be an innocent explanation."

"Maybe he knows that his fingerprints are on it and that is

why he was acting shifty this morning!"

"Now you're thinking, lad! But if Ed can provide an innocent explanation as to how his fingerprints got there, then why hasn't he come forward to tell us?"

"He looked like he had something to confess this morning. Though, maybe he is hoping we catch the killer without dragging his name into it. After all sir, he is a high-flying London lawyer, it won't do his career any good to be involved in a murder case."

"You may be right, lad," agreed Graves who set down his glass and looked once more at the roomful of people. "And then of course, there is Miss Brown. A common girl, much like these folk here. How does she tie in with the murder of Alexander Grimbourne?"

"Well, sir, we know she was an unpopular member of staff. We also know she had an unusual amount of money in her possession considering her means of income."

"Ah yes, means of income! It seems Jayne had more than one, don't you think? Yes, I would guess that Miss Brown was killed because of something she knew. Perhaps she was putting the squeeze on someone and was demanding more from them which her victim didn't have and so they felt she needed to die."

"You mean blackmail, sir? Maybe if her victim had no more money like you say sir, they would have to give something else of value to satisfy Miss Brown. Like a ruby necklace!"

Graves drank deeply and winked at his junior over the top of his glass. After wiping his frothy mouth, he said, "Now the thinking juice is working, lad!"

"Do you have any other reason to believe we will solve the case, sir?" asked Carver hopefully.

"I do. Just one more reason."

"Sir?"

"Every detective solves their first case. Now, get another round in." Graves smiled at Carver as he rose from his chair to go to the bar. He chuckled to himself, knowing how Carver was feeling, the weight of expectancy on his shoulders, the self-doubt, the anxiety, and the riddle of the locked room playing on his mind. He had been there himself on his first murder case many years before. He quaffed the last beer from his pot and smiled at the reminiscences of his early career and looked again at his young protégé standing at the bar. Yes, he thought, he'll be alright on this one.

"Look who's come in, sir," said Carver, as he set the pints of ale on the table. In the darkest corner of the inn sat Malcolm Thorpe, a puddle forming at his feet.

"He looks like he has been standing in the rain for hours, he's absolutely drenched," said Graves.

"He looks disorientated, sir, like he doesn't know where he is. Should we go over and see if he is alright?"

Graves thought for a minute before replying. "No. Let's leave him. We'll keep an eye on him mind."

"As you wish sir. Still no sign of Mr Mason, by the way."

"I doubt we'll see the good landlord again tonight, lad. William!" called Graves as the young man walked past with a cloth in his hand.

"Yes?" came the gruff reply.

"Does the vicar frequent this establishment often?"

"I don't see how our patrons' drinking habits are any of your concern, Inspector."

"Just answer the damned question, lad!"

William replied through gritted teeth. "No, not often. Will that be all?"

"Yes, go away," replied Graves without taking his eyes from Malcolm Thorpe who sat staring at the tumbler of whisky before him. Only when the pub door opened, and two newcomers entered did Graves break his watchful gaze. Carver also looked in surprise at the couple entering the Blue Boar Inn. Ed and Penelope stood on the threshold looking around the room. Upon seeing the two detectives, Penelope nudged her companion and Carver watched her mouth move in the shape of 'over there'.

"Ah Ed, we were just talking about you. Please, take a seat, join us for a drink."

"I'm afraid we are not here socially, Inspector," replied the lawyer gravely.

"Ah, well then, you must be here professionally. Perhaps you have come to tell us how your fingerprints came to be on the dagger that was used to murder Alexander Grimbourne." Ed sat stunned and looked from one detective to the other before turning to Penelope and raised his shoulders in exasperated confusion. "I-I-I don't know Inspector!"

"Oh, come off it," replied Graves, his voice thick with ale. "Tell me the truth!"

"I am Inspector, I swear!" said Ed desperately.

"I know how, Inspector." The three men turned to Penelope, each with a surprised look on their face.

"You do?" asked Ed.

"Yes. I saw you holding it in the library shortly after I arrived at the manor. You were standing by the black table. You were holding the dagger as though you were feeling its weight. You had your back half turned to me, I remember because I didn't know who you were, and my curiosity was piqued."

"When exactly was this, Miss Dunholme?"

"I told you Inspector shortly after I arrived."

"I said *exactly* Miss."

"Men are insufferable! Oh, I don't know! On Friday, in the afternoon sometime. After two but before five, I guess. That, however, is not why we're here!"

"Very well, Miss Dunholme, I am all ears. Tell me why you are here."

"There's been a terrible accident! It's George, he drowned or nearly drowned rather."

"Drowned?! Where?"

"In the lake. John found him and fished him out though nearly drowned himself. Freddie found the pair of them on the bank. John was exhausted but alright, poor George is still unconscious."

"Where is he?" asked Carver.

"He's at Treefall Manor, the doctor is with him."

"We'd better go, sir."

"I have the car outside, we'll give you a lift," said Penelope.

"Just one question before we go. Whose idea was it for you to fetch us?"

"Freddie's."

"Hmmph."

†

The rain was falling heavily as the group ran the short distance to the car. The journey was undertaken in silence, the only sounds being the chortling engine and the rain bouncing off the canopy. Peggy sat on Carver's lap and received a rub behind the ears.

Upon arrival Hodgkins was found waiting by the door with a tray of brandies which were gratefully received by all.

"Where is he? Show me the way," said Graves to everyone and no one once he had taken a glass.

"This way sir," replied Hodgkins, who took the initiative and led the detectives up the grand staircase. George's bedroom was on the second floor, midway along the corridor on the right-hand side. The village doctor was buttoning up his medical case in preparation to leave when Graves addressed him. "Will he live?" he asked bluntly. Frederick Taylor, who was sitting next to the still secretary winced as he heard these words.

"I hope so. He ingested a lot of water and I've had to pull algae out of his throat. The question is, if he comes around, will there be any brain damage? He wasn't breathing, thus getting no oxygen to his brain for a few minutes. Luckily Lord Taylor found them both almost as soon as they were out of the water and gave forced resuscitation otherwise Mr Campbell would be dead now." Graves threw a quick glance at Lord Taylor who was alone in the room with George. "It's lucky you were out by the lake,

Lord Taylor." Freddie, who was looking intensely at the patient sat unmoved for a moment until the Inspector's words finally seeped into his brain.

"What? Oh. Yes. I was out for a walk by the lake when I found..."

"Where is John?"

"I don't know Inspector."

"Come, Carver."

The two men moved swiftly along the halls of Treefall Manor with Peggy following close behind. The soft yellow lighting produced a warm imitation of calm and homeliness which was at odds with the atmosphere of the house. They found John in the library, sitting in an armchair. He was wearing silk pyjamas and woollen dressing gown with a blanket tucked around his waist. Ruth sat in a chair which she had pulled next to her brother.

Graves looked at the master of the house. John's face was pale, and his head slumped on his shoulders in feeble exhaustion, but his eyes were alive. "You did a very brave thing John. It can't be easy for you to swim," said Graves.

"No, I try to avoid it if possible." Ruth leaned closer and held John's hand.

"Do you feel up to telling us what happened?"

"Yes, though there is not much to tell really. It all happened tremendously quickly. I was out for a walk and thought I would go to the lake. I like watching the water when it rains, you see. Well, as I approached the pond or lake or whatever you wish to call it, I saw George walking very calmly but purposefully into it. I thought it mighty odd, obviously, and then of course I realised what he was doing. I scrambled as quickly as I could. By the time I reached him he was under the water, it took me several attempts at ducking to reach him. Then, well... I got him out, as you know. I'm afraid I may have passed out for before I knew it, I opened my eyes and saw Freddie pumping on George's chest. And, well, here we are. How is George now, Inspector?"

"The doctor is hopeful," replied Graves evasively. His back

was to the siblings as he was looking at the bookcase intently. "Tell me, do either of you have any idea why Mr Campbell would attempt to end his life?"

"Frankly, Inspector, I do not," replied Ruth, squeezing her brother's hand. "I can't imagine that there could be any aspect of George's life more stressful than working for my father and that, as you know, is no longer his position."

"Perhaps he was worried that with our father's death he may have lost his job," said John thoughtfully.

"Would he have?" asked Graves, turning to face John.

"I haven't thought about it to be honest, Inspector. I mean his role here might change a bit but there would always be a job at Treefall Manor for George. We are quite fond of him, aren't we Ruth?"

"Oh yes, he can be frightfully shy at times but really he is very kind-hearted. I can't imagine Treefall Manor without George."

"I see. Tell me, do you think George Campbell could have killed your father and then tried to kill himself due to a weight of guilt on him?" Graves held his brandy to the light and watched the crystal sparkle around the sepia hue.

"Oh no, Inspector," cried Ruth. "George wouldn't be capable. As I say, he's very kind and gentle."

"John? What do you think?"

"Well, Inspector, on the whole I agree with my sister..."

"However...?" probed Graves, sensing the stricken man's hesitation.

"However, I have seen a change in George recently, he hasn't quite been himself if you know what I mean."

"Since the murder?"

"No, before that, a few weeks I should say. Since he had that terrible argument with father in the study. Since then, he has been quite distracted, perhaps a bit dazed. But again, I can't imagine him capable of murder."

"Well, hopefully he comes around and I can ask him myself. Dreadfully good brandy by the way." Graves swirled the last drop around his crystal and held it aloft once again to watch the light twinkle on it like a fine diamond.

"Would you like another, Inspector?"

"No thank you, John, I think we'd better be off, there seems little more we can do tonight."

"I'll ring for Hodgkins, he will run you down to the inn."

As the two detectives walked down the grand staircase past a great window Graves remarked, "It was a close call, without luck or divine intervention we would have had another death in this case, but we didn't, thank goodness."

But Graves was wrong, for, if he had looked through the window, he would have seen a small orange glow on the horizon, where, in the village churchyard, fire was consuming the body of the Reverend Malcolm Thorpe.

14. THE THIRD DEATH

He sought his house, a sigh at every breath,
And could see no way of avoiding death.

"The Franklin's Tale"
The Canterbury Tales

Graves woke early. The rain which had fallen incessantly throughout the night continued to tap against the window, like thousands of little pebbles being thrown by an impatient lover. He had slept soundly, partly due to the amount of alcohol he had consumed, but as always, he had awakened with a clear head and a clear purpose. He sat up in the bed and fastened the top button on his pyjama jacket, which had come undone during the night. He then lit the paraffin lamp beside his bed, the grey light coming through the open curtains being miserable.

For a while he sat and stared at nothing, his mind replaying the previous day: snippets of conversation, observations, feelings which were beginning to fuse inside of him. '*Yes*,' he thought, '*the pieces of this puzzle are coming together.*'

He was still deep in thought when a shift in the air disturbed him. Somewhere close by, he could detect an energy, an urgency. No sooner had these feelings evolved into lucid thoughts than Peggy, who was lying beside the writing desk, lifted her head in the direction of the door. Immediately the sound of bounding steps could be heard. Someone was undoubtedly taking the creaking stairs two at a time, such was their haste. A loud, urgent rap upon the door was answered just as quickly by Graves.

Carver burst through the door, a dripping umbrella in one hand. His trousers from the knee down were saturated with water, where the wind had helped its ally foil man's invention. "Sir, you had better come quick!" said the constable, panting.

"Why? What has happened?"

"It's the Reverend Thorpe sir. He's dead!"

"Well, me straining my back by throwing myself out of bed in some great hurry isn't going to turn him alive now, is it?"

"No, sir," replied Carver, somewhat deflated.

"Now sit down. Good lad. Get your breath back and tell me what happened." Carver did as he was instructed. Peggy let out a wide yawn and trotted over to her new friend to greet him.

"Well sir, I had trouble sleeping, what with the noise of the rain, so I was reading *The Canterbury Tales*. After a while, I felt stiff and thought perhaps a walk might do me some good. I took a brolly from the coat rack downstairs and strolled around the village. I ventured into the churchyard and there I saw him. He was tied to the wooden cross, the smell was horrible sir, sort of sickly charred wood or something."

"Charred?"

"Yes sir. He was on the cross as I say but he was all blackened by fire."

"Hmmph. Have you told or seen anyone else?"

"No sir, as soon as I found him, I ran straight back here."

"Good. Let's go." Graves dressed quickly and within a few minutes the triumvirate were walking briskly down the deserted street towards the church. Graves held his umbrella low to keep his legs dry, but the road ran like a river and each step caused him to kick up water onto himself. Soon, he resigned himself to having a long and wet day.

Carver led the way to his grisly discovery. The remains of Malcolm Thorpe were a horrible sight. The large wooden cross was charred, though still standing. The right wrist of the vicar was in a blackened rope which was tied around the horizontal beam of the cross. The left wrist pointed to the ground; its fastening weakened by the flames the weight of the feeble body had broken through the binding. The head slumped onto the chest so that the burnt face was not visible to the detectives. Rainwater dripped off the still form ravaged by flames. Peggy, her nose being sensitive had remained at the entrance to the churchyard. Carver looked at her and thought it a wise idea. Graves gave a throaty "Hmmph," and took out his pocket watch for examination.

"Do you think it was murder, sir?"

"It looks like suicide but of course it could be murder made to look self-inflicted. Look at his right wrist, it's loose in the rope so he wasn't tied to the cross, his hand was put through the loop. Look down there by his feet, there's a lamp."

"It's broken, sir."

"Yes. Presumably he doused himself in petrol, put one hand through the rope, smashed the lamp against the post and quickly put his other hand through the rope loop before the flames really took hold."

"But why sir? It's a bit dramatic, isn't it?"

"Hmmph. Perhaps not dramatic, maybe more symbolic. There is something missing though, lad."

"Petrol cans."

"Exactly. Let's go see if we can find any."

The search proved to be a short one. The two men entered the church. It was mournfully silent and when Graves commanded Peggy to wait by the door he did so in a whisper. The two men strode slowly between the pews towards the vestry, as though to walk any faster would be an affront to the sanctity of God's house. A faint but familiar smell was in the air and as they approached the old wooden door the distinct odour grew stronger in their nostrils. Two red cans lay discarded on the stone floor of the vestry. Carver picked one up. "Empty, sir."

"Let us see if he left a note, you go check the cottage, I'll look here. Oh, and Carver, check for cups and glasses lying about, anything one can drink from."

Several long minutes passed where time was held by the soft grip of silence before Carver returned. "Nothing sir, no note and all the cups were clean and in their correct place."

"Same here, though there is a pen and blank paper."

"What was the idea with the cups sir?"

"If the vicar was murdered, he must have been poisoned or sedated then put on the cross. Either that or he was knocked out with something. The coroner should be able to help us there if he's had a bump on the head."

"What do we do now, sir?"

"I want you to inform Inspector Young about what has happened and get the body removed and examined. I am going to see how George Campbell is. Hopefully, he is in a better state than the reverend. But before that, I am going to find out what Samuel Mason is hiding from us."

"And after that?"

"After that, lad, we arrest our killer."

†

Graves instructed Carver to use the vicar's telephone to ensure privacy when phoning through to the local constabulary. He himself walked slowly through the rain to the inn, followed closely by Peggy. Ideas were revolving in his head and now finally they were gravitating towards each other, close to joining into a solid theory.

The curtains of the Blue Boar Inn were still closed, no sign of life stirred within. The place looked desolate and sad in the dark, wet morning. Graves looked furtively around, ensuring no eyes were watching him. He commanded Peggy to sit while he himself walked around the inn to the rear. Here an axe was embedded in a huge chopping block and large splinters of wood were scattered all around.

Large bushes enclosed the area to the rear, excepting a

gap wide enough for a person to pass through. It was here that Graves started his search. As he got closer, he could see through the thick rain a wooden hut with a small tin chimney on top emitting smoke. The sound of his steps was obscured by the pelting rain as he approached the hut's wooden door. Still, he tried to move as soundlessly as his bulky frame would allow. One circuit told him there were no windows through which to peek and he was back at the door with his hand on the handle. From within came low clanking sounds and pig-like grunts. Pulling the door slowly, the detective's field of vision brightened with yellow light and a wet heat lathered his face. Samuel Mason stood bending over a vat with his back to the door. In his hand was a wooden paddle and he was stirring the contents of a still, straining with every movement.

Graves pushed the door closed as slowly as he opened it and walked back towards the rear of the inn. '*Hmmph*,' he thought, '*Samuel Mason has a secret. If Alexander Grimbourne knew he was distilling illegal spirits, he could blackmail him and get the pub for a pittance.*'

†

"Really John, you ought to be in bed!"

"Ruth, I am perfectly fine, there is no need to fuss."

John was limping into the dining-room, Penelope and his sister were already seated. The table had been set for four as though everything at Treefall Manor was as right as the rain falling outside. Penelope nibbled at a piece of toast and looked hard at John from under her long-curled eyelashes. She watched his face redden, knowing that he was aware he was being observed, but Penelope wondered at herself for not taking her usual pleasure in this man's embarrassment. She looked at him now as though from afar, through a lifting fog. John had always been Ruth's older brother and had been defined by people and by himself because of his leg. Curiously, Penelope reflected, the first time she saw John she hadn't even noticed the withered limb nor the limp, despite the fact he was walking towards her. No, she remembered, it was his eyes that she had noticed, the seriousness in them, the intensity. There was a man behind those eyes and yesterday that man had nearly drowned to save another.

"How is George this morning?" asked John.

"Much better," answered his sister. "I called in on him on my way down. He came around during the night and is sleeping now."

"Did he say anything?"

"No. Freddie stayed with him, he said he awoke around three o'clock and tried to say something, but Freddie couldn't make out what it was. Then he was asleep a few minutes later."

Ruth rang the bell and Hodgkins appeared silently after a few moments. "Ah Hodgkins, would you be so kind as to ring up Mr Singh and ask him to bring a change of clothes for Lord Taylor. Invite Ed also, he must be terribly bored over there with Freddie here, we shall all have lunch together." When Hodgkins departed to his task, Ruth turned to Penelope. "Ed mentioned the other day he is going back to London tomorrow. Why don't you travel together since you are going too?" John stiffened in silence at his sister's words though the tensing of his shoulders did not go unnoticed by the peripheral vision of Penelope.

"Really, darling Ruth, your attempts at matchmaking lack a great deal of subtlety. You know perfectly well that if Ed took my fancy, he would be here now waiting on me hand and foot."

Ruth laughed playfully at her friend. "Really Penny, no one could ever accuse you of modesty."

"A beauty who pretends to be modest is a liar my darling. Now you wouldn't want me to be a liar, would you?"

"Oh, Hodgkins, that was quick, was there no answer?" said Ruth, addressing the butler who had once again glided into the room.

"I will ring presently, I was just about to when Lord Taylor found me, he wished for me to convey a message to you."

"Yes?"

"He wishes for you to know that Mr Campbell is awake and well. His brain function appears normal."

†

Carver left Constable Brent standing guard over the body of Malcolm Thorpe which was now lying on the grass covered by a single sheet. The coroner, by good fortune, had been with the constable when Carver rang up and a quick assessment had revealed no fractures to the skull. The body would now be removed and tested for traces of poison, though in its state it would not be easy to get conclusive results, he said.

Carver was glad to get away. Watching the body of a man who had devoted his life to good being left to dangle on a cross in the rain while he waited for help was much for him to bear. It had been a pathetic sight, and one which had given the young detective a lump in his throat and a sickly feeling in his stomach. He walked briskly out of the churchyard and stopped when he reckoned he was out of sight of his contemporary. He swallowed in gulps of deep cold air and tried to forget the image of the vicar that was burned in his mind. Resting against an old stone wall midway between the church and the inn he looked upward and tried to focus on individual droplets of rain as they fell from their cloudy home to the puddles their siblings had made.

He needed to stop, to take a minute, to breathe and to focus. Graves had said that they would arrest the killer, yet he, Carver, had not yet worked out how the murder was committed. Dread filled him at the prospect of failing in the task set for him. He closed his eyes to think clearer and block out any distractions. The only invasive disturbance was the sound of the singing rain.

He had always possessed a logical mind, but a man being

stabbed in the centre of a locked room by a vanishing killer was an illogical circumstance. Perhaps this was why he had not yet come up with a solution. He thought through the evidence. The dagger. The piece of paper. *The Canterbury Tales*. *The Canterbury Tales*? No. That wasn't necessarily evidence he thought. The evidence is the book as an object not the title. What was it that Graves had said? Don't judge a book by its cover? What else had Graves said?

With his eyes still shut he reimagined their conversations, he remembered the beer, he could almost taste it, and still did a little bit from the previous night. 'I'll give you a clue,' Graves had said. Dagger, paper, book, locked room, book, paper, dagger. Could it be? Yes, it made sense, there was just one thing he needed to check.

✝

"Lord Taylor is not here, sir, he is at Treefall Manor. I have just received a telephone call to take him some things."

"I know where Lord Taylor is. It was you I came here with the purpose of seeing, Mr Singh," said Graves.

"You wished to see me?" asked the servant, with some surprise.

"Yes. Nothing to get concerned about, my good man, just a few queries I need to follow up."

"Please, let me make you some tea."

The two men were in a drawing room which looked out onto well-trimmed lawns.

The servant left to complete his task and Graves watched the rain through the window. The clouds above the trees were darker than before and Graves shivered despite the recently made fire in the marble hearth. It was a very pleasant room, thought Graves, majestic yet not overly ostentatious. Simple yet expensive décor which he appreciated. Several portraits hung high on three walls. A table by the window housed several photographs. Graves picked up one of Freddie and Ed together in uniform, their revolvers buttoned to their waists. Both had the same smiling eyes as the boy in his own picture, which he now imagined, tucked in his case in the inn. He set the photograph down and picked up the next. It showed a man of about fifty who was striking in his similar appearance to Freddie. They had the same mouth and straight nose, and the shoulders were held back with the same unconscious pride.

"Lord Taylor, my first master," came a voice from the table behind Graves.

"Yes, I thought as much. Father and son look quite alike."

"Oh yes, sir. Not just look alike but are alike. Both are good men; kind men," replied Singh.

"Are? I thought the elder Lord Taylor was dead?"

"He is, sir. Apologies, sir, a habit I have yet to shake, referring to the master as if he still walks among us. I was with him for so long you see, and as you say both masters are so alike there are times when I am perhaps drifting in a daydream and young Lord Taylor will enter the room and I forget myself for a moment and think he is his father."

"I suppose that could be easily done, Mr Singh. Though from what I have heard of Alexander Grimbourne the same mistake couldn't be made between him and his son John?"

"That is correct sir, both are physically very different."

"You know them well?"

"No, not at all, sir. Of course, I have seen both men in and around the village on occasions when I am posting a letter or taking a walk, but I am in no way intimate with either man."

"But surely you would greet them here if they came to visit?"

"John has never visited to my knowledge, sir. Mr Campbell calls on occasion."

"And Alexander? Surely he visited as his daughter was betrothed to Lord Taylor?"

"I received him once. I got the impression from young

Lord Taylor that it was an unwelcome visit. It was before the engagement was announced, sir."

"How long before?"

"Only a day or two perhaps."

"Tell me of this visit, Mr Singh."

"There is little to tell sir. Mr Grimbourne came to the front door alone one evening and rang. I answered. He was in very high spirits, laughing and joking with me over nothing in particular. He requested to see Lord Taylor. I led him to this room where the two men talked for a little time. They did *not* want tea, sir! When they had finished their discussion, I was rang for and I led Mr Grimbourne back to the front door."

"How was Mr Grimbourne's demeanour when you saw him out?" asked Graves, before sipping from the steaming cup in his hands.

"If anything, sir he was giddier than when he arrived."

"And Lord Taylor, how was he?"

"He seemed a little distracted sir, a bit off. Though he does have occasions when he is not quite himself. The war was awfully hard on him, you understand."

"Yes. Yes, I do," replied Graves, again thinking of the picture in his suitcase of the boy in uniform.

"Was there anything else, sir?" added the butler, seeing the detective lost in thought.

"Eh, yes. Did you say you were going to Treefall Manor?"

"Yes, sir."

"Mind giving me a lift? Excellent tea by the way."

"Thank you, it's chai."

†

"I've done it sir! I've cracked it!"

"Cracked what lad?"

"I know how the murder of Alexander Grimbourne was

committed!"

"Good, now we just have to tie up the loose ends."

Graves had seen Carver walking up the long driveway to Treefall Manor and had instructed Singh to stop and pick him up. Carver, in the presence of a stranger struggled to withhold his jubilant admission and had fidgeted for the few minutes' drive to the house, oblivious to the wanting look of Peggy.

They were now in the library, happy to be out of the rain and sheltered from the oncoming storm. Hodgkins who had led them there had departed to prepare coffee.

"What were you seeing Lord Taylor about, sir?"

"I wasn't. I asked Lord Taylor to pass the night here and keep a watch on George, which he did. I wanted to see his manservant, Mr Singh. A delightful chap, he makes an unusual spicy tea which is not too bad at all." Carver, showing confusion on his face was about to ask for an elaboration on this statement when Hodgkins returned carrying a silver tray.

"Is there anything else you would like, Inspector?"

"Yes, Hodgkins, could you please ask Miss Grimbourne to come here, thank you."

Lifting a hot china cup, Graves continued, "Now we are getting to the crux of things, my lad, I will have the truth out of this lot!"

Ruth came into the room and looked expectantly at Graves without speaking.

"Miss Grimbourne, I am afraid I have the unfortunate duty to tell you that the Reverend Malcolm Thorpe was found dead this morning." The beautiful pale complexion of the lady turned paler still.

"Oh Lord, it is as I feared then."

"Feared? Feared what Miss Grimbourne?"

"Not this, certainly, but when I saw Malcolm yesterday morning, he looked different, so... old and worn, like he was burdened by some terrible fear. Tell me Inspector, how did he die?"

"I believe he died by his own hand."

"Oh no! Oh heavens!" The lady sobbed openly and without

embarrassment.

"Miss Grimbourne, I am going to ask you some very simple questions and you are going to give me very simple, very truthful answers. Do you understand?" Ruth froze, her mouth shut tightly, and Carver thought he could read fear in her tear-stained eyes.

"I take your silence to mean you acquiesce. Now, firstly, are you having a relationship with William Hopkirk?" Graves received a faint murmur and a slight nod of the head in response.

"Right. On the night preceding your father's death, did you during the early hours meet William?"

"Yes, Inspector."

"At what time did you get out of bed? Two o'clock or four o'clock?"

"How did y—, it was four o'clock, Inspector."

"Your father knew of this relationship and sacked William from his position because of it didn't he?"

"Yes."

"You also met William on the same evening in the garden, didn't you?"

"Yes. I told William not to come, that it was too risky, but he would not listen. He said he needed to see me. I met him briefly by the rhododendrons before dinner and told him to come again at four o'clock in the morning when we could be sure to be alone and not seen by anyone."

"But you were seen, weren't you? Jayne Brown saw you," continued Graves, his tone becoming kinder with each truthful word spoken.

"Yes. I had no idea she saw us but then she hinted in front of everyone when you were interviewing Mr Roberts." Ruth produced a silk handkerchief and blew into it. "She said something about being in the gardens and the amazing things you see early in the mornings. She looked straight at me, and I knew that she saw myself and William. Later, as I was going to bed, she confronted me and told me that if I didn't give her my necklace, she would tell you our secrets and William would be arrested."

"Why was her hatred towards you and William so great?"

"Because she was in love with William, and he rejected her. Then when she discovered our relationship, she began following us. One day she followed us to the shed behind the inn…"

"Ah! And she told your father about your relationship with William and about the illegal distilling operation?" Ruth nodded slowly, her head still bowed. Peggy, sensing her distress nuzzled softly against the young lady's leg. "Your father forced you into a marriage with Lord Taylor when he found out about you and William and paid Miss Brown for her information, didn't he?"

"Yes."

"Your father told you that if you didn't marry Lord Taylor, he would have William arrested for brewing illegal spirits along with his uncle, did he not?" Ruth burst into sobs.

"Yes, he was a monster. He would think nothing of blackmailing anyone. But you must understand, Inspector, things have been hard for Mr Mason since the war, the inn has not been making a profit and with William losing his job here it has been even more difficult!"

"I understand, Miss Grimbourne, I am here to solve two murders not a moonshine operation. Is there anything else you wish to tell me?"

"I've been so worried, Inspector! William is a good person! I know he can seem a bit off at times but really, he is the best of men. He would never kill anyone, not even a devil like my father!"

"Miss Grimbourne, you do not need to worry about me suspecting William. I know he didn't murder your father or Jayne Brown."

"Oh! thank you, Inspector, really! I have been so frightened and when Jayne was killed, I thought…"

"You thought I would suspect William."

"Yes, I mean, who could want to kill my father *and* Jayne?"

"That I shall reveal to you very soon." Ruth fled the room leaving a trailing echo of grateful sobs.

"Now we are getting somewhere, lad. Miss Ruth has helped us by finally revealing her truth. If only everyone in this blasted case could do the same."

"Now what, sir?"

"Now, before we go any further, we make sure our ducks are lined up in the same way. Tell me how the murder was committed." Graves listened carefully as Carver told him in a low, excited voice the steps the murderer had taken. The young man's voice trembled in anticipation of the senior detective's reaction, though he needn't have worried. Graves smiled at the conclusion and clapped Carver warmly on the back. "You are quite right, lad, very good. Now tell me, who killed Alexander Grimbourne?"

"I-I don't know sir" stammered Carver, taken aback.

"But of course, you do, lad! You've just told me!"

"I have?"

"Yes! The way you describe the murder taking place is spot on, but only one person could have committed the crime in that way. Don't you see yet?"

"I'm sorry sir, I don't."

"Never mind, lad, onwards we march together, nevertheless."

"And where are we marching to sir?"

"To see George Campbell."

"I hope the chap passed the night peacefully and is better today."

"Blast the night and the day! We are going to get the truth out of him! You were right, Carver, *The Canterbury Tales* being left at the crime scene was intended to incriminate Mr Campbell and rightfully so! Now we seek his confession."

15. THE TRUTH

If you are not afraid to hear the truth
I will be open and expose to view
Your monstrous lies. Authority forsooth!

"The Second Nun's Tale"
The Canterbury Tales

The room of convalescence was deathly quiet when the two detectives entered. The curtains were only slightly open, revealing streaks of tears streaming down the window.

"Lord Taylor, would you be so kind as to leave Mr Campbell alone with us? And thank you for doing as I requested last night." George Campbell, who was sitting upright in the bed glanced upon his companion with a questioning look as the detective spoke these words. Freddie met his glance with an embarrassed smile as he obeyed the request and rose to leave.

"Of course. I am probably needed downstairs," he said as he stepped over Peggy and into the hallway.

"Indeed you are," continued Graves. "Please gather everyone in the library and await me there."

"As you wish, Inspector."

"And now we get to the crux of the matter," exclaimed Graves squarely at the bedridden man.

"Inspector?" asked George, his face creased with worry.

"Mr Campbell, I am going to recite to you a history, a recent history. If at any time you feel that I have spoken an inaccuracy, or misrepresented the facts, please correct me. However, I am sure that you will not do so as I am about to speak the truth which you have deliberately kept from me." Carver watched as the pale, cadaverous cheeks of the stricken man filled to scarlet at those ominous words.

"Inspector, please… I…"

"Hush, and let my words unburden you."

Carver listened in wonderment as the weight of deception was lifted from the room. The words poured from Graves in a slow, calm stream and the young detective watched as George Campbell nodded unwittingly at what he heard. After what seemed an age, Graves had finished, and George, with red-rimmed eyes muttered, "It's true. Do with me what you will, Inspector."

†

The tread of Graves's step was not heard as he entered the library, for the first crash of thunder sounded as he stepped into view of the assembled household. Lord Taylor, who stood by the ebony table had done as commanded: Ruth sat between John and Penelope. Elsie Barter stood shaking by the window: her shredded nerves being soothed by Hodgkins.

"Good afternoon," boomed Graves, echoing the thunder, "I see we are nearly all here. Mr Campbell won't be joining us I'm afraid."

"Ah! Here you all are," said a voice from the doorway.

"Just in time," replied Graves.

"For what?"

"For you to be arrested for the murders of Alexander Grimbourne and Jayne Brown."

Peggy, knowing her master's tone growled at Edmond Osborn.

†

"But sir, there are still one or two points that I don't understand." The two men were sitting in their now familiar chairs by the fireside of the Blue Boar Inn. Peggy, whose coat glistened with raindrops from their walk from the manor, lapped at a bowl of nutty brown ale.

The oppressiveness of the darkness and lashing rain outside was held at bay by the bright glow of the burning logs and homely smells emanating from the invisible kitchen.
The curtains were pulled closed, yet the occasional flash of lightning revealed chinks in their armour. The warmth of the inn lessened the effect of the terrible weather which terrorised the village and hovered over the minds of the merry patrons.

"Well lad, all you need to know is here in Ed's confession," said Graves, tapping a brown envelope on the table. Carver looked upon the letter longingly and thought bitterly towards Graves, who had not let him sit in on the interrogation of the murderer. Instead, Graves had commanded him to stand watch over the rest of the household under the dubious authority of 'procedure'.

"But let us start at the beginning," continued Graves. "The first striking aspect of the case was the circumstances in which our first victim was found. Alexander Grimbourne was stabbed in a locked room by enormous force with a book in his hand and a folded piece of paper found lying next to him. Now, you commented upon inspection of the corpse that the dagger was thrust through the body in such a powerful manner that it was unusual. You were correct: it *was* unusual, yet, because you couldn't find a logical reason to explain the excessive force you ignored it to look for other evidence that would support a theory you could form. Lesson number one, lad. Never try to make the evidence support a theory, make the theory support the evidence!"

"Lesson learnt, sir."

"Good. Next was the piece of paper which was from the blotting pad in the library. It showed an imprint of a love letter. The words which had been written (though interesting from the perspective of the relationships in the house) were completely irrelevant in terms of how the murder was committed. The important piece of evidence was the material paper itself. Next, we had the coin which lay beside the dead man's pocket. Finally, we had the book. *The Canterbury Tales*. These four pieces of evidence told us how the murder was staged but not the identity of the killer. Tell me, lad, what was the significance of the book?"

"Well, at first I thought the authors initials were pointing to George Campbell as our killer..."

"And you were right, that is what we were supposed to think."

"But then later I saw the inscription in the book from Malcolm Thorpe to Alexander's wife and I wondered if there was some secret love affair which lay at the heart of the matter. That, coupled with the fact that Reverend Thorpe had spent time in the Canterbury parish made me suspicious that he could be the killer."

"Thus, it made no sense. If *The Canterbury Tales* being left at the crime scene was meant to implicate George Campbell for sharing the initials of Geoffrey Chaucer, then why would the killer attempt to implicate Malcolm Thorpe using the same book? Unless..."

"Unless the killer was unaware of the inscription in the book and therefore not aware that the light would be cast upon the vicar!"

"Precisely. So, we can determine that the murderer was trying to frame *either* Malcolm or George but not both."

"So, how can you be sure it was George who was intended to be framed and not Malcolm?"

"You heard yourself why during our conversation with George today, but let's not race ahead, we'll get there. First, how the murder was committed. Time was the most important element. It was what bothered me from the beginning. The whole thing seemed like a charade, a stage-managed piece of theatre that made no sense. Why murder someone in a locked room? Why not wait until they were alone in a field or a hallway and blow their brains out? The answer it seemed was the simplest one. The killer had no choice… they had no time to do otherwise. Let me take you back to the evening before the murder. We know from the testimony of the individuals involved what occurred to some degree of accuracy.

"The group gathered for an evening meal where Alexander Grimbourne stated quite frankly that his solicitor was coming the next day to facilitate the making of a new will. Certainly, this is interesting for us to hear, but it would be a grave leap into the boggy depths of assumption to render this as relevant to the murder. Next, we know that the meal has moments of frosty atmosphere, and that George Campbell leaves the room to give instructions to Hodgkins. Importantly, George does not return. At the end of the evening, Alexander takes Ed for a tour of the wine cellar and, as they stand chatting beneath one of the mini towers, what happens? A slab of rock falls, narrowly missing Alexander. Or does it? Do we assume it misses Alexander because he is subsequently murdered the next day? What if the stone misses Ed? Picture it, Alexander Grimbourne, a man who is master of his estate, a man who instils fear in those around him is talking to the lawyer from London. They are standing idly, the younger man has no idea what is about to happen and seemingly no reason to be afraid, until… the tone of Alexander's words change, and he is spewing hateful bile towards his guest. Ed's secret has been unveiled and, with a piece of theatre worthy of the West End the crashing crescendo is a falling rock to crush the skull of the man Alexander hates so much. And yet, George, the terrified would-be murderer misses with his aim. His conscience deflects the flight of the stone as it leaves his grip, and the piece of masonry falls with a thud between the two men. He is like a footballer taking a penalty who, caught in two minds as to which corner to kick the ball hits it straight down the middle into the safety of the goalkeeper's arms. And now you see why time was the most important element of the case: why the murder was committed in the way it was. With a click of two fingers the back door is flung open, and the other members of the household appear. What do they do? Each of the two men is now wearing a mask of deception. Ed, so close to death is in a state of shock, yet he cannot denounce his would-be murderer because then the reason why Alexander wants him dead will be revealed. Alexander thinks the more quickly of the two:" he claps Ed on the shoulder thanking him for pushing him out of the way of the falling stone thus saving his life.

The situation is diffused for the moment but now we have two prize-fighters sparring, working out the weak spot for the killer blow. Ed values his reputation as a lawyer more than anything else, he acknowledges to himself this is now kill or be killed, and so his mind races.

We will never know the thoughts that possessed Alexander, for of the two he drew his gun slower, as it were. Ed goes to bed amid the celebrations of heroism, but he knows time is short, he must act. So, he lies in bed, and he plots, he works out every detail, he thinks over what he has seen of Treefall Manor, what he has heard.... He remembers the conversation between Ruth and William by the rhododendrons that afternoon, he remembers standing on a rake, how the head came off, he remembers the dagger, the weight of it in his hands. In his mind's eye he sees the hilt of the dagger slot into the shaft of the rake where the head came off like a hand in a glove. He gets out of bed, eager to test his experiment. John wakes at two o'clock as Ed creeps past his room. He goes to the library and takes it to the shed, it doesn't fit! The handle of the dagger is thinner than where the head of the rake fits in. But wait! He remembers the blotting pad on the library table, if he takes a piece of paper, he can fold it as many times as is necessary to fill the gap between the handle of the dagger and the inside if the rake shaft. The dagger will be held tight! He has fashioned a spear almost. The idea is forming fully now in his mind, but he needs to consider what can go wrong. He knows after the events of the evening Alexander will be on his guard and in all probability lock the study door. He also knows the barred window will be locked shut due to the coldness and the time of year. Therefore, to gain access to the study where he knows Alexander spends his mornings, he must be able to open the window."

"Hence the coin we found beside Grimbourne's body."

"Exactly, Ed opens the study window from the inside during the early hours. He turns the window handle retracting the latch bolt and places a coin over the bolt housing. He pushes the window shut. The spring which works the bolt is then working against the coin preventing the bolt slotting into its housing giving the appearance that the window is locked when in fact it is not. Elsie, who cleans the windows the next morning is unlikely to notice the deception unless she pushes on the window from outside causing it to open, which we know she does not. So far, so good. And now to the book. Standing at the crime scene, I looked around at the evidence at my feet and tried to slot the pieces of the puzzle together, yet there was one thing that did not fit: *The Canterbury Tales*. I looked and looked and knew that something was wrong, and yet I could not see what it was even though the answer was staring me in the face. The book should not have been in the room. I could see the gap where the book had seemingly been removed from, that lonely slot in the row of books and yet I knew I was being tricked. Sometimes, lad, you must take a step back to see what you are looking for up close. I looked at the other books on the case and they all had one thing in common: they were by Italian authors. *The Prince* by *Machiavelli*, *The Decameron* by *Boccaccio* et cetera. *The Canterbury Tales* should not have been amongst them. I knew then there was a significance and slowly I realised the full extent. We agreed that death would have been instantaneous, the dagger having been driven through the heart."

"Yes sir, that's right."

"So, it would have been impossible for Alexander Grimbourne to be stabbed and then search among his books for one whose initials were shared by George Campbell, pick it up, then drop down dead?"

"Agreed."

"And so, Ed, having seen *The Canterbury Tales* in the upstairs library that day, takes it that night and replaces it with a book from Alexander's study to make it look like no book is missing from the library."

"You were staring at the shelves in the library when Miss Dunholme disturbed us earlier, sir!"

"I was, and if you look in between *A Study in Scarlet* and *The Hound of the Baskervilles* you will find *Triumph of Death* by *Gabriele D'Annunzio*. But to continue… after using the coin trick to set up the window, he takes Chaucer's work to the shed along with his weapon and goes to bed and waits for the morning. Everything is in place. When the morning comes, he must act normal and wait for his opportunity, yet he knows he can't wait for long as he doesn't know what his victim is planning. After breakfast, he goes for a walk in the village, probably making sure he is seen by a few people, thus establishing an alibi. He then races up Poacher's Lane to the shed. Alexander, as suspected is sitting at his desk, Ed slowly pushes the window open and through the gap in the bars tosses *The Canterbury Tales* onto the floor a few feet from the window. The small coin falls as the window is opened and rolls to the middle of the study where Alexander's body will soon fall beside it. Don't forget lad, we found that Alexander kept his coins in the desk so why would he have one in his pocket? Alexander then looks up at where the noise of a falling book has disturbed him and goes to pick it up to put it back on the shelf. Had his mind not been so consumed with his new problems, he may have queried how the book came to be there; after all, some force must have knocked it from the shelf, but we can surmise Alexander was too distracted to think of this. Now, Ed strikes like a cobra. He thrusts his makeshift spear between the bars with all the force he can muster. Alexander stumbles back, driven by the impact and falls stone dead in the centre of the room. As he falls back, the dagger sticks in his chest. The packing piece of paper dislodges, and the rake shaft remains firmly in Ed's angry grip. Ed then pulls the window closed where the latch bolt locks in place and Alexander has seemingly been killed by a ghost. I'll have another pint lad," finished Graves with a long gulp.

16. THE WHOLE TRUTH

Thy Child thou sawest slain before thine eyes;
My little child lives still and seeks thy aid

"The Man of Law's Tale"
The Canterbury Tales

"But sir!" said Carver after hastily retrieving two amber jars from Samuel Mason. "Why? Why Ed?"

"Ah! Indeed the 'who' has proved harder than the 'how', and it took until today for me to see the absolute proof needed. You see, lad, there were circumstantial pieces of evidence which pointed to our young lawyer throughout our investigation. For one, he never gave us an alibi for Grimbourne's murder. If you recall, Lord Taylor interrupted our interview on the night of the murder and told us that he and Ed were together at the time of the crime was committed. So, I asked myself, what if Lord Taylor was lying and he had unwittingly given an alibi to the murderer? After all, he was unlikely to suspect his best friend, unless he was in on it too."

"I see, sir, but hardly anyone had a solid alibi, why did you focus on Ed?"

"Because of Malcolm Thorpe. You remember the difference in the man? When we spoke in the graveyard, he was amiable, chatty, possibly eccentric but certainly full of life. Then when we saw him here before he killed himself, the difference was extreme. He looked like a ghost and Ruth said the same."

"But what has that to do with Ed?"

"I think we should let him explain." Graves picked up the envelope from the table and handed it to Carver who tore at it like a starving wolf.

Inspector Graves,

As requested by yourself I am writing this letter as a confession of my crimes, not out of remorse for the murder of Alexander Grimbourne but for the death of Malcolm Thorpe.
I suppose the beginning is always a good place to start…
When I was a boy, I committed an act of childish foolery. They said one should not play with matches lest they get burnt. Alas, it was not I who got burnt. The result of my actions was that I no longer had a family, and another family no longer had a mother.
Fortunately for me, the person who found me that night had a kind heart and, knowing the fate that would befall an orphaned child, he hid me away for two days until he found a family willing to take a young boy in and raise him as their son.
Of course, I have never forgotten what happened that night nor the actions I took, but time twists and distorts memories and gradually my guilt at what I had done was replaced by guilt at feeling less guilt than I used to. I was in the embrace of a loving family, I was enjoying my schoolwork, after a while I could even attend church and pray without tears wetting my face. In summary, I grew, and the world opened up to me. I excelled at English and History at school and decided I would become a barrister, to serve the law not as some perverted joke but as a penance for sins committed in what now seemed a previous life.
Fate: it sleeps but does not die.
When the war broke out, I took a commission and was soon contemplating whether a German bullet or bomb would serve the sentence which should have been carried all those years before. It

is strange the things one thinks when they live with death as a constant companion. The poor boys falling around me could not have committed greater sins than I, yet the bullets kept on sailing past me.

After a particularly costly battle, I was reassigned to a battalion near Amiens. It was here that I met Freddie Taylor. We hit it off immediately and, you know, the funny thing was we enjoyed months of friendship before I even thought to ask where he hailed from. "Swinbridge," he said, when I finally asked, "though I doubt you will have heard of it." "No." I lied. Swinbridge. Lord, what were the chances? I reasoned to myself, was this why the bullets wouldn't touch me? Was fate waiting to punish my soul and not my body? Of course, Inspector, you must remember that Freddie's father was Lord Taylor then and though as a child everyone in the village knew of those who lived in the 'big house' the man in the trench beside me was simply Captain Frederick Taylor.

Our friendship grew and, like us, survived the war. Whenever Freddie invited me to visit at his ancestral home, I always found some reason to decline and would see him when he was in London. And so, I continued with my invented identity, blissfully arrogant that I could run faster than the past. That is until one day a few weeks ago when I was sitting in my London club and a letter was delivered to me on a silver platter. Unbeknownst to me, it was a death warrant disguised as a wedding invitation. As you know, the letter was sent by Alexander Grimbourne, and I don't mind telling you I had a sleepless night fretting over whether I had been discovered. The letter contained no open threat or clue and yet a feeling gnawed at me, I smelt danger.

To assuage my fears, I reassured myself with facts and played the situation in my head like a court case. After all, it had been many years since I had set foot in Swinbridge and though I was somewhat familiar with Alexander as a child (his wife visiting us often), I knew that my appearance had changed dramatically since I was a boy. If my secret had been uncovered, would Alexander waste any time denouncing me to the authorities or the newspapers? My star was rising, as they say, due to my recent successes in court, it would have been the ruin of me to be revealed as a killer even if my age when the crime was committed would spare me prison.

After much deliberation, I decided to accept the invitation. I reasoned that, on balance, my secret was probably safe, and I could not miss the wedding of my best friend. Really though, I guess I accepted because I needed to know whether I was still safe. And so, I travelled to Swinbridge but decided to ignore Alexander's instruction to seek a lift from the station porter. I wanted to test the waters before taking the plunge. I went to the Blue Boar Inn where I was happily treated as a stranger by Mason and that old crone Elsie Barter. She used to tell all the children off for no reason when we were young and if anyone should have been able to unmask me it was that old hag, and of course Malcolm. When I met him the morning after talking to you, Inspector, I could see he recognised me instantly and he knew then who had killed Alexander Grimbourne.

But, as I say, the Barter woman was ignorant of me, and I felt comfortable then. I set off for Treefall Manor after the pub. I was going to walk but John saw me and gave me a lift. Coincidentally, I remembered not to take the shortcut up Poachers Lane as this would give me away as a local should anyone see me. Then, stupidly, I directed you that way a few days later when my mind was swamped with doubt. Anyway, nothing untoward occurred until after dinner when Alexander insisted on showing me the wine cellar. We chatted pleasantly but I was on my guard, and I wondered if my tension was perceived by that horrid man. As we walked back to the house he stopped and stared at the sky, then his voice changed, and he unleashed all my secrets in a torrent of hate filled speech. I was dumbstruck, all my fears were realised, and I froze to the spot when out of nowhere a great slab of rock landed between us. Before I had time to compute what had happened the others rushed out of the house and Alexander was hailing me as a hero.

And so, he had to die.

I must confess (though I don't expect you to believe me), had Alexander not been such a devil I may not have committed the act that I did. I could see the terror he caused his household and perhaps I told myself I was freeing his children from tyranny and that in some

way this made up for robbing them of their mother.
I then planned the murder exactly as you have just described it to me, Inspector.
I must admit I thought it rather clever, bravo for working it out. I do feel bad about trying to frame Mr Campbell, but an eye for an eye and all that. Jayne Brown on the other hand, well, I'm afraid that was most regrettable. I had no idea Ruth got up in the night to meet her lover, so when Jayne spoke to us all about what she saw the night before Alexander's murder, I naturally thought she was directing her remarks at me. Later that night, I sought her out and suggested we meet in the woods the following morning. She seemed quite pleased at the idea. I only realised what a fool I had been when we were in the forest and I spoke to her, implicating myself. The horror on her face told me that she had not seen me at all, but I had just confessed to her so naturally she had to be silenced. There was a rock lying at my feet - well, you know the rest.
I'm afraid fortune has not smiled upon me; it all could have been so different if it wasn't for that damned book: The Canterbury Tales! I now join thousands of schoolchildren in cursing Geoffrey Chaucer forever.

Yours sincerely,

Edmond Osborn

"But sir, how did *you* work out that Ed was the killer?"

"As I was saying, after we left the church, we met Ed coming in the opposite direction and Ruth talked to Malcolm less than an hour later when he was in a morose state. It would not be too much of a stretch to suppose that the catalyst of this change was that Reverend Thorpe met Ed after we left him. And so, I asked myself why, and then the words floated together in my mind… Edmond Osborn; Desmond Broon."

"The two names are an anagram sir!"

"Precisely. Ed is really little Des, who supposedly perished in the fire that killed Alexander's wife. And don't forget, lad, as

Ed says in his letter, he directed us up Poacher's Lane to the manor. Only a native of the village would know of this path."

"But he said Freddie showed him the path, sir!"

"Freddie couldn't have, remember? Freddie told us he was walking with Ed at the time of the murder, but if Ed is our killer, then that isn't true, is it? So, when could he have shown Ed the path?"

"Ah, I see. So why the change in Malcolm? Well, we know that Malcolm was first on the scene at the fire, imagine he finds little Des standing with a box of matches in his hands, what does the reverend do? After all, we are talking about a child. Does he give him to the authorities for Des to be reared in a horrible, stinking workhouse, or does he take pity on the boy who has just made himself an orphan, and believe in redemption, and maybe that the boy's act was unintentional? Does he hide the boy away until he can find a family far away who wish to raise a son and cannot have children of their own? It is a moral dilemma facing Malcolm Thorpe and it can't have been made easier by the fact that his dear friend Mrs Grimbourne also perished in the flames, although he might not have known it at the time. Still, he has a decision to make, and he makes one. He hides the boy in the vestry where the child draws the flames on the wall which we saw and mistook for a child's imagination of eternal damnation. And so, Malcolm lets the world believe that the child is dead. And he may as well be to the village of Swinbridge until the day Malcolm Thorpe sees the grown child walking towards him and he knows who killed Alexander Grimbourne. Thus, Malcolm feels that he is responsible for the worst of all sins, he hid the truth, and the truth has grown into a deadly force. A man lies buried because of Malcolm Thorpe, or at least that is what he believed."

"When we looked upon his charred remains you said there was something symbolic about the scene. I thought you meant that a man of God should die on a cross, but you didn't, did you sir?"

"No lad, I meant the fire. If Malcolm Thorpe openly

condemned Edmond Osborn he knew he would be sending him to the gallows and another life would be taken because of him. He was facing the same dilemma as twenty years before. So, he cleansed his guilt with flames and at the same time gave us a clue of the murderer's identity."

"Like George attempting suicide over his guilt at trying to kill Ed?"

"Yes. Both men felt the only way to atone for their sins was to offer up their souls, one with fire, the other with water. George was racked with guilt and disgust at his weakness that he would do whatever Alexander commanded. The Georges of this world lead a hard life lad, living in a society where they cannot live or love openly and honestly. Oh! Don't look at me so surprised lad! I know you think me to be a cantankerous old git, but it shouldn't surprise you that I know something of the world. Men have lain with one another since the dawn of time, hell, even the Spartans would practise fighting in the morning then go behind the chariot sheds at lunchtime.

"George and Lord Taylor are an item and Jayne Brown told Alexander this. He blackmailed them: George was to murder Ed and Freddie was to marry Ruth, otherwise their secret would be revealed, and their lives ruined."

"What a terrible thing to blackmail someone, sir!"

"What's terrible lad is that people are judged because of who they love. If there was no stigma, Freddie would not have had to lie about his alibi saying he was with Ed when really, he was with George, and we may have caught our killer quicker. Perhaps there may not have been any murders to solve."

"And the piece of paper, the love letter…"

"From George to Freddie. Probably how Alexander discovered the affair. We shall never know."

"There is just one more thing I don't yet understand, sir?"

"Go on."

"How did Alexander know Ed's real identity? Did he know before he invited him to the Treefall Manor?"

"Ah, that is what it took until today for me to verify! You

remember the newspaper we found in Alexander's desk?"

"Yes, it was a few weeks old was it not?"

"Correct. In the newspaper was an article on Edmond Osborn and a picture of the young lawyer. I suspect the face was familiar in a rather distant sort of way, but Alexander was a crossword enthusiast, his foremind will have deciphered the anagram of the names in no time. He will have found himself staring at the boy who was supposed to have died in the same blaze that killed his beloved wife. But what to do with this information? Well, an opportunity presented itself that very day through cruel fortune. Alexander visited Freddie to blackmail him into marrying his daughter. When standing in the Lord's drawing room who should he see staring at him from a picture frame? Edmond Osborn. Standing proudly on the Western Front next to Lord Taylor. 'Who is this?' toys Alexander. 'My friend Ed,' replies Freddie, sensing no danger. 'Friend, eh? Well, he must attend the wedding, Freddie! How can I find him?' 'I shall give you the address of his club,' or words to that effect. You see, it all fell into place for Alexander, or so he thought. He forgot what a rat will do when it is cornered."

17. AND NOTHING BUT THE TRUTH

My sovereign lady, only of your grace –
Yet in a garden yonder, at such a place
You made a promise which you know must stand
And gave your plighted troth into my hand
To love me best, you said, as God above
Knows, though I be unworthy of your love.

"The Franklin's Tale"
The Canterbury Tales

The storm raged throughout the night, weakening towards the dawn. By the early morning the day shone clear and bright, the dark clouds scattered like a defeated army leaving a blue sky and autumn chill. Treefall Manor stood as it had for centuries, its spires pointing to the heavens, its walls solid and forbidding, unruffled by the recent events.

The kitchen smelt of buttery toast and strong coffee. Elsie Barter sat gasping for breath between slurps of tea and floods of sentences. "And I said Betty, didn't I say it were him! The devil he looked the minute he arrived! Strolled into the Boar like some puffed up prince, he did! I said to Mr Mason then, the moment I clapped eyes on the scoundrel, I said Samuel Mason! Trouble has arrived in Swinbridge! You mark my words and mark 'em well! And wasn't I right! Murder no less!" No amount of soothing sounds that Betty mustered could stem the torrent of outraged exclamations being expressed by Mrs Barter. Hodgkins, who heard this outburst as he approached the kitchen door thought that perhaps he was needed elsewhere and promptly changing direction, glided quickly down the hall. "Oh Lor' I hope that is all the young master's troubles over now Betty! It were bad enough having a father he disagreed with but then to have him murdered in cold blood by a lawyer, no less! Lor' I don't know what the world is coming to. I hope he can find some happiness now."

✝

George Campbell sat in bed in the same position as he had the previous day when Inspector Graves of Scotland Yard had told him his own secret thoughts and deeds. Then, he could feel his head swim and his stomach tighten with overwhelming fear and shame. Now, he felt a fraction of that fear as he thought of what he was going to say to the man next to him who was gently holding his hand. "Freddie, I don't know what will happen next in my life, but it can't continue another minute without me getting something off my chest."

Lord Taylor looked into his eyes and gave a weak smile. "Go on."

"You see Freddie, as you know yesterday the Inspector asked me a few questions. Questions he already knew the answers to it seems. He asked me about my argument with Mr Grimbourne and about my relationship with you. He also made clear that he knew who threw the stone the night before the murder. Oh, Freddie, it was me! I did it!" George looked down and focused on a loose thread coming from his pyjama jacket, unable to meet his lover's eye.

"Are you worried I will cast you off over this revelation?"

"Of course that is what I fear."

"Then fear not. What's done is done. Ed was the only person here who murdered, and I have my own share of responsibility in that. He was my friend after all and would not have been here if he did not know me. Let us move on and never speak the names Alexander Grimbourne nor Ed Osborn ever again."

"That sounds good to me, but where do we move on to? We still have our secret to keep, the Inspector did not give us away even though he caught me trying to enter the study in an attempt to find the letter I wrote to you, the one which Jayne found and gave to Alexander."

"No, he denounced the killer in our midst very skilfully. He's more exceptional than he looks, that old detective. Anyway, my estate is rather large and there is a dreadful amount of work to do which, in all honesty, I have been struggling with recently. Why don't you give up your position here and come and be with me? Of course, I shall ensure John is properly remunerated for losing such an efficient secretary."

"That sounds wonderful, and, really, I don't think John will mind losing me too much, I imagine he will want to run Treefall Estate in his own way and be rather more hands on than he has been."

"That's settled then, if you are feeling better tomorrow, we can move your things over."

"I think I'm feeling better now."

†

"The lawyer fellow? But why?" asked William incredulously. He was sitting on top of a beer keg, his legs dangled gaily as he looked into Ruth's smiling eyes.

"We don't know everything yet. Inspector Graves was rather cryptic, he said the important facts would be revealed at the trial and that there were other personal matters which needn't be recounted. Then that Constable Brent came in and whisked Ed away in a pair of handcuffs to be interrogated in the dining room." Ruth pulled her shawl close around her neck; the damp beer cellar causing her to shiver.

"I see," said William thoughtfully. "Well, I'm glad it wasn't anyone we cared about, although I was hoping it was Elsie Barter. I guess we shall have to continue listening to her loud gossiping for years to come."

"Oh William, you are dreadful," laughed Ruth. "Poor Elsie is traumatised by the whole event; she still can't go near the study to clean."

"She loved every minute of it, the old witch, and don't you think otherwise!" Ruth stifled a laugh and looked deep into her lover's eyes.

"Speaking of household tasks not being done, I noticed there are a lot of leaves that need collecting and weeds that need pulling. I spoke to John this morning and we think we need to employ a gardener. Well? How about it?"

"Sure, I'll take my old job back, on one condition."

"Which is?"

"Your wedding goes ahead… with me as the groom."

✝

Penelope Dunholme listened to the squelching sound the sodden grass made beneath her feet. She was standing by the still lake which seemed to be resting after being thrown about relentlessly during the storm. Her mind so enraptured in thought, she was oblivious to the uneven gait approaching her from behind. Only the familiar voice woke her to the present.

"I wondered where you'd be. Doesn't your train leave soon?"

"In a few hours. Ed had suggested getting the early one together but as he will no longer be boarding, I see no reason to rush myself."

"Were you fond of him?" asked John.

"No. I thought him rather an arse, actually. He was typical of the men I encounter in London really: smart and smug, rather full of themselves, all alike and invariably rather dull."

"Maybe you should look for a man outside of London."

"Who said I am looking for a man? Why should I look for a man? Why shouldn't I look for a nice country house to live in and take my pleasures from the beauty of the English countryside?"

"If that is what you desire why don't you live at Treefall Manor?" They looked each other in the eye.

"Do you mean that, John?"

"I do, but only if you will be the lady of the manor and be Mrs Grimbourne. I love you, truly I do."

"If you had have asked me that a few years ago I think I might have said yes, but you dithered in shyness and as a result I must say no. However…"

John saw a mischievous sparkle in her green eyes.

"I will be lady of the manor and Mrs Dunholme-Grimbourne. It's what my father would have wanted. Are my terms agreeable?"

"My darling, they're wonderful!" After a loving embrace Penelope cantered back through the mud to find her soon to be sister-in-law to share the exciting news.

John stood gazing at the water, happiness warming his bones from the autumn breeze. On the far shore of the lake a heron beat its majestic wings. It lofted itself into the air and disappeared over the trees towards the village stream.

John sat on his favourite stump and took his pencil and pad from his pocket. The words flowed from his head, through his veins to his hand and onto the page.

Exalt! Exalt! The King is dead!
Long live the Queen!

. . . .

†

Inspector Graves stood in his room in the Blue Boar Inn beside his half-packed suitcase. He was looking down at the photograph in his large hands, a sad smile on his face. A timid rap on the door caused him to hurriedly place the picture frame in his case before he issued a tentative, "Come in."

"Ready to go sir?" asked Carver, who appeared in the doorway. "The train leaves shortly."

"Yes, lad, nearly packed."

"Sir, there was one thing which I still don't quite understand. The imprint of the letter we found in the study. It said: 'will to think about' on it; yet the case turned out to have nothing to do with Alexander Grimbourne making a new will."

"Ah, but did it say that?"

"How do you mean sir?" asked Carver, confused.

"I asked George what he wrote in the letter. Don't forget, parts of the sentences were missing. And the piece missing in that sentence is what is missing in every cold-blooded murder case: *good*. Here, read for yourself." From his pocket Graves took a handwritten copy of the letter George had sent to Freddie.

Dearest one,

Oh, how I wish for us to be together. I hate Alexander with all of my being and long for the day when we can live side by side without that tyrant towering over us! Oh, what folly am I speaking! I am trapped here in this prison. There is no way out!
The old man must die for us to be free, there is no other way. If only he died before the wedding all our troubles would be solved! An accident, a sudden illness, anything to free us from his grip! But how

selfish of me to even dream. This is not only about us, there is poor Ruth to also consider. No doubt she longs for the day she can marry you and she has been so sweet to me I have her goodwill to think about. Yes, it is not just us under the yoke of Alexander Grimbourne!

All my

love, George

EPILOGUE

*'God knows it's true that children in the main
Are much unlike their elders gone before,'*

"The Clerk's Tale"
The Canterbury Tales

Superintendent Hill leaned back in his chair and looked out of his window at the familiar sky whilst he waited for Inspector Graves. He had received a short telegram the previous day stating that the murderer had been apprehended, that sufficient evidence had been amassed to conclude a successful trial and that Graves and Carver would be returning by the eleven o'clock train. The Superintendent looked at his pocket watch when he heard the clicking of familiar footsteps coming down the corridor. Graves removed his hat as he entered.
"Take a seat Graves, take a seat."
"Thank you, sir."
"Well done on solving the case, a tricky one, it seems. I've had Inspector Young on the telephone thanking us for our co-operation. He ran through most of the details as he understands it."
"Very good, sir."
"Tell me, how did young Carver get on?"
Graves allowed himself a hint of a smile before replying. "He'll do sir, he'll do fine."

†

An envelope had been left on Graves's desk. He picked it up and examined it. The postmark read Swinbridge. It was addressed to Detective Inspector Graves, Scotland Yard. London.
He tore from the corner and read the short letter.

Inspector Graves,

I hope this finds you well. I will be dead by the time you read this letter and I have no doubt that you will have correctly deduced my death to be suicide. I also have no doubt that you will have solved the murder of Alexander Grimbourne. However, if I am wrong and you have not (which, having judged your intelligence, I think unlikely) I am sorry to say that I cannot reveal the name of the person who perpetrated the deed. What I can say is what I mean to say: that I am sorry for the sins I have caused. Though I did not wield the knife that struck Alexander Grimbourne dead, I feel I am just as responsible for his death as the person who did.
For too long I have harboured a secret love which has haunted me. I have never confessed this to anyone and do so now to unburden myself before God's judgement.
Many years ago, I fell madly in love with a woman when I was doing the Lord's work in Canterbury. This lady was from the local area, and we would spend our time touring the ancient city. She shared her knowledge of the place with myself, a newcomer, and a stranger. After a few months of bliss together my world was shattered when her mother became seriously ill, the result being that my love and her mother moved to Scotland where there was an extended family who could better care for the poor woman. We agreed that our hearts would mend sooner if we did not write and instead try to forget one another. This seemed to me to be the best course of action and indeed over time my longing for her warm touch faded ever so slightly so that eventually life seemed to be worth living again.

A few years later, my calling took me to the small village of Swinbridge where I was soon shocked to see the woman I had loved living there. She was married to a local landowner. I believe you can guess to whom I refer. Anyway, much against God's will, we resumed our relationship in secret, and she became pregnant. She bore a son and named him John. I believe God saw fit to punish us by inflicting a deformity upon the child, a constant reminder of our sin. The love affair ended instantly.

Please understand why I did what I did, I believed in second chances, perhaps I was wrong.

May God have mercy on my soul.

Firstly, thank you for buying *The Mystery of Treefall Manor*, I hope you enjoyed reading it as much as I enjoyed writing it.

The book world is a competitive place, and because of that, I hope you'll excuse me taking the liberty of kindly asking you to leave a review on Amazon, Goodreads, or wherever you bought this book. It is reviews which ultimately influence an author's success, and which bring their books to a wider audience, so thank you.

More importantly, however, don't forget to keep an eye out in future for the next Inspector Graves mystery!

Printed in Great Britain
by Amazon